KAMALU

M. J. HARDY

Other Charlie Taylor Mysteries

Sleep Baby Sleep (75 – 76)

Wende,

Wishing for you all the happiness in the world.

M. J. Hardy
10/21/21
Englewood, CO

Dedication

I n memory of Margaret, Kimberly, Helen, Mayumi, Vicki, Regina, Denise, Louise, and Linda and my thoughts and prayers go to their families.

Acknowledgments

As always, to my own family, Aera, Paige, Aeran, and Alex, who've brought me more riches than I ever imagined. We've already covered several continents, numerous countries, and vast miles. Our journey continues.

To Martha Powell, Ellen Copeland Buchine, Larry and Marilee Fisher, Michelle Fisher, Jen Dunne Tew, Mary Fitzgerald Feola, Barb Daniels Niblock, Margaret Weissman, Harriet Tresseder Clark, Christine Blackshear, Cisco and Carola Barreto, Kevin and Kelly Loubert, Jenni Newman Rockoff, Ben Pardieck, Lisa Biondo, Shantel Wells, Michelle Pierce Carter, Jacalyn Beckers Goforth and the members of the "Let's Get Lit" book club, and Gabrielle Jones— my dreams have been kept alive by you and all my other terrific friends whose love and friendship have been the fuel to keep the fires burning. Your support and encouragement with both *Sleep Baby Sleep* and this mystery are so appreciated.

To my outstanding associates at Booz Allen Hamilton: Dennis Gibson, Bob Lietzke, Andy Gilbert, Regina and Jay Irwin, Julie Hong, Nate Aikens, and Christen McCallister and the Booz Allen Book Club members—humbled.

Ramy Vance, my writing coach, and the team at Self-Publishing School— your timely kick in the butt was where and when I needed it the most. Sharon Reaves, my social media expert on Upwork— thank you!

To my editors and the team at The Artful Editor—Denise Logsdon, Jennifer Kepler, Naomi Kim Eagleson, and Jackson Palmer—thank you for your patience and guidance.

Finally and most importantly, I so greatly appreciate the readers and fans who gave *Sleep Baby Sleep*, the first book in the Charlie Taylor series, a try and left a review. Your words of support and encouragement are both heartwarming and humbling. If you enjoyed this story, please leave a review on Amazon. Reviews (good, bad, or indifferent) are not only indispensable for authors to succeed but, more importantly, make me a better writer.

Vr
M. J. Hardy
MJ Hardy, LLC
www.readmjhardy.com
amazon.com/author/mjhardy

Contents

Introduction

This is a scary admission, but as a writer, I feel inept trying to find the right words to capture the essence of the Hawaiian Islands. Despite their incredible beauty, breathtaking sunsets, mountain ranges, waterfalls, and the magnetic pull of the ocean's formidable waves, how do you find words to capture the aloha spirit?

Ground yourself by walking along the beach with your feet immersed in the sand and water. In the evening, when you look up into the sky, the stars seem so close that you feel like you can reach up and touch them. Hawaii is a mystical, therapeutic, and compelling place. Simply, it has to be *experienced*. Hawaii has it all.

But paradise was not immune to evil, either. What follows is a fictional account of events that changed the lives of not only the victims and their families but all the citizens of Oahu. In 1985 and 1986, a series of murders began that would introduce Hawaii's first serial killer.

The first victim, Vicki Gail Purdy, age twenty-five, an army wife, kissed her husband goodbye, left their home in Mililani, and went down to Waikiki to meet up with her friends for a night of fun. Regina Sakamoto, seventeen, a Leilehua High School senior, called her boyfriend from a pay phone to let him know that she had missed the bus and was running late for school. Denise Hughes, twenty-one, wife of a sailor, had an enjoyable dinner the night before on her husband's ship. The next morning, she got ready for work and headed to the bus stop near Leeward Community College, like she always did. Louise J. Medeiros, twenty-five, had just returned in the evening from a family visit to Kauai and was waiting for a bus near the airport—she was anxious to be reunited with her children. Linda Pesce, thirty-six, had left her job at McCaw Telepage around six thirty in the evening. Her car was found on the Makai shoulder of the Nimitz Highway viaduct to the H-1 freeway near the airport.

They were all Caucasian, attractive, and young. They were found with their hands bound behind them, strangled, sexually assaulted, and near a body of water. The Honolulu Police Department (HPD) created a task force after Denise Hughes's murder based on the similarities in the first three cases. Although a suspect was brought in for questioning for the kidnapping and murder of Linda Pesce, he was eventually released.

On November 17, 1975, sixteen-year-old Margaret Hauanio was leaving Leeward Community College. She had just finished class, called her sister to let her know that she was on her way home, and started for the nearby bus stop. She never made it back. Although Margaret has never been associated with the Honolulu Strangler, the circumstances surrounding her case are eerily like those five murders.

In my desire to achieve a certain amount of authenticity and mood, I've used the information made public through various sources that the reader can find at the end of the story. Thus, some of the locations, times, dates, and events surrounding the crimes are as close to the actual events as possible; however, names of victims and family members, persons of interest, characters, and incidents are the product of my imagination or used fictitiously.

To date, these murders remain unsolved.

Ka Pule a ka Haku
(The Lord's Prayer)

E ko makou makua i loko o ka lani,

E ho'ano 'ia kou inoa

E hiki mai kou aupuni;

E malama 'ia kou makemake ma ke honua nei

E like me ia i malama 'ia ma ka lani la.

E ha'awi mai ia makou i keia la, i 'ai na makou no neia la.

E kala mai ho'I ia makou i ka makou lawehala 'ana,

Me makou e kala nei i ka po'e i lawehala i ka makou.

Mai ho'oku'u 'oe ia makou I ka ho'owalewale 'ia mai,

(aka)

E ho'opakele no na'e ia makou i ka 'ino;

No ka mea, nou ke aupuni,

A me ka mana, a me ka ho'onani 'ia a mau loa aku.

'Amene.

Leeward Community College
Monday, November 17, 1975

I stare into the dark abyss.

"Maddie, see ya Wednesday."

The last of my classmates wave goodbye and disappear into the night. The lecture hall, once filled with energy and commotion, is now quiet and abandoned. I push my hair behind my ear and look at my reflection in the window glass. A freckle-faced strawberry blonde looks back at me. Goose bumps pop up all over my skin, and I rub my bare arm, trying to get my blood flowing.

The phone receiver smells like my high school chemistry teacher's bad breath. I look around the foyer at the odd posters about academic and health assistance, campus news, and membership drives. My right leg quivers. I absently twist the phone cord around my finger. *Come on, answer the phone. Shit, the bus is going to get here any minute.*

The only sound is the distant ringing at the other end. I stare at the ceiling. *Why won't anyone answer?*

"Sis, thank God. I thought you'd never answer."

"Maddie?"

"Ya, ya, I just finished the class. I'm on my way."

"Maddie, what time is it?"

"The teacher kept us late."

"Okay, be careful."

"I know, I'll be safe. Hey, I need to get going or I'll miss the bus."

I hang up and run out of the building and into the dark. As I walk-jog to the bus stop, I feel excited about my future. College is nothing like high school, but I am so glad that I finished early and can study something I like and can use to help children with disabilities so they no longer feel ashamed. I know I can help.

It's black out tonight. Where are the damn lights? The bus stop is just a little way ahead. *I need to get there before I miss the bus, or I'm screwed. I'm almost there.*

"Hey, where are you going?"

I turn to see a guy in a car looking at me. "Home—sorry, I can't talk. Gotta go."

"Hey, princess. What's your hurry?"

I shiver. The hair on my neck and arms rise, a sour taste seeps into my mouth, and my stomach gurgles. *Just keep moving and don't pay any attention.* I start to run a little faster. I hear the door slam and footsteps running toward me.

A searing pain goes through my shoulder and down my arm. He spins me around. "Hey, I'm asking you, what's the hurry?" he says calmly.

"Oh, that hurts. What are you doing?" My head is on fire. He has my hair wrapped around his hand and shakes my head back and forth, forcing me down to my knees. "Stop, please, stop!"

"Princess, I asked you nicely what's your hurry. How old are you?" he asks quietly, pulling my face closer to his.

"I'm . . . I'm sixteen. Please don't hurt me."

He twists my hair harder. My eyes well up from the excruciating pain of my hair being pulled out by the roots.

"Princess—so sweet. I've got just the thing for you."

Pam Adair's Story

Blue Water Café, Waikiki
Wednesday, May 29, 1985

"**S**hit." My pager is full of notifications. Paul keeps calling me, but I'm not in the mood to talk. I don't know why I'm so pissed off. I'm out clubbing and wearing my go-to outfit, the one that he drools over, the one that makes everyone notice me. My mind is racing with frustration and anger. Paul is so needy—I wonder if he suspects. I've missed the linkup with the girls. I find everyone in this place so annoying. I thought Hawaii was going to be this magical place, but the longer I stay here, the more I hate it.

"I think you're a diamond in a coal mine. Are you looking for someone? Because I think you found him."

I look up from my pager and turn around to see the owner of those slurred words. Usually, I find these simple come-ons at least humorous, but tonight is different. I look at him with complete disgust. He's in a faded Hawaiian shirt that's a size too small. His gut and shirt are in a wrestling match, with his gut cruising to a comfortable victory. I glance over at his table. His friends are laughing, slapping each other on the back, and giving high fives. I look back at him.

"Please leave me alone. I am not in the mood."

"Ya, ya. Baby, I am just the guy to put you in the mood." He turns to look back at his buddies for reinforcement.

"Cute, really cute. Please go back to your table." I turn back to my drink, using the decorative umbrella to stir the watered-down tequila sunrise in front of me.

"God, you're hot. Love that jumpsuit, but what I wouldn't do to see you out of it. Do you know if it's girlfriend material?" His blurry eyes molest my body.

I stare at my drink as I swirl it. "Please leave now."

"Come on, me and my buddies, we're just looking for fun."

I feel my face flush, and my heart pounds against my chest. I grit my teeth and grip the glass harder.

"How 'bout a dance?"

"How about taking 'no' for an answer?"

"What's the harm? Come on, one little dance," he says, slightly teetering.

"Why don't you go home and get your rocks off with your old lady?"

He grabs me by the wrist and starts to dance in place. "Come on!"

I pull the umbrella from my glass. "Better yet, how about if I stab you in the eye with this? Now get the hell away from me!"

"Hey, I only want one little dance." He tries to pull me closer to him.

I take my drink and throw it in his face.

A roar of laughter comes from his table of buddies. I leave him staring in disbelief with the drink dripping down onto his shirt as I grab my bag and storm out of the bar.

I look up and down the street for a taxi. I see one down the street and flag it. The driver pulls the car up alongside me, and I open the door and look back at the bar to make sure the dumb shit or one of his buddies hasn't followed me.

"Shorebird Hotel." I reach into my purse, pull out my cigarette case, and shake a cigarette loose. After rolling down the window, I strike a match, and my nostrils flare at the smell of sulfur. I draw hard on it and blow a stream of smoke as the taxi pulls away and makes its way through Waikiki. I sit back.

The warm breeze feels good against my face. I watch the tourists, military, and locals walk along the sidewalks looking for something to eat or purchase or just a good time. I blow a stream of smoke out my nose as I look at my pager again—still nothing from the girls or him. *That prick, he promised tonight was going to be our night. Why haven't I heard from him? Adding to my frustration, God, Paul, leave me alone.*

The taxi finally arrives at the Shorebird Hotel parking lot. The driver looks back at me and smiles. I hand him the money and shake my hand as I hold it out.

"Change."

He looks at me with disappointment and mutters while he gives me my money. I couldn't care less what he thinks. God knows how hard we work for our money. I toss the loose change into my purse.

I dig for my keys in my bag as I walk toward the parking garage stairwell. "Gross!" The smell of urine is overpowering. I climb the stairs as quickly as possible, trying not to be overcome by my gag reflex.

I hear the metal door below me slam shut as I continue to make my way up the stairs. I listen to the footsteps on the cement stairs below me. I think it must be a man because it doesn't sound like heels. He's moving faster. The noise of the steps is getting louder.

The heavy metal door to the garage floor squeaks loudly as I push it open. For some reason I begin to walk faster. I smile and shake my head. I'm like one of those typical blondes who get murdered in the opening scene of every horror movie, the audience yelling at the screen, "Run, get the hell out of there! What the hell is she doing?" I hear a long squeak from the door opening behind me. I'm about to look back when I notice a new dent in my rear bumper.

"Damn it! I can't believe this night. Can it get any worse?" My knuckles are white, and I can feel the key ring dig into my palm. I insert the key into the lock. A strange sense comes over me. I hear the footsteps quickly approaching me. I open the door. Fear begins to replace my frustration.

"What do you want?"

"Whoa, whoa, I'm here with good intentions. You seem stressed, and you look like you could use some help. I was just asking a simple question: Can I help you?"

"No, no, I'm all right. Sorry for being a bitch." The pounding in my heart slows down.

"Bad day? Night?" he says, so calmly and quietly. I move closer to hear him.

"A little of both. Second thought, this night has kind of sucked. I was supposed to meet up with some friends, and that didn't happen. I was hoping to run into someone else, and that didn't happen. Then this drunk asshole starts pawing me, and now the dent. Could this night get any worse?"

"Given everything that you've been through, I hope not."

"Thanks. I think that I'd lose it."

"Take a deep breath and exhale. Let all the bad air out," he says jokingly.

I imitate his movements of a lousy yoga instructor.

"Maybe we can salvage the night. How about getting a drink with me?"

"Thanks again, but I'm fine."

"You're right. I know that we just met, and I didn't want to seem like I was coming on to you. I'm sure you get plenty of that."

I nod my head and smile.

"Okay, I understand. My girlfriend got pissed at me, and my ex-wife is driving me up the wall, so I thought that maybe we could commiserate by going and having a drink."

"You too?" I look at him, the dent in the car, and then my pager.

He starts to walk toward a parked car.

"Wait," I say, and he turns and looks at me. "You're right—the night is young, and maybe I can salvage it," I say encouragingly.

"I'd hate to see your car get another dent, so why don't we take mine?"

"Sure. By the way, I'm Pam."

"Princess, your chariot awaits you." He smiles and bows.

"Please, can we do without the cheesy remarks?"

"We can definitely do without them. The car is just over here."

Mililani
Thursday, May 30, 1985

"Nine-one-one, what's your emergency?"

"My wife, she hasn't returned home this morning."

"Sir, your name?"

"What? My wife, she hasn't returned home this morning; this isn't like her."

"Sir, your name?"

"Adair, Paul Adair . . . I'm worried as hell."

"Sir, I need you to calm down. I'm sure she's fine. What's her name? Can you describe her? What was she wearing? When did you last see her?"

"I'm sorry, I'm sorry. I just got home from PT."

"PT?"

"PT, PT, physical training. I'm in the army. We do it every morning."

"Thank you. Her name? Please describe her?"

"Pam, Pam." His chest expanded and collapsed with each breath. "She's about five feet, six inches. I don't have a clue how much she weighs. Blond hair, and she was wearing a yellow jumpsuit."

"Thank you. When was the last time that you saw her?"

"It was about five thirty last night. I'd just gotten home from work, and she was getting ready to go downtown to meet up with some friends and go clubbing."

"How was she going to get there? Was she riding with friends?"

"No, no, she was driving her car."

"What's the color and make?"

"It's a blue Ford Taurus."

"Do you know the license plate number?"

"No, I'll have to go looking for it."

"Okay, transferring you to the police department now."

"Honolulu Police Department."

"Yes, yes, my wife is missing!"

Waikiki
Thursday, May 30, 1985

"We're homicide, for Christ's sake! What are we doing canvassing local establishments for a missing haole?" Detective Dennis Williams asked as he slammed the car door.

Detective Frank Tanaka swallowed his tobacco spit. "Maybe if you hadn't pissed off the captain, we wouldn't get this crappy detail."

"She probably drank too much, and she's either passed out on the beach or shacked up with some guy. We'll get a call in a couple of hours that all is well."

A young woman with a dark tan, wearing a bright orange crocheted bikini and leather sandals, walked past the detectives as they made their way through the hotel lobby toward the restaurant and bar. Williams caught the woman's faint scent of coconut suntan lotion as he spun around for a glance at her bottom. "Like two pigs in a gunnysack—the universe has achieved balance. I have to admit these haoles have some cute butts—not like our wahines that are too flat."

Tanaka shook his head in exasperation. "Can you stay focused? This is what Griffith was talking about. You gotta watch your behavior. Mac, I'm serious. Your obsession with women—it's going to get you into trouble."

"Sorry, bra, ya know me by now. Just can't pass up a nice body, but I'll try. It's hard to pass up tail." He slapped Tanaka on the back.

The restaurant was decorated in teak furniture and pastel wallpaper. "Good morning, my name is Detective Tanaka, and this is my partner, Detective Williams." Tanaka opened his wallet to expose his badge. "We are canvasing the area to see if a young lady meeting this description, about five feet, five inches to five feet, seven inches tall, blond, wearing a bright yellow outfit, was here last night."

"Aloha, Officers. Oh gosh, I'm sorry. I wasn't working last night, so I couldn't tell you if she was here or not. I'm sorry. I hope she's all right." The middle-aged hostess stopped rearranging the silverware.

"Mahalo. If you could ask the night crew when they come in? If they happen to remember something, please contact us." Tanaka handed her his business card.

"This is going to be painful, trying to track her movements last night. Ya know this is a lost cause." Williams sighed.

Tanaka frowned at his partner.

"Where next?" Williams asked.

"Let's check out the hotel parking lots to see if we can locate her car."

"What are we looking for?"

"A Ford Taurus, blue."

The detectives continued their sweep of Waikiki, driving in and out of the hotel parking lots until they spotted a car that matched the description of the missing woman's vehicle.

"Slow down. Over there." Tanaka pointed.

"And it looks like we're not the only ones showing an interest in it, either," Williams added.

The detectives got out of their car and walked toward the man standing next to the vehicle and peering inside it.

"Sir, I'm Detective Tanaka, and this is Detective Williams, with HPD. Can we see some identification, please?"

Startled by the voices behind him, the man jumped and turned around. The two detectives carefully studied him: Caucasian, muscular, in his late twenties, faded blue jeans, Reebok tennis shoes, and a polo shirt.

"What's your interest in this particular car?" Williams asked.

The man's hand trembled as he reached into his back pocket, pulled out a nylon camouflage wallet, and withdrew his ID. He handed the card to Williams.

Tanaka glanced at the ID. "Mr. Adair, have you heard from your wife?"

"No, no. I haven't heard from her since last night when she left our place."

"Mr. Adair, is this your wife's car?" Williams asked as he started walking around it.

"Yes, sir. Have you found her? Have you seen her?"

"No, we haven't seen her yet. How did you know to look here for your wife's car?" Tanaka asked as he handed back the ID card.

"I didn't. I've been searching all over town for it."

"Is this dent new?" Williams asked as he continued his inspection.

"It must be. I've never—" The man's response was interrupted by a message coming over the police radio.

Ke'ehi Lagoon, Honolulu
Thursday, May 30, 1985

Everything about him was old and tired. The mechanic parked his faded red Ford pickup, grabbed his dented lunch pail from the passenger seat, and pushed the lock button down. Dust flew in and outside the cab when he slammed the door. He wished it was Saturday and he had a fishing rod in his hand. *Why are the best days to fish workdays?* He couldn't wait to retire so he could go fishing whenever he wanted. He sighed and shuffled along.

The slight breeze ruffled the remaining strands of his gray hair, which he took as a good sign that today wouldn't be hot and sticky. A perfect spring morning. He smelled the ocean air and looked at the clear blue skies, just wisps of clouds in the air. And then he heard the thunder.

He looked toward the airport as the noise grew louder and watched the jet scream down the runway and lift off. He was always glad to see the planes depart, taking the tiresome tourists with them, but he knew another plane would arrive shortly with a fresh load to invade his island.

He wondered if people in Las Vegas felt the same as he did. Hell, he and his buddies were crazy to go to Vegas any chance they could get. He smiled, remembering the last time they went. He didn't know of anyone from here who didn't vacation in Vegas. The lights, food, women, and slots—now, that was heaven.

His mind wasn't on anything particular. "What's that?" He wasn't sure what drew his attention to the water, maybe the sound of the birds or a flash of something bright that he saw out of the corner of his eye.

He walked over to the edge and looked down the rocky embankment to the water. An object bobbed up and down as the small waves came rolling in. He rubbed his eyes and saw a mannequin dressed in bright yellow, its blond hair floating. He closed his eyes and opened them again, focusing. He slowly backed up in horror, turned, and ran.

Honolulu
Saturday, June 1, 1985

The detectives pulled off Iwilei Road and drove under the overhang to the medical examiner's building and parked in a stall. Tanaka grabbed the soda can from the holder and, with his tongue, pushed a black wad of tobacco into it.

The building smelled of various cleaning solutions and a faint trace of formaldehyde. Tanaka's cowboy boots clacked, and Williams's rubber-soled shoes squeaked on the bright white-and-gray-speckled linoleum floor.

"Aloha, Mac." A small, captivating Filipina nurse in a starched white uniform walked past and smiled.

"Aloha, Joyce," Williams replied, turning to watch her walk down the hallway. "What can I say?"

"How about not saying anything?" Tanaka asked.

"You're just jealous. How long have you been married?"

"What's that have to do with anything?"

"I'm serious. How long? I mean, I love spicy tuna poke bowl, but damn, don't you get tired of eating the same fish day in and day out?"

"My wife and I are happy, and yes, I enjoy the same meal every day and night—there's comfort there. This job brings enough excitement. Besides, I can live my life vicariously through you and not have to worry about catching any diseases." Tanaka pulled open a heavy glass door with *Examination Room* printed on it in gold letters.

"Dad, I wear a trench coat every time. Aloha, Doc," Williams said with a smile as they stepped inside.

"Is it raining?" the doctor asked, looking at the detectives' clothing.

"Hell no, it's another gorgeous day out there. I've just been telling my partner that I take the necessary precautions when engaging with the fairer sex," Williams said proudly.

"You better—there are some diseases and viruses now that don't respond to our antibiotics or protocols. While you're at it, please stay away from my nurses." The doctor pointed a scalpel at Williams's crotch.

"Doctor, what can you tell us about the victim?" Tanaka asked.

"Female; age twenty-five; five feet, six inches tall; one hundred forty-three pounds; excellent health."

"Except she's dead," Williams quipped.

"Yes. Her death was due to asphyxiation. You can see the bruising on her neck for yourself." The doctor pointed at the various dark brown, blue, and gray marks on the victim's neck.

"Sexually assaulted?" Tanaka asked.

"There's evidence of being physically and sexually assaulted, but the water played havoc on the body, so it's hard for me to determine the degree. She was partially clothed but missing her shoes, and some personal effects were found," the medical examiner said, pointing to a bag on the counter. Tanaka walked over and picked it up. He examined the yellow jumpsuit for a moment and then passed the bag to his partner.

"There are deep lacerations around her wrists and ankles. Her hands were bound behind her back." The doctor pointed to another bag on the counter.

Williams picked it up and examined it. "Nylon rope certainly does the trick," he said as he handed the bag to Tanaka.

Tanaka examined the contents. "It looks like standard-issue army OD 550 cord or parachute cord."

"OD?" the medical examiner asked.

"Olive drab," Tanaka said.

"I'd speculate that she died between ten and twelve last night and her body was dumped shortly afterward."

"Can I assume this is our missing girl?" Williams asked.

"We are waiting for a positive ID from the husband, but yes, we believe she was the missing person. Pam Adair, twenty-five, Kuahelani Avenue, Mililani."

"We've already met him," Tanaka said, staring at the body.

"Who?" the doctor asked, continuing his examination.

"The husband." Tanaka picked up the plastic bag containing the nylon rope again. "We have plenty of military around here, so not a stretch for them to get their hands on this, but how easy is it for locals to get it?"

"Shouldn't be a problem at all. I use it all the time," Williams replied.

Honolulu
Saturday, June 1, 1985

"I never thought you were capable of an actual date, with dinner at a nice restaurant to boot." Joyce smiled, slowly unzipping her black dress and letting it slide down her body to catch on her curves before it dropped to the floor.

"Beautiful, I'd never pass up an opportunity to spend an evening with you," Williams said as he lay naked on his bed, rubbing his belly.

"Usually we never go anywhere. All we ever do is . . . you know, this," Joyce said. She started to take off her black, spiked heels.

"Stop—what are you doing? Leave them on, and the rest of it too. You look hot in that whole outfit," Williams said, sitting up.

Joyce flipped her luscious black hair with her hand, slowly turned around, and showed off her black lingerie. Her hands slowly caressed her body, framing the lace bralette with spaghetti straps accented with O-rings and a high-waisted, strappy garter belt with more O-ring accents, matching panties, and thigh-highs.

"No tying me up this time," she said. "It hurts, and it's not much fun. Last time I had bruises on my wrists and ankles, and it was hard to explain to my family and coworkers how they got there."

Williams jumped out of bed, grabbed her from behind, and wrapped an arm around her waist. "You know I go crazy when I don't get what I need, and you know I'm going to get it. Somehow, some way."

He placed his other hand around her throat and gently squeezed. He threw her down on the bed and pulled her hips toward his groin, pressing his hand against the back of her neck. "Beautiful, you've been a bad girl." He slapped her butt hard.

"Mac, you're crazy." She giggled.

Waikiki
Friday, September 13, 1985

He could feel tiny streams of sweat run down the back of his neck and begin to pool at his lower back. He ran his finger between the collar of his starched white shirt and his neck. He scanned the audience in front of him and thought, *How fitting—Friday the thirteenth. They don't know what horrors await them. It's only a matter of time. They won't have the resources or experience to deal with this type of killer. Beautiful weather has a way of attracting the lunatic fringe.*

He had seen the worst of humankind, driven by rage, hate, jealousy, and sexual desires. He subtly adjusted his tie, trying to gain some relief from the heat even in the air-conditioned room. *So this is a paradise, and even paradise can't escape evil.*

Leo Griffith, the Honolulu police chief, tried to introduce the guest speaker while competing with the usual banter, laughter, and clinking of glasses. The Prince Kuhio Hotel ballroom was filled with over two hundred attendees for the Hawaii Hotel Security

Association luncheon. "Now it's my pleasure to introduce you to the director of the FBI's Behavioral Science Unit."

The man stood while the polite applause continued. He waited at the podium, adjusted the microphone, and breathed out slightly before he spoke. "It's only a matter of time before Hawaii has its first serial killer—there's a price to be paid for living in paradise. I've been part of investigations of the Atlanta Child Killer, Hillside Stranglers, and now the Green River Killer. These killers, who we refer to as 'serial killers,' are attracted to pleasant weather and an easygoing lifestyle, and from everything I have witnessed and experienced," he said, pointing to his sweat-stained collar, which drew light laughter from the audience, "you have plenty of it around here."

After the formal presentation and question-and-answer period, the ballroom emptied quickly, with a few exceptions.

Tanaka looked over his shoulder at his name being called out. "Rice, Mac, come on over here. I'd like you to meet Special Agent Ron Bowen," Chief Griffith said, waving the two detectives in his direction. Tanaka and Williams broke away from their conversation with a group of colleagues to meet the FBI agent.

"Special Agent Ron Bowen, I'd like you to meet Detectives Frank Tanaka and Dennis Williams. They are our most experienced homicide detectives. I realize they aren't much to look at, but they're competent."

"Ron, Frank Tanaka, and this is my partner, Detective Williams. It's a pleasure to meet you." Tanaka gripped Bowen's large hand and shook it.

Bowen remarked to Griffith, "I thought I heard you address them by different names."

Tanaka smiled. "In recognition of my Japanese and Williams's European heritage. I'm the scoop of white rice, and Williams, the creamy macaroni salad, side by side, found on the popular island luncheon plates served in almost all the restaurants around here. Thus, I'm Rice and he's Mac.

"It's our running joke in HPD that when Tanaka and Williams arrest someone, the perp got served the lunch special. However, joking aside, they're respected and capable detectives." Griffith placed his hands on his hips and smiled at his detectives.

"Do you have a preference?" Bowen looked at Tanaka and Williams.

"We answer to just about anything, especially when the chief is calling for us," Williams responded, smiling.

"Tanaka and Williams work best," Tanaka said. "Thanks for making the trip all the way out here. We enjoyed the lecture, but it started me thinking. How likely do you really think we are to have a serial killer on the island? I'm not afraid to say it—we're not equipped to handle something like the Atlanta Child Killer or the Green River Killer."

"Agent Bowen, I'll be honest," Griffith said. "Frank is correct—we're not equipped for anything like these crimes. Ya, we see our fair share of murders, but most times, they're stabbings and the occasional shootings associated with drugs, robberies, or family disputes. But we are woefully unprepared for this type of killer."

"Love, hate, jealousy, or money is what we do best on the island," Williams said.

"Don't feel bad—you're not alone. Most local law enforcement isn't prepared for this type of killer. Sorry to say, but I think the likelihood is certain—it's a numbers game. The odds of you eventually having a serial killer on the island are very great. I get your remoteness, but why the fiftieth state would be exempt from the same experience that all forty-nine other states have is hard for me to comprehend. You have a large transient population with the military and tourists." Bowen looked at the three officers. "Trust me, I pray to God that it doesn't happen, but those prayers seem to have gone unanswered lately. Matter of fact, we've been running into more cases associated with serial killers."

"Chief, what do you think?" Tanaka asked.

"You're right, we don't have the experience to handle a situation like this, so we are going to have to get creative. Special Agent Bowen, any suggestions?" Griffith looked apprehensive.

"Please call me Ron. We could set up a series of trainings with local agents here. Additionally, I would recommend that when it happens, you consider using all the available resources that you have on the island, and do not hesitate to use us. I understand how sensitive it can get between feds and locals, but this will be your show. We won't take it over, but we can provide some additional resources."

Everyone nodded in agreement.

"I like to avoid the tourist traps, so where can I go to get an authentic meal and a drink?"

Williams was about to respond when Tanaka spoke up. "I'll pick you up in front of your hotel at six thirty, if that works for you. You don't want to go anywhere with my partner. No telling what dive he'd take you to."

"Hey, he asked for authentic, and all my hangouts are nothing but the most authentic," Williams said, feigning hurt feelings.

"The man is not here to get food poisoning or in a fight with some hotheaded local. Frank will take good care of you," Griffith said.

Ichika Satu's Story

Honolulu
Wednesday, November 27, 1985

*H*awaii is supposed to be warm. I slip on my black jeans and a black sweatshirt. I whisper to my jet-lagged, groggy husband, "Otto, honey, I be right back." I grab some money out of his wallet and put it in my pants pocket. I run the shopping list through my mind: *diapers, milk, and something to eat.* I tenderly kiss my baby. I look at the two of them sleeping on the bed as I close the door and move into the hallway. *Our little family, so cute.*

I take the elevator down to the tiny, shabby, but brightly lit lobby. I jump in at the end of the line of customers waiting to check in. I finally make it to the counter, and there's a large lady standing behind it. She's like a sumo wrestler—her frizzy black hair pulled back in a bun, a broad face and large nose, great hands, and enormous girth. "Excuse me; I need some milk, diapers, and things for my baby. Store? Is a store nearby?"

I'm embarrassed about my broken English. She gives me an unpleasant look and then smiles wide.

"You're a tiny thing. Ya, ya, go out the front door. You see that main road? That's Nimitz. Cross over the main road, and you'll see a road called Camp Caitlin. Follow the dirt road, and you'll see a small store there. Hey, what's its name? Keiko, what's the name of that mini-mart?"

"Halsey Terrace."

"Ya, ya, follow the dirt road until you see the store."

"Thank you." I bow out of habit, only understanding a little bit of what she said.

I wait at the busy intersection, watching the cars zip back and forth. The light changes, and I dash across the big road before the light changes again. So far to get across.

I didn't understand her directions and can barely read the English signs, so I look for the dirt road and find it. This isn't my first time in the United States, but still, we just arrived on the island, and everything is so foreign to me. I'm scared. The States are so big compared to Japan. I look at the dark sky, the stars, and the dense bushes along both sides of the road. I see the light just ahead; I hope it's the store.

I open the door, and the little bell tinkles above me. A couple of customers and the clerk all turn toward me. I blush with embarrassment. They all return to what they're doing. I walk up and down the aisles. There's a continuous tinkling of the bell as customers come and go. I pick out a small package of diapers, some juice, and doughnuts.

I continue to browse. The packaging is dull—boring. There is nothing healthy to eat here. At least in our convenience stores, you can find good, healthy food. *No wonder all Americans are so fat compared to thin Japanese.*

"Arigato." I stuff my change into my pocket and collect the plastic bags. The bell tinkles above my head to announce my departure. I walk along the dirt road, and my eyes try to adjust to the darkness. The lights from the car behind me make my shadow appear so much taller. The bushes along the side of the road look like little monsters ready to grab me.

I run, the plastic bags banging against my thighs. I need to get back to my family. I feel the hands grab me from behind. *My family!*

Wahiawa
Monday, December 16, 1985

The homicide detective out of the Wahiawa station arrived at the stuccoed front building at 50 Wilikina Drive just off Kam Highway next to Wilson Bridge—the gateway to downtown Wahiawa. He got out of his car, stretched, and looked across the road at the fence with the barbed wire on top. On the other side was the military housing of Wheeler Air Force Base.

A patrolman walked up and greeted the detective.

"Officer, what do we have?" the detective asked.

"Sir, two women, Catherine Daniel, fifty-six, owner, and Christine Flynn, thirty-six, an employee, found stabbed multiple times to death. It appears to be a robbery. Signs of a slight struggle, but for the most part, everything is intact. Both women were clothed, last night's cash receipts missing; however, there was an envelope containing cash on the floor. The store had been locked, but some of the other employees broke in to check on one of the employees."

"The name Daniel sounds familiar."

The officer flipped through his notepad. "She was arrested last year and put on a year's probation for selling pornography."

"That's right, but there's something else too." The detective rubbed his temples. "Think, think . . . I know—that military spouse who was murdered and her body dumped in the lagoon. If my memory serves me right, she worked here too."

"Sorry, I don't remember that one. This place must have some bad juju." The patrolman looked back at the storefront and then down at his notes. "The building contains an adult bookstore, video club, and family amusement center. Fun for the whole family."

The detective raised his eyes to the patrolman. "Continue, please."

"The bodies were discovered about two thirty when an employee from the other video store just across the way came over here to see one of the women. When she found the door locked, she went to the bookstore to ask if her friend was there. They told her that she was next door in the video store. She complained that the door was locked, which everyone found strange since most days it's open at nine. So they went back to the video store and eventually forced the door open and found the victims."

"Who saw them last, and what time was it?"

"One of the store employees said they saw Flynn about one thirty."

"Did anyone hear or see anything?"

"Not a damn thing. I guess that stuff on the walls makes them virtually soundproof." The officer pointed to the stucco.

The homicide detective looked down at the older woman's body as the medical technician inspected it.

"We'll know more after the official examination, but it appears she was stabbed in the back and it punctured her heart," the technician said. Pointing to Flynn's body, he merely said, "Stabbed in the throat."

"Thank you. Please let me know when you're going to conduct an autopsy."

"Will do," the technician said and went back to his work.

The detective looked around at the technicians going about their business, dusting for fingerprints, measuring, and taking photos. He shook his head, knowing that it was going to be a challenging case. Adult video stores were notorious for disgruntled employees and transient clientele.

"What's back there?" the detective asked.

"I'll show you," the patrol officer answered as he pulled back the curtain.

"I guess she wasn't too concerned about her probation," the detective muttered as he looked at all the shelves containing pornographic videos.

He walked out of the store and returned to his car. As he unlocked it, his eyes swept the area. He looked for inspiration and tried to imagine which way the perpetrator had come and gone.

He looked at Wilson Bridge, across Kam Highway, and saw the familiar homeless man standing on the traffic island near the light, panhandling the cars waiting to either turn left on Wilikina Drive toward Schofield Barracks or North Shore or go straight on Kam into Wahiawa. His eyes swept over Wheeler Air Force Base and then down Kunia Road. He opened the car door and jumped in. "It's probably a soldier—what a mess."

Rebecca Saito's Story

Waipahu
Tuesday, January 14, 1986

"Mom, I've gotta go." I push open the screen door and run down the street as fast as I can. In the distance, I can see the bus just pull into the stop. "Wait, wait, stop, stop!" I wave my hands, jumping up and down. "Wait, please. Please, wait." The bus begins to pull slowly away. "Please, please . . ." I hold my hand against my chest, my heart pounding, and try to settle down. I take a few deep breaths.

I arrive at the empty bus stop and watch the traffic speed along Farrington Highway. I begin to feel desperate, not about being late for school, but about making Tony upset. My stepdad hates the way he treats me and says that I could do better, but he doesn't understand how hard it's to be a haole. Before Tony showed an interest in me, my life was hell.

I look around and see a phone booth at the edge of the parking area. I push open the door. "Disgusting," I mutter. The ground is covered with cigarette butts. I dig out loose change from my pants pockets and purse, lift the receiver of the pay phone, and start pumping coins into the appropriate slots. *I can't believe I missed my bus again! God, Tony is going to be furious with me. I'll try him at home. Please be there.* The phone stops ringing as I hear a click on the other end.

"Ya, ya."

"Hi, baby. I'm sorry, but I missed my bus, and I'm going to be late for school."

"You sure there's no other reason?"

"What do you mean?"

"You know what I mean. You sure you weren't with anyone else?"

"No, no, I'd never do that. You know that I love you."

"You'd better not. I'd teach you a lesson you'd never forget if I ever thought that you were fooling around on me."

"Honey, you got to believe me. I'd never do anything like that. You got to believe me. I'll give you some sugar later to prove it to you."

"Ya, your sugar isn't that sweet. There's a lot of hotter girls that I could be with than you, and they beg me to do it with them all the time. Maybe I should do them."

"Honey, please don't say that. You know how much you mean to me. Please, I'll give you whatever you want."

"Ya, ya, get your ass up here quickly before I decide to change my mind."

"Sure, honey. I'll get there as quickly as I can."

"Just get your ass up here."

The phone goes dead. I hang up and push open the door to the booth. I wipe the tears from my eyes. I feel so sad as I run to the bus stop. *Why does everyone hate me?*

I'm chewing on my lower lip when I hear someone yelling.

"Hey! Where are you heading to?"

I look around to see who the guy's yelling at, figuring it isn't me.

"No, you."

I point to myself.

"Ya, you. Where are you going?"

"Going to school."

"Where?" he asks as he opens the front passenger door.

"It's not around here."

"Just tell me where."

"Leilehua High School."

"Where?"

"Leilehua, it's in Wahiawa."

"You're in luck. I'm heading that way. Jump in!"

"I don't want to be a bother."

"Princess, your chariot awaits you. Come on, jump in."

"Okay." I run to his car, thinking to myself, *I won't be late for school anymore.* I smile as I get in. "Thank you—this means a lot to me."

"It's my pleasure, all my pleasure." He smiles.

I settle back into my seat and pull on the seat belt. Disaster avoided.

Ke'ehi Lagoon
Wednesday, January 15, 1986

Frustrated, the Japanese fisherman checked on his five poles with their lines lying flat in front of him. He dropped the word search magazine and stubby, fat pencil to the ground and stretched his arms above his head. He shook his empty thermos to see if there was anything left. He sighed, tilted his head backward, and pulled his stained white bucket hat over his eyes. Retirement had looked so promising—no more work, getting away from the wife and noisy grandkids. Was it too much to ask? He longed for peace.

He had been at this since early morning and not a damn hit. What had seemed like a great idea had turned into a colossal waste of time. He looked at his watch; it was almost ten. He decided to call it a day and pushed himself out of his aluminum folding chair. He picked up the first rod and reeled in the line. He completed the task and laid it down by his chair.

He shuffled back to the second rod and started the process again. He saw her floating among the other lines. "Hey, you all right?" he yelled. She didn't respond. He yelled again, "Hey, miss! Miss!" His dentures shifted as his mouth gaped wide open.

Honolulu
Thursday, January 16, 1986

"What's wrong?" Charlie asked. Annie had walked into the family room, sat in front of the fire, and started sobbing.

"Garrett somehow found out about us. He's threatened to take the kids away from me unless I move back in with him and stop seeing you."

"That asshole. How did he find out?"

"I guess he overheard the kids talking about us and thought something didn't seem right, so he hired a PI to follow us. He's got pictures."

"So what? He's got pictures. What can he do? He's a jackass husband and an unfit father."

"I talked to a lawyer, and he can do a lot. Most times, the court will take kids away from a lesbian, even though the guy is a jackass husband and an unfit father. The court seems to think that a jackass husband and unfit father who spends all his time and money on hookers is a better role model than a hardworking and dedicated lesbian mother."

Charlie sat down and put her arm around Annie. "We'll work something out. I'm not giving up on the first loving relationship that I've ever had."

"I love you so much—I don't want to lose you, either, but Charlie, I'm not like you. I'm not strong. I can't risk losing my kids. I'm sorry, I can't lose my kids . . . I just can't." Annie laid her head on Charlie's shoulder and continued to cry.

Charlie's head suddenly snapped forward. Her subconscious registered the voice over the intercom system. "Stewardesses, prepare for landing." She tried to wake herself up, but every part of her body voiced a complaint.

Her neck was sore, and her mouth felt like it was stuffed with vulgar-tasting cotton balls. Her eyes were dry and painful. The rest of her body didn't want to move. The red-eye from Detroit to Honolulu had seemed like a good idea at the time. Charlie massaged her temples and the back of her neck. She took a sip of water from the plastic cup and swirled it around in her mouth.

The stewardess walked past and corrected the passengers on their landing violations. Charlie watched the passengers adjust their seats and store their items under the seat in front of them. Some opened the window shades to get a glimpse of the ocean. She looked at her carry-ons: a large purse stuffed with a sweater, a brightly decorated bag containing a gift for her auntie, and a plain wooden box.

She slid open the window shade, and the sun blasted in. Her eyes shut tight as a reflex. It was Charlie's first real vacation in a long time, and she was looking forward to it. She needed this. She wanted this. She was exhausted from the emotional drain. Work had provided no relief, either. The novelty of the first snow of the season had worn off a month ago. Now it was just dark, ugly, and freezing, the snow along the roads black from the exhaust, the potholes that were sprouting up all over jarring her every time she hit one, leaving her wondering about the damage to her car.

She had leaped at the opportunity when Auntie Barbara had suggested a visit. She was excited to see her—her mom's lifelong best friend. Charlie hadn't been back to the island for a long time, and she missed it. She remembered the Christmas and summer vacations spent there with family when she was growing up.

She looked forward to shedding all her heavy winter clothes, throwing on a bikini—*better make that a one-piece, damn cellulite*—and heading to the Royal Hawaiian, the beautiful pink icon of Waikiki, to sit on the beach. Getting sunburned sounded like a brilliant idea.

The plane began its descent. Charlie yawned to try to reduce the pressure on her eardrums. She looked over the landscape: rugged green mountains and lush valleys with roads carved into them. The aircraft flew along the windward side of the island. The water was an incredible blue green, the crests of the waves white as they rolled toward the shore. *Sure beats Michigan this time of year.*

She could make out a few surfers waiting for just the right wave. She thought about getting on a surfboard again. How long would it take her to get the feel? She knew how strenuous surfing could be on the upper body. She massaged her arm and shoulder. Ten years later, she could still feel the pain. She looked at the scars on her arm from the shotgun pellets.

She could see the military planes in the hangars at Hickam Air Force Base and thought about her dad serving there during WWII. How frightening it must have seemed with the Japanese dive-bombers dropping their ordnance, the machine-gun bullets zipping through the air, indiscriminately tearing everything apart. Her father had once taken her on a tour of Hickam. She had seen firsthand the large bullet holes that remained in some of the buildings.

Charlie tried to imagine what it must have been like that quiet December Sunday morning. Everyone still sleeping and recovering from a night of partying in Waikiki, enjoying a delicious breakfast on the lanais of their plantation-style homes, or going for an early morning swim when the Japanese bombers dropped from the cover of the clouds, coming through Kolekole Pass and using the terrain for navigation. They dropped their bombs on Wheeler Air Force Base, then pushed their way toward the ultimate prizes: Hickam Air Force Base and Pearl Harbor.

She thought about her dad leaving her mother to get back to the base. What was he thinking, feeling, when he arrived? Chaos all around him, friends either dead or writhing in pain, heat from the fires, the smell of burning fuel, and the large black plumes of smoke coming from Pearl. He would have watched the last few bombers climb into the sky and disappear into the clouds as quickly as they had appeared.

She asked her dad about his war experience, but he would never share with her. He always remained silent. It was only when he'd had one too many that he might let a little out, but those were the rarest of occasions. He had been one of the lucky ones.

Charlie wondered how he'd felt when he returned to Hawaii after the war, what her dad and mom might have said to each other the first time they met again. Was he torn, conflicted, because he'd survived? She was named for one of his door gunners. Maybe it was his way of paying tribute to him and others. She was the son he'd never had. He and her mother were such an odd couple, so opposite in so many ways, but they had made it work. Despite the arguments and disagreements she had with them especially her mother, she loved them.

The opening of the landing gear brought Charlie back to the present. The plane's speed seemed to increase as they approached the landing strip. The passengers bounced slightly in their seats as the aircraft touched the ground. Charlie pushed back as the pilot applied the reverse thrust. The plane eventually slowed down and begun its taxi to the gate.

She felt slightly annoyed by the overly enthusiastic travelers who got out of their seats too soon to retrieve items from the overhead compartments, immediately followed by the pilot's announcement for everyone to remain seated until the plane had stopped at the gate and the seat belt light had been turned off.

When the plane stopped at the gate and the stewardess opened the door, Charlie was hit with the warm, humid air and started to sweat. She felt like a wilted flower and smelled like a wet dog. She looked forward to stripping out of her clothes and taking a shower. The passengers in front of her started to stand, retrieve their belongings, and make their way up the aisle. Charlie picked up her purse and bag carefully, trying not to disturb the contents.

A rotund man with a loud Hawaiian shirt, wrinkled shorts, white socks, and sandals stopped to let Charlie into the aisle. Like the passengers in front of her, she managed her packages and began shuffling up the aisle, gaining speed the closer she got to the door. There was the requisite "Aloha" and "Thank you for flying" from the crew as she stepped through the door and onto the ramp.

She walked into the waiting area and looked around. She could see the joy on the faces of family members and friends as they hugged, kissed, and laughed. The passengers had beautiful pink, white, and purple leis placed around their necks, followed by more hugs and laughter. Other passengers crowded around a young woman dressed in a vibrant purple dress, holding up a sign that read *Hawaiian Islands Tours*.

Charlie spotted Auntie Barbara standing off to the side. Almost sixty, she looked stylish and youthful. She was tanned and fashionably dressed in a pink floral Hawaiian dress. She smiled, shifted her orchid leis into the other hand, then waved warmly and called out to Charlie.

Charlie smiled, walked up to Barbara, and gave her a warm hug and kissed her cheek. She could smell the fragrance of the leis mingling with the lilac of Barbara's perfume. Barbara wrapped her arms around Charlie and held her tight. "Oh, my baby is here, finally." Charlie felt a glow inside. "Oh my goodness, it's so good to have you here. I have missed you so much," Barbara said, taking Charlie's face in her hands.

"Auntie, I've missed you too. It's been way too long. I'm sorry I didn't come back sooner."

"Never mind all of that. It's great to have you here, and we have so much to catch up on."

"You look sensational," Charlie said admiringly.

Barbara stepped back and looked at Charlie. "Oh my God! You look bad, really bad. You were such a beautiful girl, even in your awkward teenage years. What have you been doing to yourself?"

Charlie didn't flinch at the honest and brutal observation. She had grown used to older Korean women pointing out her flaws. She knew Barbara wasn't mean-spirited, just expressing a form of tough love. She bowed slightly as Barbara placed the leis around her neck.

"I know, I know, I see it every morning when I look in the mirror. I look like an extra from *Night of the Living Dead*."

"Well, I'll take care of that! Some sunshine, rest, and good food will have you back to your old self in no time."

"I can't wait. I've been dying especially for some of your delicious Spam musubi and fresh pineapple."

Her auntie scoffed. "Spam musubi? That's just snack food. You need real food inside you. Let's go get your bags." She put her arm through Charlie's.

"I was so sorry to hear about Uncle Bennie. I still can't believe that he's gone."

"It was tragic—the poor man never had a chance. He survived WWII, but that pancreatic cancer just ripped through him. One day he was complaining about his back, and within weeks he was gone."

"I loved him. He was always so much fun to be around. His laughter, his bad jokes, and playing his ukulele. He was special."

"Oh, honey, Uncle Bennie loved you too. You were always like a daughter to him, to us. The house doesn't seem the same without him."

Charlie and Barbara walked arm in arm along the outside walkway. On the right, planes were parked at the gates with carts zipping among them, loading and unloading baggage—all the flurry of activity that it takes to run an airport. On the left were parking lots, palm trees, and Highway 1. They followed the signs and the escalator down to the baggage claim.

Charlie recognized some of her fellow passengers circled around the conveyor, anxious to get started on their vacation. By evening, their pasty faces and bright white legs would all be varying shades of red from overdoing it on their first day.

After she grabbed her bags, Charlie made small talk with Barbara as they walked to the parking structure. When they found Barbara's old Honda, Charlie lifted the bags into the trunk and jumped in. They left the airport and followed H-1 until they exited the highway and began to climb the hills to Barbara's house in Manoa.

It was a quiet residential area near the University of Hawaii, tucked away in a valley known for its lushness and rainbows. Charlie started to feel at ease. The island always had a restorative effect on her.

"What is it exactly that you do? The way your mother described it, it sounds just dreadful."

Charlie shook her head in frustration, sighed, and looked out the window. "My mom hasn't ever really understood anything I did. You know me, I'm an eclectic personality, always traveling to the beat of a different drummer."

"Aigoo, how old are you? You don't know by now that she only wants the very best for you? She wants to see you happy. She doesn't understand why you can't be more like your sister, Susan—a doctor, married, with children. You've always been so brilliant in everything that you did. She had such high hopes for you."

"Everyone seems to conveniently forget that I'm a doctor too. But what she means is for me to be more typical and reasonable."

"I think she means a more traditional doctor like a surgeon, pediatrician, or general practitioner. Wandering around in another person's head, it doesn't sit well."

"I'm well regarded in my profession. I choose not to have the whole husband, kids, nuclear family." Charlie tried to choose her words carefully and not snap at her auntie. She turned and looked out the passenger window to take in the landscape.

"Tradition, a family—is that so bad? You're my daughter too, and all we want is the very best for you, to see you happy."

Charlie turned back to Barbara. "Everyone seems so consumed with my happiness—a little acceptance and understanding would go a long way." She looked out the window again. "I'm sorry for being snippy. I'm just tired."

Barbara reached over and squeezed Charlie's shoulder. "Honey, it's understandable. You've been under enough pressure without me adding to it. You haven't been here more than five minutes, and I've already screwed up." She glanced at Charlie.

"Kamsahamnida, auntie. I know everyone means well. It's hard to explain. It's something deep inside of me that drives me. Auntie, we're so similar. You're a college professor—a professional woman. You've got a great life. In fact, I'm very much like you, with the only difference being that I haven't met the right person yet. Did people ask you why you didn't have kids? Did they pressure you?"

"In the beginning we got asked about it all the time. We talked about it. We both wanted kids, but it never happened. One of life's unexplained mysteries." Barbara shrugged as she flipped on her turn signal and made a left.

"I'm sorry if I overstepped my boundaries."

"Don't give it a second thought. I started this whole discussion in the first place."

Charlie stared straight ahead and let her mind wander.

"Roll over," Annie demanded. Charlie obeyed. Annie sat up, straddled Charlie's naked butt, and began to massage her shoulders.

"Oh my God, that feels so good. I'm sorry, I'm so sorry. Really. You're the one that's been so sick lately. I'm the one that should be providing you with the tender loving care."

"Nonsense, you did plenty for me. You're always doing things for the kids and me. It wasn't your fault that I got so sick. My damn husband is the one that gave me this bug. God, it was terrible—I thought I was going to die. I couldn't keep anything down. It was either coming right back up or right through and out the other end. It seemed like it would never end." Annie bent over, her breasts resting on Charlie's back, and nibbled on her ear. *"This is the best medicine possible,"* she whispered. *"I've missed this—just spending time together."*

"Speaking of your charming husband, where is he? How did you get out of the house?"

Annie continued to knead Charlie's shoulders. *"He's visiting his girlfriends."*

"Girlfriends?"

"When Garrett tells me he's going to visit his folks in Detroit, that's code for meeting with a few of his favorite prostitutes."

"What an ass!"

"You're telling me?" Annie moved off Charlie, knelt beside her, and drew small circles on Charlie's firm buttocks with the tip of her tongue. Her teeth just scraped Charlie's skin as she bit her gently. *"Besides, it's an opportunity for us to be together, and I've wanted this for so long."*

Charlie rolled onto her back and pulled Annie toward her. Their mouths parted in a passionate kiss.

"Charlie?"

She smiled. "Sorry, jet leg. It's a long flight, and I've been up all night."

"If you don't mind, please explain to me this terrible thing that you do."

"It's not terrible and not so awfully different from your work. You look for clues among broken plates and vases and try to determine how a culture lived. I work for the Michigan State Police and help them solve crimes. I look at the victim's behavior, and I look at what was done to them by the perpetrators. I make an assessment of what type of person that killer might be, and with that, along with outstanding police work, we're able to apprehend the perpetrators. I try to make the detectives' jobs easier by identifying or eliminating potential suspects."

"That sounds gruesome," Barbara said. "I know you're doing important work, and I'm sure that the victims' families are incredibly appreciative of all the things that you've done for them."

"They are, but it only alleviates a small part of the pain and anguish they feel. At best, it may give them some closure."

"Very thoughtful. Speaking of which, if you admire my life and career so much, while you're here, why don't you think about staying? I have this idea, and I think it's brilliant, if I may say so: You could stay here! Why not? Maybe as a professor at the university in the psychology department, become a consultant to the HPD or some other police organization that needs you. You'd be just like—"

"My dear Dr. Yamamoto, it's elementary. I already have a job. I love being with you, and the island has always felt like home, but it's ten hours of flying to get anywhere. Besides, I don't feel like starting all over again. University politics and competing for tenure just don't sound appealing."

"Your job is burning you out. You look like you've lost a lot of weight, and you just don't look like your old self. Are you sick?" Barbara glanced at Charlie again and then turned her eyes back to the road.

"I don't know," Charlie said, shaking her head. "Granted, I see the very worst in humanity, but I also see some of the best. It's hard to leave or let go of something when it's been such a big part of my life. I know Mom is right in some regards, that I'm not normal, because there's a part of me that finds the work exhilarating."

Barbara nodded in agreement. "Okay, how about a compromise? You could request a sabbatical from the state troopers and stay here with me. Give the island a try. If you like working for the university, then you can submit your resignation. Who knows, you might meet some fabulous military or island guy."

"What is it with you Korean women? You and Mom can never take no for an answer, especially when it's from a daughter. Most importantly, there is no one as fabulous as Uncle Bennie or my dad, so the odds of meeting someone fabulous just dropped to zero." Charlie smiled and took in the sights. It had been too long since she'd seen sunshine and the ocean.

"You're right, honey. Your uncle and dad are the best, but I'd really appreciate it if you would consider my offer. Stay with me and work here. It'd mean so much to me."

"It sounds fabulous and a generous offer, but I've just begun my vacation, so let's not dwell on what I should do or don't do or need to do. Auntie, this is my vacation. I don't want to think about anything. I want to spend it with you, and I can't imagine meeting anybody more special than you."

"Thank you, honey, but please consider it?"

"Auntie, I'll consider it."

"Really, will you consider it? Really?"

"No promises."

"Great. Well, we're here." The Honda made its way up the driveway to Barbara's quaint little home.

Charlie grabbed her luggage out of the trunk, careful to keep the bag with the gift and box safe. Before following Barbara in, she paused for a moment and looked at the familiar house. She thought back to running out the screened front door with Susan and letting it bang behind them, racing to the car to get shaved ice or go to the beach. She smiled as she came back to the present and walked up the sidewalk.

"Something the matter, honey?"

Charlie shook her head. "Reliving wonderful old memories."

Barbara opened the front door and was greeted immediately by two miniature, long-haired, dappled dachshunds barking and scurrying around them. "Salt, Pepper, get down and out of the way. The female is Salt, and her brother is Pepper."

Charlie bent over and held out her fist so the dogs could sniff her. She patted them and rubbed their sides, much to their delight. "They're adorable."

"They're a nuisance, but good companions. After Bennie died, they've provided so much relief. Honey, your room is just over here on the right side, like always."

Charlie walked into her room, and a bright greenish-brown gecko scurried across the wall and out a small crack between the jalousies. The slow-spinning bamboo ceiling fan produced a faint breeze. The wallpaper with bright green flowers against a white background, the brass bed frame—it hadn't changed one bit. *I love this room.* Salt and Pepper, nails scratching the tile floor, ran excitedly in and out, trying to decide where they wanted to be.

"I'm sure you could use a shower. I'll make us breakfast while you freshen up."

"Auntie, a shower and breakfast sound great. I'm famished—airplane food is not that good. And I can't wait to get out of these gross clothes. They're soggy and smelly. Wait, I have something for you." Charlie pulled out a brightly wrapped gift.

"Honey, thank you. You shouldn't have," Barbara said as she unwrapped the package and opened it. "It's beautiful, exquisite, and way too expensive." She held up a sapphire Calvin Klein silk blouse. "I know that I should visit you more, but I can't stand being held captive on the planes for so long. I get claustrophobic after a while. California is about as far as I'm willing to fly and on occasion maybe Vegas. I feel bad for your mother, but that's why I never come to see her. I hate flying." She folded the blouse neatly and placed it back in the box.

"Mom understands. Besides, she's always considered Hawaii home, no matter how long she's lived in Michigan, so she'd much rather come here for a visit, especially during this time of year—the winters are brutal. I think Mom would retire here if it weren't for Susan and the grandkids."

"To have you and your mother here would be an answer to all of my chanting. Now go shower."

Charlie carefully removed the leis from her neck, inhaled their intoxicating fragrance, and then hung them on the bedpost. She lifted her suitcase onto her bed, opened it up, and began to put her belongings in the dresser drawers and the small closet. She placed the wooden box on the shelf in the closet for safekeeping.

They cuddled on the sofa like spoons. "Tonight is our night! The kids are with my folks, and Garrett is staying in Detroit. So what are we going to do about it?" Annie asked.

"I don't feel like going out to eat. Do you mind if we stay in tonight? These nights are few and far between, and I'd prefer it if we made dinner together. I find doing those simple things together brings the greatest pleasure. I love it when we just hang out." Charlie started to kiss the back of Annie's neck.

"That's torture." Annie wriggled away and smiled. Charlie looked confused. "Wait till after dinner, and then you can have all the dessert you want."

Charlie laughed. "That's the most pathetic but enticing line I've heard."

"Yes, but so deliciously true. Now let's get dinner started so we can get to the dessert," Annie said as she jumped up and raced off to the kitchen.

Charlie closed the door reverently, peeled off her clothes, and left them in a mushy pile on the floor. She walked into her bathroom, pulled the shower curtain back, and stepped in. She welcomed the soft, warm water pouring down and covering her body. She stood under the showerhead while the water pelted her face, embracing the slight discomfort as some bizarre form of self-flagellation.

Charlie thought about her life, the pressures of her job, and the possibility of her illness. She wished she could scrub and wash away all that ailed her, but hard as she tried, she knew that it was only a temporary escape and relief.

Charlie picked up the pink bar of Camay to her nose and smelled the familiar fragrance. She was instantly brought back in time to when she was in the same shower as a teenage girl—a better time, a better life? She felt finally she belonged.

Reluctantly admitting that she had finished her shower, Charlie reached for the towel, wrapped it around herself, and looked down. Pepper stared back at her with curiosity. "Pepper, you have to give a girl some privacy. Just like a boy—we only just met, and you're already trying to get a peek. You stinker, go play with Salt."

Barbara yelled from the kitchen, "Pepper, get out of there! You rascal, leave poor Charlie alone." Pepper looked over his shoulder and then back at Charlie. Grudgingly, he padded out of the bathroom.

Charlie emerged feeling refreshed. She adjusted the fluffy pink towel wrapped around her and looked in the mirror. She tugged on her gaunt cheeks. Her auntie was right. The dark circles around her eyes, her skin gray white—an unflattering look. *I've become what every woman dreads—forty years old. Middle-aged. Getting old sucks.* She felt slightly thankful that the term "spinster" wasn't used anymore because she had nailed it.

Charlie continued with her self-inspection and winced at all the streaks of gray in her hair. She ran her fingers through it. *Maybe I'll start with a new cut and dye job.* But she couldn't see herself in any of the current hairstyles: crimped, permed, big curls, or, God forbid, a mullet. *It's a lost cause.* Despite everything being bigger and bolder in the eighties, Charlie was determined to buck the trend—no surprise there. *It's going to be something shorter, lightly feathered, and softer. I'll embrace the gray!*

Charlie was about to put on her bra, but she paused. *This is a vacation, lose the bra.* She tossed it toward the bed, but Pepper leaped in the air, caught it, and ran off with his prize. "Pepper, you little shit, go ahead and keep it." She pulled on navy shorts and an oversized white Eygptian cotton shirt with long sleeves.

She looked down at the pile of discarded clothes on the bedroom floor. *Is this emblematic of a new life?* She looked at herself in the full-length mirror. *What a great feeling.*

She was going to make this vacation special. *No work, absolutely no work.* She briefly thought about Barbara's suggestion. *I could see myself living here.*

She walked into the kitchen and saw Barbara busily preparing their breakfast. "Can I help?"

"Perfect timing. No, this is a labor of love. It feels great to be able to prepare food and have a meal with someone."

Charlie pulled out a chair and sat down. She took a swallow of fresh pineapple juice.

"Here you go, honey."

It smelled delicious. Sunny scrambled eggs, a small portion of salad with carrot-ginger dressing, a scoop of white rice, and three perfectly fried slices of Spam.

She laughed. "Yes! Spam, the devil meat, has appeared!"

Barbara laughed and shook her head. "I don't know why your family always makes such a big deal about it. We grew up on it. Everyone eats it here."

"I know, I know. Spam used to be a running argument between my mom and dad. My mom loved to eat Spam, so did Susan and I. She would fry some up with rice, and instead of salad, she occasionally served it with kimchi. My dad would look at his plate and usually let out 'really,' followed closely by 'evil.'"

Barbara laughed. "That was all he ate during the war, and it was probably served cold and greasy. No wonder he thought it was evil."

Charlie picked up the *Honolulu Advertiser* and browsed through it while taking bites of her breakfast. It had the usual national news about President Reagan, the economy, and the Philippine president, Marcos.

Her breakfast almost finished, she pinched a small portion of scrambled eggs and held her hand out underneath the table. Salt nibbled at and then licked her fingertips. Pepper pawed Charlie's leg, looking for his share.

"Bennie spoiled them too. They'll never give you any peace." Barbara wrinkled her brow as she picked up the *Star-Bulletin* and flipped through the pages. She began to mutter quietly to herself.

"Auntie?" Charlie drank her juice.

"What's this world coming to?"

"What is it, auntie?"

"They found another woman, a girl in Ke'ehi Lagoon. Only seventeen, murdered."

Charlie stopped chewing.

Honolulu
Thursday, January 16, 1986

The detectives entered the elevator and pushed the button for the basement, where autopsies took place.

"Seventeen-year-old Leilehua senior. She lived on Awanei Street in Waipahu," said Williams.

"What's a Waipahu girl doing going to school up in Wahiawa?"

"Not sure. Witnesses last saw her at a city bus stop off Farrington Highway across the street from the diner. Reports have her calling her boyfriend from a nearby phone booth stating she had missed the bus and would be late for school. A local fisherman found her around ten near the Diamond Head end of the reef runway floating in the Ke'ehi Lagoon, partially naked. Aloha, Doc. We've really got to stop meeting like this!" Williams said as the detectives pushed through the heavy steel doors and entered the examination room.

"Aloha, gentlemen."

"Is this our girl?" Tanaka asked.

"Yes, seventeen years old, dark blond hair, hands bound behind her back with rope, raped, sodomized, and strangled to death. You can see the petechial hemorrhaging, which caused the red pinpoint marks on her face, eyes, and eyelids," the doctor reported. "Additionally, you can see the deep ligature groove where the rope had dug into her neck, and note the extensive bruising."

"Shit, a regular trifecta." Williams examined the teenager's body.

"Clothes?" Tanaka asked.

"She was found wearing only a blue sweatshirt with *Hawaiian Island Creations* printed on the sleeves over a white T-shirt, pearl stud earrings, and a white sports watch," the doctor said.

"Rope?" Williams

"Same as last time." The doctor pointed at the plastic bag on the counter.

"Same as last time?" Tanaka repeated.

Williams held up the bag. "OD 550 cord, a popular choice among the military and sports enthusiasts. As my partner will attest, I'm not the sharpest tool in the shed, but I'm in agreement with the doctor. This reminds me of the other woman that we had in here—the military spouse." He examined the rope more closely and then handed it to Tanaka.

"Pam Adair," the doctor answered as he turned over the papers on his clipboard and stopped at a specific one.

"Doctor, I don't like jumping to conclusions, and I don't believe in coincidences, but as both you and Mac have observed, this sounds eerily similar to our other case last spring," Tanaka said.

"Detectives, I don't like jumping to conclusions, either. I report the facts, but I believe we have enough medical similarities to be concerned."

"What did that FBI agent call them?" Williams asked.

"Serial killers."

Honolulu
Wednesday, January 22, 1986

"Excuse me, I'm looking for Professor Yamamoto."

The student in the hallway paused. "I believe her office is the third door down on the left."

"Thank you." *When did junior high girls start attending college? Where did time go? When did I become so old!* Charlie moved down the hallway, saw Barbara's nameplate outside the door, and knocked.

"Come in."

Charlie opened the door. "Aloha, auntie."

"Charlie, perfect timing. I was about to join a couple of the other professors for lunch. It would be a great time for you to meet and get acquainted with some of the faculty."

"Sounds nice, I'd like that." Charlie watched Barbara file the remaining papers on her desk in colored folders and place them on various levels of the stacked desk tray.

"I'll be the first to admit the amount of paperwork seems to grow each year exponentially, and it's definitely my least favorite part of the job," Barbara said, grabbing her lunch from the bottom drawer. "Now I'm ready. Let's go."

Charlie held the door open. "Auntie, I thought we might be going out for lunch and didn't pack anything," she said as she closed the office door behind her.

"Don't worry, I packed enough for the two of us. Most times, lunch turns into a potluck event, and everyone just shares."

"So sixties—so Asian."

"Well, I won't deny that we're a little behind the times. We have a tendency to go at our own, slower pace. But we're more communal and family-oriented too. Which aren't all bad things, I might add."

"It's definitely part of the charm."

Charlie watched the students make their way to and from classes.

"A lot of professors hate instructing and look upon it as a necessary evil; however, I really enjoy working with the students. It's great when you create a connection. I think that I get as jazzed as they do. It makes me feel young, like I'm an undergraduate all over again."

"You look like you could be confused for a student." Charlie watched another one walking past and waving to a friend. "I really enjoy learning, but I do have a reputation for not being the most patient person in the world, so I'd be nervous that I might go off on a student who wasn't as passionate as I thought he should be."

"You have tremendous energy, which the students will feed off of, and you'll have some excellent real-world examples to back up the academic parts of your instruction—trust me, you'll be a natural, and in no time, the most popular professor on campus."

In the courtyard, other professors were sitting around cement tables. Charlie was introduced to everyone and listened in on the discussions. Most of the professors were complaining about the lack of interest and limited learning abilities of their students. Eventually the conversation turned to Charlie.

"What do you do, Charlie?" one of the professors asked.

"I'm a psychiatrist."

"Aha, a real doctor," another said.

"And in psychiatry too. You must make the big bucks."

"Do you have a specialty?"

"I specialize in criminal behavior and work for the Michigan State Police," Charlie answered.

"Doing what?"

Now the questions were coming from all directions, and a lively discussion ensued. Charlie smiled and responded as quickly and as thoroughly as possible before the next one was asked. She didn't have to worry about not bringing a lunch because she never had a chance to take a bite of what Barbara had prepared.

"I assist them in identifying criminal behaviors that may help in the apprehension of the perpetrators."

"She's amazing," Barbara said. "She has solved many crimes."

"My husband works for the HPD in the Homicide Division. The two of you should talk. He's working on a case right now that he could probably use your help with. Don't tell him that I told you so," said a Japanese-looking woman with shoulder-length light brown hair.

Her colleagues laughed.

"I'm sure that he doesn't need my help. Besides, I'm here on vacation."

Barbara chimed in, saying, "I'm trying to convince Charlie to stay here. She could be a great addition to our medical school or our psychology department. Kim, she could even help Frank out at HPD." She put her arm around Charlie and squeezed her shoulders. "She's like a daughter to me."

The conversation continued for a little while longer until a man approached the group.

"It's McCloud," one of the professors yelled out.

"The Marlboro Man," another said.

The distinguished-looking man removed his cowboy hat, revealing jet-black hair with just a touch of silver at the sideburns. He wore an untucked navy-and-green Hawaiian shirt, creased blue jeans, and polished cowboy boots.

"Perfect timing, honey. You know everyone here," Kim said. The man nodded at the group. "Come over here—I'd like you to meet Barbara's niece. Charlie, this is my husband, Frank Tanaka. You should talk to her. She could help you."

Tanaka shook his head in frustration. "Honey, I told you not to discuss my work with others."

"Hush, you're as stubborn as one of those mules from your westerns. Charlie is a doctor and works for the Michigan State Police. Barbara was telling us how she's solved all these crimes. She's amazing."

Tanaka made his way around the group, shaking some hands and greeting others, until he reached Charlie. He held out his hand. "Detective Tanaka."

"Pleased to meet you, Detective. Charlie Taylor." Charlie stood up and took the detective's hand.

"Okay, I'll bite, Doctor—what do you do for the Michigan State Police?"

"I'm a criminal psychiatrist. I assist their investigations with developing profiles." Charlie sat back down.

"Visiting Barbara? On vacation or another reason?"

"I'm here on vacation, so don't worry about me meddling in any of your investigations. I've promised my auntie and myself that I wasn't going to get involved in anything."

"Well, it was nice meeting you, and enjoy your vacation," Tanaka said. He bent over to kiss his wife's cheek. "I've got to go.

I just came by to say a quick aloha, because I probably won't be home until late."

The chatter resumed around Charlie as she watched Tanaka and his wife walk away from the group.

"I can see you're in one of your moods again. You know, that dark, brooding look you have when you're on a case. That deep, dark place where no one can reach you, not even me. Honey, it's not healthy. I worry about you," Annie said.

"What?" Charlie asked.

"You proved my point exactly!" Annie laughed and tossed her head back. Her red hair fell onto her bare white shoulders.

Honey, not this time. Not this time.

"Charlie, Charlie, yoo-hoo, Charlie . . . I think she's still suffering from jet lag," Barbara said.

"Yes, auntie. I'm sorry. Could you repeat the question?"

Manoa
Saturday, January 25, 1986

Charlie had settled into her vacation. The jet lag had almost completely evaporated. Gone were the mornings of waking up and staring at the ceiling at three—it was now closer to five. She got up and went for a run while it was still dark and calm. She had the streets to herself.

She climbed the hills to watch the sun rise over the city. She enjoyed listening to the invasive parakeets as they flew chattering overhead from one part of the island to another; they returned each evening at sunset. After her run she would take Salt and Pepper for a walk, all followed by a filling breakfast with her auntie.

Charlie enjoyed being with Barbara. Most nights, they walked through the quiet campus with the dogs leading the way. They stopped at the replica of a Japanese tea house that sat at the top of a small knoll surrounded by a small Japanese garden and a stream. Barbara pulled out her juzu beads, a mixture of green and red aventurine, rainbow agate, and gold.

"My practice helped me, especially when Bennie was dying. Are you still a practicing Catholic like your mom and dad?"

"Another one on my long list of crimes and sins. No, I haven't been to Mass in years. I never seemed to get much satisfaction. Maybe I'm being too harsh, given my job and everything else going on in my life, but I could never seem to find any hope or peace."

Barbara took out another set of beads and placed them in Charlie's hand. "The juzu beads are similar in nature to a rosary. Instead of praying to Mother Mary, you are chanting. We don't believe in a higher deity—our power comes from within us. These were your uncle's. I know he would want you to have them."

"Auntie, thank you, but I don't know. I'm definitely not a religious type of person, and frankly not the faithful kind, either." Charlie tried to hand the beads back to Barbara.

"Just give it a try while you're here. You'd be surprised what this practice can do for you. We tell new practitioners to test the faith. Ask for something. Something tangible. You'll be surprised how the answers may come to you, in ways that you may never have imagined. Please."

The sandalwood beads felt comfortable in her hands. Barbara showed her the proper way to hold them.

"Just repeat after me, 'Nam-Myoho-Renge-Kyo.'" Charlie was amazed at how fast Barbara could repeat the words. She sounded like a bumblebee buzzing.

They returned home in silence, comfortable in each other's company. Later that evening, after Barbara and the dogs had gone to bed, Charlie leaned back in the large padded desk chair in the little makeshift home office that once was a bedroom. Charlie re-read the postcard she had written and put it down.

She studied the tan IBM Selectric III typewriter and turned it on. The typeball rotated and pivoted to the correct position as Charlie's fingers moved swiftly over the keys. Years of piano had provided her with the dexterity needed to type accurately and efficiently. She stared at the paper, read, and reread the letter.

She reached the end of the page and pulled the paper from the machine, folded it into thirds, and slid it into an envelope. She ran the tip of her tongue along the glue edge and sealed it. She pulled a pen from a cup and addressed it, then opened a drawer, rummaging for a stamp and not finding one. *It's probably best I don't find one. I better make sure that I'm not being headstrong. God knows, if anyone is prone to being stubborn, it's me.*

Manoa
Tuesday, January 28, 1986

"I was in my apartment, studying with the TV on. I can't remember what I was watching—some soap opera or other—when Walter Cronkite interrupted the broadcast with a special announcement that President Kennedy had been shot. I'll never forget that day and where I was in that little apartment. I could hear people outside screaming and crying. I curled up in a ball and cried. I wonder if people will remember this tragedy the same way," Barbara said.

Charlie put her arm around Barbara as they watched President Ronald Reagan address the nation:

"Ladies and gentlemen, I'd planned to speak to you tonight to report on the State of the Union, but the events of earlier today have led me to change those plans. Today is a day for mourning and remembering.

"Nancy and I are pained to the core by the tragedy of the shuttle *Challenger*. We know we share this pain with all of the people of our country. This is truly a national loss . . . but they, the *Challenger* Seven, were aware of the dangers, but overcame them and did their jobs brilliantly. We mourn seven heroes: Michael Smith, Dick Scobee, Judith Resnik, Ronald McNair, Ellison Onizuka, Gregory Jarvis, and Christa McAuliffe. We mourn their loss as a nation together.

"For the families of the seven, we cannot bear, as you do, the full impact of this tragedy. But we feel the loss, and we're thinking about you so very much. Your loved ones were daring and brave, and they had that special grace, that special spirit that says, 'Give me a challenge, and I'll meet it with joy.' They had a hunger to explore the universe and discover its truths. They wished to serve, and they did. They served all of us."

"Christa McAuliffe, a teacher—she was going to be the first civilian in space," Charlie said as she held Barbara's hand. Charlie bowed her head and prayed.

Debra Harris's Story
Pearl City
Wednesday, January 29, 1986

"Hi, honey. Yes, I made it home safely. I had a great time and I'm glad that we were able to have dinner on your ship tonight. I don't know why you complain so much. Everyone was very nice," I say, smiling as I start to undress while holding the phone between my ear and shoulder.

"They were just nice because you were here. You don't see these jerks day in and day out, like I do. Most times, they're uptight assholes. Besides, you're nice to everyone."

"Anyways, I thought they were nice." I kick off my dress.

"Anyways, have you given any more thought to having a kid?"

"Listen, Romeo, we've been riding a whirlwind. I come here for vacation, we meet, you propose, we get married, and I move here, all in about eight months. I'd like to have a little more time together before we start having a family. I want to have some fun! I love my mom, but I don't want to be like her. She was seventeen when she had me. Babies are a lot of work. I just met my biological father for the first time a few years ago—I don't want the same thing happening to us." I make my way into the bathroom.

"All right, but when we do, we're going to have a lot of boys."

I laugh. "Don't be so sure of yourself."

"Anyways, let's say, in my family, we only have boys. Well-hung boys, I might add."

"Anyways, you're such a knucklehead. Hey, I'm tired, and I've got to get up early to catch the bus downtown, so I need to get some sleep."

"Get to bed and be safe."

"I will. I love you."

"I love you too. Sweet dreams."

Snohomish, Washington
Thursday, January 30, 1986

The images ran through her subconscious. She sat up, breathing heavily. She couldn't shake the visions from her nightmare—a man chasing her and her beautiful daughter. Something horrible happening to her daughter.

She tried to resist the image. She strained so hard to fight the evil that seemed to be after her daughter, but she couldn't keep the darkness away. She couldn't protect her. She saw the light of her daughter vanishing, slowly fading away until it was gone.

Leslie peeled the cold, wet sheets from her frail body and swung her legs over the side. She looked at the phone and then the clock. It was three hours ahead—too early to call Debra. She'd have to wait till later in the morning. She spent the early morning hours staring at the clock, praying to God that nothing had happened to her daughter.

As soon as the clock struck the appropriate time, Leslie reached over and dialed Debra's number, but there was no answer. She hung up, dialed again, then again, and again. She kept at it, but the results were the same—there were never any answers. In her mind she tried to justify it. Debra was busy getting ready for work and didn't hear the phone ringing, or she didn't have time to answer.

Pearl City
Thursday, January 30, 1986

I look at all my cosmetics, my hairdryer, and my brushes spread across the bathroom counter, the wet towels and small puddles of water on the floor. Luckily, I'll be home before Bill and can get this placed cleaned up. I look in the mirror and see the clock and turn to confirm the time. *I'll be late.*

I glance at the mirror one last time and smooth out my dress. I'm overdressed, but this job is important to us. I look at the mess and run for the door. The phone starts to ring. *I'm sorry, I can't stop to answer it. Please call back later.* I close and lock the door.

I move down the stairs as quickly as I can in my heels and start walking down the sidewalk toward the bus stop. By the time I reach it, I'm out of breath. Either I'm early, and no one has arrived yet, or I'm late, and the bus has already come and gone. I have a sinking feeling that I'm screwed.

I look at my watch and try to calculate which scenario is most likely.

"Which way are you going?"

I look up. "Into town."

"Jump on in. I'm heading that way."

"Thanks, but the bus will be here shortly."

"You just missed it. Besides, you look like a princess. You're dressed too nicely to be riding a crappy city bus."

He has a point. I look at my dress and then back at his car. I've ridden in worse-looking cars and with scarier drivers when I used to hitchhike. "You sure it's no problem?"

"Positive. Besides, we'll catch up and eventually beat the bus with all the stops it has to make."

"You're right about that," I say, laughing. "Thanks, I appreciate this."

"Princess, it's my pleasure, all my pleasure," the man says. He smiles as he opens the passenger door.

"As long as you know I already have a Prince Charming."

"Your chariot—let's get going."

Pearl Harbor
Thursday, January 30, 1986

"Seaman Harris."

"Hi, this is Betty, Debra's boss from Hawaiian Telecommunications. Debra hasn't shown up for work today, and we wanted to make sure that everything was okay."

"What do you mean she hasn't shown up for work? I spoke with her last night, and she was planning on going."

"Hmm, I'm sorry. I'm sure everything is all right. Maybe she had to go to the doctor's and forgot to tell us about her appointment."

"Maybe, but that's not like her."

"I'm sure she's all right, and I'll have her call you as soon as she gets here."

Honolulu
Friday, January 31, 1986

"Homicide, Tanaka . . . Why are we getting this call? Homicide doesn't take care of missing persons . . . I see."

"What was that about?" Williams asked.

"More coincidences. Military spouse; twenty-one; five feet, eight inches; light brown hair. She went missing yesterday—no sign of her."

Honolulu
Saturday, February 1, 1986

"Ya, ya, I'll set the ring down there. Hey, come over here," the teenager said.

"What's up?" a second teen asked.

"Look over there! Don't be stupid, bra—not there, there! Blue tarp, bra!" The first teenager pointed at the object in the irrigation canal. "What do you think it could be?"

"Don't know, don't care," a third teenager said as he prepared his crabbing rings and nets.

"You look."

"Not me, bra," the second teenager said and picked up his rings.

"You two losers. I'll go look," the third teenager said. He threw his equipment down on the ground next to his old car.

Honolulu
Saturday, February 1, 1986

"Hope you brought a change of clothes. Are those boots waterproof?" Williams asked. He smiled at Tanaka and turned on the emergency light and siren in their unmarked car.

"Where was the body found?"

"We have a woman's body found on a mudbank of a drainage canal on the Moanalua Stream behind MidPac Lumber's Mapunapuna industrial tract yard at the Koko Head end of 2729 Mokumoa Street," Williams recited as he maneuvered around the traffic pulling out of their way.

"Who found the body?"

"The victim's body was found at about one fifteen by three local teenagers who had been crabbing on the stream bank nearby.

They were curious when they saw a bright blue tarp and went over to investigate it. The tarp was smeared with mud and contained the body."

"You know my next question."

"We don't know yet. The victim was wearing a navy-blue dress, possibly a party dress. The first reports indicated her clothing was intact, her hands tied behind her with a rope."

"Rope?"

"Pretty sure it was our favorite—OD 550 cord. Like I said, she was wrapped in a thin blue plastic tarpaulin, and it appears her body was rolled down a seven-foot embankment."

Williams parked the car, and the detectives made their way toward a group of officers and emergency technicians.

"Wounds?"

"She'd been beaten pretty badly."

"Not to speak ill of the dead, but she didn't catch a break. Maybe we'll catch one."

Manoa
Sunday, February 2, 1986

Pepper occasionally looked back and then resumed tugging at the leash while Charlie and Salt walked side by side. They made their way through the deserted campus until they got to the Japanese Tea Garden. Charlie sat down, and the dogs sat peacefully next to her. Salt laid her head in Charlie's lap while Pepper forced his way onto her lap and tried to lick her face. "Pepper, enough. I love you too."

Charlie pulled out her uncle's beads and looked at them—they felt comfortable in her hands. She sought answers to questions that had plagued her for a long time, answers that she hadn't found in her own faith. Her mother had insisted that she try harder and not give up on God, that he had a plan.

> "Umma, I just don't get anything from going to mass," Charlie explained.

> "You think that because you're a doctor that you are smarter than me." Charlie's mom applied her usual psychological warfare.

> "Of course not. I'm not saying that at all. Mass is boring; the priests have little to say, and they're so out of touch with reality."

> "Mass is not to entertain you. If you want to be entertained, then go to the movies. Mass is there to bring you closer to God."

> "Okay, if there is a God, that loves and cares for us, then why does he put us through so much pain?"

> "Aigoo, we've spent so much money on you attending Catholic schools to have an excellent education. You still don't get it?"

> "Umma, I appreciate all the sacrifices that you and Dad have made for me."

> "Charlie, you need to have more faith that this is part of your journey. How can you look forward to heaven if your life is too easy here? One step at a time. Just like Jesus carried the cross for us one step at a time, we must carry our own crosses one step at a time."

Remembering her strict Catholic upbringing and attendance to Catholic schools, Charlie felt a slight pang in her heart, as if she were being disloyal to her own faith. She looked around like some teenager about to try her first cigarette, as she began to chant. She asked for answers and relief for her troubled mind and soul.

Back home and showered, Charlie sipped pineapple juice at the kitchen table and rubbed the dogs' tummies with her foot. She was flipping through the pages of the paper when she saw a headline about the body of a woman found along a stream bank. She shivered and tossed the paper to the far end of the table, trying to distance herself as far as she could from the news. This was not the answer she had hoped for.

Honolulu
Monday, February 3, 1986

"Detective Williams, do you know this is our fourth murdered woman associated with the military?" the doctor asked.

"Yes, but they're all unrelated," Williams responded, looking around the room in hopes of seeing Joyce or another nurse.

"Doctor, what we want to know is if she's related to the others," Tanaka said.

"I can't say with one hundred percent certainty, but I think we have our third."

"Shit!" Williams exclaimed.

"We're still waiting on fingerprint comparisons to try and make a positive identification, but what we do know is that she is Caucasian; five feet, eight inches tall; and one hundred and fifty-four pounds, with a fair complexion and short light brown hair. She was beaten, raped, and strangled."

Honolulu
Monday, February 3, 1986

"Are we entirely sure?" Griffith asked, running his hand through his graying hair.

"Chief, we've all been at this for a long time, and you know how I hate jumping to conclusions, and I don't believe in coincidences, either, but there are just too many similarities to ignore," Tanaka said, spitting black slime into a Coke can.

"Do we think this goes beyond the three that we know of?" Griffith asked.

"As of right now, we don't think so," Williams said, crossing his leg over his knee and adjusting his notepad on his lap.

"What does the district attorney think about all of this?" Griffith asked, looking at the man leaning against the filing cabinet in the corner, his arm draped on top of it.

Phil Crawford, deputy city prosecutor, stepped forward. "I've spoken with the district attorney, and he concurs with your assessment that a task force should be created. Are we prepared for all the calls and information that are going to start coming in? We don't want to lose out on important or critical information because we don't have the proper procedures or equipment in place."

How does he stay so pristine? Tanaka thought, spitting into the can again and adjusting the wad to the other side of his mouth.

"Who are you putting on the task force?" Crawford asked.

"A combination of homicide and sex division detectives," Griffith said, looking at a list of names. "You know we're going to need additional funds for all of this."

"Are Rice and Mac the leads?" Crawford nodded toward Tanaka and Williams. "What about the FBI?"

"I've spoken with the local agent, but he doesn't believe there's enough to officially bring them in. However, he will assist in any way he can."

Tanaka scratched the back of his head. "I met a doctor the other day at the university. She's vacationing here from Michigan. Barbara Yamamoto, her auntie, is a professor with Kim. This doctor is some kind of criminal psychiatrist that works with the Michigan State Police. Maybe she could help?"

"Is this wise?" Griffith asked.

"Maybe we can use her in some sort of consultant capacity. She doesn't have to be an official member of the task force," Crawford said.

"Fair enough. The FBI agent who spoke with us last September said that we should take advantage of all resources," Griffith said.

"Who is she? What's her name?" Crawford asked.

"It's a man's name . . . Frankie, Billie? Shit, it'll come to me."

"Is it Charlie, Dr. Charlie Taylor?" Crawford asked.

"Ya, ya, that's it. You know her?" Tanaka leaned over and spit in his Coke can.

"Do you have to do that in my office? You know I think it's a disgusting habit." Griffith frowned.

"I don't know her, but I've met her, and I know of her reputation. I highly recommend that you do whatever you can to convince her to help us," Crawford said.

"Who is she?" Griffith asked.

"I met her at a conference hosted by the DOJ and FBI a couple years back. Just a few women were in attendance. An attractive woman among a hundred guys? She stood out like a sore thumb, and I think every guy in the room tried to make a run at her, but she wasn't having any of it. She has an impressive record in these types of cases. I've heard that she'll literally kill herself in pursuit. She doesn't know how or when to quit. She's a machine. Clearly skills we lack on the island."

"I don't care how good she is, I'm not crazy about bringing a haole into an investigation. She'll turn the locals off, especially up in Waipahu. Up there, they hate haoles with a passion," Williams said.

"Mac, I think she's hapa. All the victims were white and non-locals," Tanaka countered.

"Partner, I still don't think it's a good idea. I don't like the idea of an outsider snooping around in our business."

"You two give it a break. You sound like an old married couple," Griffith said, frustrated.

"There will be immense political pressure to get this resolved quickly," Crawford added.

"We're up against more than city hall—" Griffith started to say.

"A serial killer," Tanaka said.

Honolulu
Tuesday, February 4, 1986

He had ditched his whole Hawaiian cowboy persona. In a button-down shirt, paisley tie, and gray suit, Tanaka stood at the podium to speak to the press. "We've identified the victim as Debra R. Harris, twenty-one, wife of a Pearl Harbor sailor. She lived off Kamehameha Highway in Pearl City.

"It is our understanding that she had dinner with her husband on his ship on January 29. She returned to their apartment sometime in the evening. Her husband called her later that evening, around ten thirty or eleven, to check on her. They talked briefly. We believe that she remained home for the rest of the evening. In the morning she got ready for work, left their apartment, and went to the nearby bus station.

"She usually went to work by bus. She apparently used a bus stop near Leeward Community College and the Waipahu interchange. She worked as a secretary for a telecommunications company downtown. However, she never reported to work that morning.

That day at noon, her employer called her husband aboard the ship to ask why she hadn't shown up to work. Currently, that is all the information we have. We are not taking any questions today, but there will be another briefing tomorrow."

Honolulu
Tuesday, February 4, 1986

Tanaka relaxed into his leather chair, staring absentmindedly at the TV screen. On his lap was the latest issue of *Sports Illustrated*, the cover emblazoned *Paradise Found* and showing Elle Macpherson in a revealing blue-green one-piece swimsuit. He had one foot propped up on the matching ottoman. On the end table next to his chair was the usual soda can and a glass of iced tea dripping condensation onto a waterlogged *TV Guide*.

"How did the briefing go today?" Kim asked, sitting down on the sofa next to him. Frank continued to stare at the TV screen. Kim picked up the magazine and flipped through the pages. "God, she's gorgeous! Think I could wear something like this to the beach?"

"Thirty-five years ago." Frank raised his right eyebrow slightly.

"Bastard. Getting old is not much fun, and the students seem to get younger every year."

"That's because they are." Frank adjusted his position.

"How did the briefing go today?" Kim asked again. "Did you dazzle them with your ability to say a lot but not give away anything?"

"It went fine. All I had to do was lay down what little facts we have on the latest young woman's murder, and I didn't have to answer any questions, which always makes things a lot easier. We have another one tomorrow—we'll announce the creation of a task force, and then we'll take questions, which will be brutal."

"Just by yourself again?"

"No, it'll be Griffith, Crawford, and me."

"It's that bad?"

"Ya, it's that bad. We have no clues. We're inundated with calls all day long. Everyone is concerned. We get calls from the governor and the mayor, the DA's office, the tourist board—and that's not even taking into consideration the concerned and grieving family members, the press, and anxious citizens." Tanaka sipped his iced tea.

"Who'll be in charge?"

"I'll be lead, so you won't see me until we resolve this case."

"I understand, but what's really bothering you? I can see it on your face."

"Do you remember that case from a couple of years ago? The one that went all to shit? Luanda, nineteen years old. The only difference is she wasn't a Caucasian."

"Frank, you will nail this bastard." Kim took hold of his hands.

"We have to do better this time. We can't afford to be seen as a bunch of screwups again." Tanaka rested the perspiring glass on his knee and turned his head away in frustration.

"None of that was your fault!" She placed her hand on his arm.

"Thanks, but I was part of homicide at the time, and we didn't do a damn thing right. We spent a tremendous amount of time and money on the whole maniac cop conspiracy that proved to be bogus. We had this idea that it might have been Luanda's boyfriend because he supposedly had scratches on his face and had failed two polygraphs, but we could never find any concrete motive or evidence, so we moved on from him very quickly.

"Then we received one tip that a witness claimed to have seen a woman slouched over in a car on the night of her disappearance, but we never followed up, which was just another indication to the public of our incompetence. We even went as far as exhuming her body to determine how she died, but all we found was an unwashed body covered in dirt and leaves and haphazardly wrapped in a police body bag. We looked no better than the killer—we'd dumped her body into a hole and moved on." Tanaka took a sip of his tea and looked at Kim.

"If that wasn't bad enough to fuel the conspiracy theories, the medical examiners managed to look at some parts of her and were still unable to ascertain how she died. And do you know what happened next?"

"No." Kim took the glass out of Tanaka's hand, wiped it off with a napkin, and sipped from it.

"We lost the damn body parts! They somehow seemed to have disappeared. It's incredible."

"You're a smart guy. What can you do differently this time?"

"Well, Crawford and I want to bring Barbara's niece on to the task force as a consultant. Griffith is indifferent but wants to make sure we're showing the city and the governor that we're doing everything possible. Mac is dead set against it." Tanaka sat back in his chair.

"I don't get it. Why wouldn't Mac want the additional help?" Kim curled her legs underneath her on the sofa.

"He can be really weird sometimes, a real control freak when it comes to women, and like a lot of us, he's concerned that she'll see firsthand how incompetent we're capable of being, and then the word will get out that nobody is safe, that we can't protect our own or the tourists."

"Aren't you getting ahead of yourself?"

"Probably. I don't even know if she'll accept."

"I think there's a strong possibility that she will. Barbara and I orchestrated her visit and the opportunity to meet you at lunchtime. Barbara wants her to stay on the island—she loves that girl—especially now that Bennie is gone, and I want you home sooner."

"Really, you think so little of me?"

"Listen, cowboy, I fell in love with you the day we met in third grade, and I haven't stopped loving you all these years. I know that you are the best detective and officer they have on the force, but you can't do it alone. Mac is a jackass to think that way. He can be a real Neanderthal, and the rest will only do the minimum. So, yes, I'm doing it for Barbara and me—and for you."

"Damn, girl, when did you get to be so tough?" Tanaka smiled and winked.

Honolulu
Wednesday, February 5, 1986

Despite the open windows and the soothing breeze, the Honolulu Police Department public affairs room remained hot and stuffy. Reporters were jammed in with all their equipment. They listened intently as they waited for their opportunity to grill the panel for more details that Griffith, Crawford, and Tanaka would be unwilling, if not unable, to provide. They needed to keep specific facts out of public knowledge so they could eliminate the crackpots who were sure to arrive at the station following the news reports.

They sat at the table with microphones in front of them and announced the formation of a task force to address the recent murders. Tanaka adjusted his glasses and his tie for the umpteenth time. *I hate these damn things—ties, news conferences. Shit, two days in a row. I can't believe this.* He began to read the prepared statement in front of him.

"We are here to inform you that we have established a task force with officers from the Sex Crime and Homicide Divisions to look into the murders of three women. All three crimes are similar in some instances: the women were young, white, strangled, and dropped off in relative proximity to each other either in or near bodies of water. However, we do not have conclusive evidence that ties all three together. We'll take a few questions."

Waikiki
Wednesday, February 5, 1986

Charlie dove headfirst under the wave. Her eyes stung from the salt, but the water felt invigorating. She popped up and tried to get the saltwater out of her eyes and mouth. She'd forgotten how strong the taste was.

She watched a fleshy man's boobs jiggle near her as he bounced up and down in chest-high water, waiting for the next big wave to come rolling toward them. He leaped up and stretched out. Unlike most newbie bodysurfers, he had impeccable timing—he caught the wave.

Charlie watched, and then she noticed all the little things that started to go wrong. The softer white waves disappeared into larger ones crashing hard against the shore. She could see the strong undercurrent pulling swimmers out into the ocean. The wave continued to pick up speed. Charlie watched, suspecting it would end badly, like a gawker about to witness a terrible traffic accident.

The surfer's head and shoulders had dipped too low. The wave grabbed hold of his legs and began to push them up over his back, toward his head. His body contorted into an unnatural, painful position that resembled a scorpion. His arms and legs flailed as the wave threw him viciously against the beach. He rolled around, trying to gain his balance, and began to sit up on his knees when another wave smacked him in the head, knocking him over again while the undercurrent started to suck him out again. He made a great impression of a beached beluga whale.

Some sunbathers suppressed their laughter, while others, concerned for his safety, ran to the man's aid and pulled him up out of the water before another wave sucked him out and repeated the beating.

Charlie adjusted her tight-fitting black one-piece, stretched, and looked around. She wished she had her fins. She lowered her shoulder and turned her body perpendicular to the waves to allow them to pass by. She was patient, but sometimes she had to play her hunches. She saw the formation of a wave with good potential. She bobbed, watching and waiting for the wave to approach. She readied herself and pushed off the ocean floor, swimming with strong strokes, waiting for the wave to pick her up.

She lowered her head and shoulders so her legs and feet were slightly higher. She stopped swimming and straightened her body like a surfboard, but the wave fizzled out and didn't carry her more than five feet. *Shit, pay attention!*

Facing the shoreline, Charlie spat saltwater again and pushed her hair back. Determined, she turned back to catch the next wave. The wall of water was right on top of her. She dove, arms pointed straight ahead, her body taut. The giant wave picked her up, and she rode the crest of it. Her adrenaline kicked in—fear was a great motivator.

The shore was fast approaching. Charlie started to prepare mentally and physically for what was coming next. She let the wave's momentum lift her body up and over the lip to exit. She felt her feet touch the sand and landed in a crouched position, timing her jump out of the shallow water to avoid the undercurrent, pleased that she only stumbled slightly as she ran up onto the shore.

Charlie smiled as she caught her breath. She watched the cute Japanese girls in their bright bikinis giggle with pleasure as they tried to mimic her actions. She stood at the water's edge and took in her surroundings: majestic Diamond Head and the Royal Hawaiian. She never got tired of beauty, man-made or natural.

She hurried across the burning sand and plopped down on her towel. Wiping her face, she put on her black Wayfarers, rolled up her top as a makeshift pillow, and lay down. She felt the sun begin to broil her face and body. She closed her eyes and fell asleep as quickly as the water on her body evaporated.

She ran her fingers through Annie's red, frizzy hair and looked into her soft hazel eyes. Annie closed her eyes, and her lips parted as she gently kissed Charlie's mouth. Their embrace became more intense and passionate. Charlie's heart was pounding, and she could feel the urge deep within her.

"Excuse me, auntie."

Charlie woke and felt a presence over her.

"Sorry to disturb you, but your auntie said we could find you down here."

Charlie opened her eyes. Through the glare from the setting sun, she could barely make out the female officer standing over her.

"Yes?"

"Detective Tanaka would like to speak with you."

Charlie looked at the officer's name tag. "Officer Urada, may I ask what this concerns?"

"Ya, ya. Auntie, I'm not sure. I was told by Detective Tanaka to find you and bring you downtown."

"You are very persistent. Am I being arrested?"

"No, no, auntie, nothing like that. Detective Tanaka would like to meet with you."

"But I've already met Detective Tanaka, and he didn't seem like he was very interested in meeting with me."

"I think things may have changed." Urada took a knee alongside Charlie.

"Officer Urada, you do understand I'm on vacation? Nothing personal, but I'm trying to stay as far away from work as possible."

"Auntie, I know! I'm so sorry. Your auntie explained every-thing, but Detective Tanaka said he has to speak with you, like urgent, like now."

"What's your first name?"

"Lani."

"All right, Officer Lani Urada. You found me, so I'll strike a deal with you. Well, sort of."

"Thank you, auntie."

"I haven't told you what the deal is yet." Charlie smiled, pulled off her sunglasses, and sat up.

"I'm sorry."

"No need to apologize—I'm definitely not trying to shoot the messenger. I'll meet with Detective Tanaka at my auntie's house this evening. In the meantime, I'm going to take advantage of this incredible sunshine and try to stop doing my best impression of a vampire." Charlie put her sunglasses back on and lay down.

"Oh, thank you so much, auntie." Lani smiled and awkwardly made her way back through the sand.

Charlie knew precisely what Tanaka wanted, and she wanted no part of it. She sat up and bowed her head, and the sunglasses fell off between her legs. She exhaled. *I don't need this. I don't want this. Why do I even feel compelled to meet with him and possibly cave in to his demands?* She looked at the sliver-thin white scars on her wrists and the larger BB-sized dots and streaks on her shoulder and arm. She rolled over to expose her back to the sun and tried to regain her evaporated peace.

Overcome by anxiety and feeling drained from the sun and swimming, Charlie gathered up her things. She piled them into her beach bag and made her way to the parking lot and her auntie's weary Honda. Charlie looked at the car, the heat pouring out of it as she opened the door. *I need to do better.* She climbed into the hot vehicle, her skin sticking to the worn cloth seats. She rolled down the windows and blasted the AC.

Manoa
Wednesday, February 5, 1986

After her shower, Charlie applied cold aloe vera gel to her hot, reddened skin. She decided it would be too painful to put on a bra and went with a comfortable white sundress. Salt and Pepper were waiting for her when she opened the bathroom door and followed her into the kitchen to help Barbara prepare dinner.

"Auntie, we're going to have a guest tonight," she said as she chopped the water chestnuts.

"I figured as much. Kim came by to ask how to reach you. She said it was important that Frank speaks with you today. Then an officer came by asking how she could find you. I told them you were on vacation. But they didn't seem to pay any attention to that."

Charlie laughed. "A persistent group, aren't they?"

"Honey, I'm sorry if I messed up your vacation."

Charlie put down her knife, walked over to Barbara, and hugged her. "You could never ruin my vacation. I owe all of this sunburn to you."

Barbara leaned her head against Charlie's shoulder. "It's just these dreadful murders. Those poor women! What can the police do?"

"I saw on the news that they're forming a task force to try and find the killer. Pretty standard procedure. We've done it in cases like Ted Bundy, Wayne Williams, and now they have another one, the Green River Killer, in Seattle."

"Do you think there could be a killer here like those evil men?"

"I don't know with one hundred percent certainty, but there's a distinct possibility. From what I've gleaned from the papers and the radio, there seem to be enough similarities in the deaths to warrant suspicion." Charlie scooped up the vegetables on the cutting board and tossed them into a glass bowl.

"Oh my God, here I'm asking you questions about killers—I'm no better than the rest. Honey, I'm sorry. I really thought you'd get a chance to get away from all the evil. Let's enjoy the meal," Barbara said, picking up the plates and making her way toward the dining room table.

"Sounds great. I'm famished."

"I spoke with the provost this afternoon." Barbara passed the salad bowl.

"Really? How did that go?" Charlie spooned a large amount of salad onto her plate.

"At first he was reluctant because you aren't coming from an academic background. The man can be such an imbecile."

"You know, he's right." Charlie spun spaghetti onto her folk with the aid of a spoon.

Barbara sipped her merlot. "Ya, ya, but you are such a great practitioner. You'd bring a considerable amount of experience. The other thing is this island is bleeding to death. Kids are leaving to attend different schools, and they don't return, because we don't have high-paying jobs or career opportunities, and real estate is getting more expensive by the minute. The Japanese are buying everything in sight, and it's driving the market bonkers. They can't afford to live here." Barbara waved her hands in frustration.

Charlie was about to respond when Pepper and Salt started barking. She looked over at the front door to see what the commotion was about and then heard the doorbell ring.

Barbara got up and opened the door. "Kim, Frank, come on in." She tried to shoo the dogs out of the way.

"Sorry, Barbara, is this a good time?" Kim asked.

"Sure, we're just finishing our dinner." Salt and Pepper ran around, excited.

"I told you we should have waited longer." Kim looked at her husband in disapproval. "Barbara, I'm so sorry. We can come back later."

"Salt, Pepper, hush, you two. No, no. It's all right. Please, come in. Have you had dinner? We've got plenty. I can fix you a plate."

Tanaka was about to respond when Kim interrupted. "Thank you, but we've already had dinner." She slipped out of her sandals.

"Salad is not dinner. It's an appetizer, or a first course, or something on the side to go along with dinner, but it's definitely not dinner." Tanaka struggled to peel his cowboy boots off.

"Do I need to remind you what the doctor said about your diabetes and blood pressure?"

"Then let me die joyfully and not in fear." Tanaka joined the women in the dining room.

"Detective, auntie, it's good to see you again. Please sit down," Charlie said.

"Kim, it's just some spaghetti, bread, and salad. Frank's so thin, I'm sure a small plate will not adversely affect his health." Barbara made her way to the kitchen.

"It's the damn job. It will be the death of him," Kim said.

Charlie followed Barbara into the kitchen, and they returned shortly with plates of spaghetti, silverware, and glasses.

Their casual, pleasant conversation covered everything from weather to baseball to local gossip, carefully avoiding the real topic that was front and center in everyone's mind.

"Kim, could you give me a hand clearing the table? And we can make the coffee and get the desserts prepared while Charlie and Frank talk," Barbara said as she started to pick up the plates.

"Mahalo, Barbara, that was a delicious dinner. And, I might add, a dinner that had a main course, bread, and salad. And now dessert. Perfect." Tanaka sipped his wine thoughtfully.

"You're impossible." Kim picked up a knife and pointed it at his gut. "We'll take some coffee, but no dessert. We've got to cut back on our sugar intake too."

"Come on, I had a piece of toast and coffee for breakfast and missed lunch. This is the first decent meal that I've had in weeks. I really would like some dessert too."

While Kim and Barbara cleared the table and made their way to the kitchen, Charlie observed Tanaka as he walked around the living room, looking at the pictures and the books stacked on the coffee table and packed onto the shelves. He stopped at one particular photo. "You?"

"Yes. My mom grew up on the island, and our family often came back for visits when I was a kid." Charlie took a sip of her wine.

"But your mom and Barbara are not related, are they?"

"No, they're just best friends." Charlie could remember when the photo with Barbara and Bennie was taken.

"There's a resemblance there." Tanaka stared at Charlie.

"We'd get mistaken for not only mom and daughter, but sisters too." Charlie smiled.

Tanaka nodded and smiled and turned back to the photo. "I'm sorry for your loss. I didn't know your uncle well, but the times that I did meet him, he was always likable and outgoing."

"He was a fun person. He could chase away the blues in a heartbeat."

Tanaka continued his examination of the room. "I shouldn't be surprised. Our house is stacked with academic and reference books too." He picked up a book and looked at the title. "I prefer westerns. You know, Zane Grey, Louis L'Amour. Sometimes I wish I could live in one. It seemed like a much simpler time—straightforward, good guys wore the white hats; bad guys wore the black hats. You could tell who was dangerous. Now we can't even tell if the bad guy is living right next door to us." Tanaka put the book back in its place and turned around.

"Detective?" Charlie said, standing behind a kitchen chair with her hands resting on the top.

"Apologies. I was trying to reconcile the picture of the girl with the woman standing in front of me."

"It's the same person. The years and experiences haven't always been the kindest." Charlie pulled out her chair and sat back down.

"I've never been to Detroit, but I would imagine there aren't a whole lot of hapas running around. Catch hell?" Tanaka joined Charlie at the table.

"My dad would call my sister and me Komericans, but that never seemed to make us invincible to our peers' cruelty.'"

"For the most part, I was pretty fortunate. I looked a lot like the other kids, but there would always be some haole from the base that thought my relatives were responsible for Pearl Harbor."

"I grew up in a beautiful neighborhood, but there were very few Asians and no mixed races. So I'd get my personal favorite: 'Where you from?' When I'd say, 'Here,' they'd go, 'No, where are you really from?' I tried to explain that my mom was Korean, which was futile because they'd still think I was either Japanese or Chinese. Sometimes it's hard to convince people, even with facts."

Tanaka smiled and nodded. "Guilty as charged. How's the vacation going? I've heard that you might consider joining the university faculty?"

"I've thought about it, but I've heard the provost and dean think that I wouldn't be a good fit."

"Minds can be changed. Well, mahalo for seeing me tonight."

"Do you know that you're a lot like Detective Tanaka on *Magnum, P.I.*? Was his character based on you?"

"I look nothing like him," Tanaka said defensively.

"I'm not talking about looks, but the way you act. You're more like an Asian Columbo. You take a circuitous route, but there's reasoning behind it. Deceptive."

"I've been called a lot of things, but I think this is a first—an Asian Columbo." Tanaka chuckled. "But, to answer your question,

I did some limited technical advising for the show, but no, they didn't base the character on me."

Charlie nodded. "It's not a stretch. Charlie Chan was based on Chang Apana, a Honolulu detective, and Steve McQueen's character Frank Bullitt was based on a real San Francisco homicide detective named Dave Toschi."

"I like to think of myself more like Dennis Weaver's character McCloud or Clint Eastwood's Walt Coogan in *Coogan's Bluff*." Tanaka nodded toward his cowboy boots by the door. "A cowboy detective working in a big city."

"Ah, then you're a true paniolo?"

"Impressive! You're familiar with us Hawaiian cowboys. I grew up on the Big Island and worked on the ranches with my dad and uncles. It was a great life, and I miss it sometimes."

"So how did you go from being a paniolo to a homicide detective?"

"I saw the movie *Seven Samurai*, and something clicked about the injustices that I'd witnessed and protecting those who couldn't protect themselves. So one day, I gave up my horse and lariat for a Harley and a gun." He smiled. "I'd like to think that I've got a certain amount of authenticity."

"Do you still ride?"

"Unfortunately, not very often. My time and places on Oahu are limited, so I'll occasionally go for a weekend to Hawaii. When I can convince Kim, I've even vacationed in California, Arizona, and Texas, but by far, Montana is my favorite place—Big Country is what it's all about." Tanaka pulled out a can of Copenhagen from his back pocket.

Charlie watched him intently as he held the can, with the lid facing him, between his middle finger and thumb and flicked his wrist so his index finger slapped against it. He repeated this motion several times.

Tanaka looked up. "I know, a nasty and disgusting habit. Believe it or not, I stopped for a long time, but this case seems to be reigniting bad habits. It helps me think." He twisted off the top of the can, pinched out a dab of packed snuff, and strategically placed it between his right cheek and gum. "Yourself?"

"Like you, I saw a lot of injustice going on. As an extra incentive, I had some shitty things happen to me. Plus, trying to fathom the human thought process fascinated me. So, not a stretch, and similar in a lot of ways to other law enforcement personnel that I've spoken to over the years." Charlie smiled. "What do you want with me?"

"I'm sure that, even on your vacation, you've been following the recent murders. We now believe they're connected." Tanaka leaned forward in his chair.

"I have." Charlie nodded.

"What do you think?"

"I'm sure that you've held back some key pieces of evidence so you can eliminate the false confessions, so my response would be pure speculation. I can't make an informed analysis based on a few newspaper articles."

"But if you were to speculate?" Tanaka rubbed his hands together.

"I'd say you have a difficult and complicated task ahead of you, and I don't envy you at all. Even with hard work and dedication, most times, you'll catch them by accident. One day, a patrolman will stop a car for running a traffic light or rolling through a stop sign, and something won't sit right with him. He'll ask the driver to get out of the car—and voilà. Sometimes it comes down to pure luck."

"I don't know if we can wait for luck. We really could use your help." Tanaka looked Charlie in the eye.

"Detective, I can sympathize with you, and I know what difficulties you're up against, but I'm really trying to avoid all of this." Charlie shook her head.

"Please call me Frank. What happened there? One of those shitty things?" Tanaka pointed at the white scars on Charlie's arm and shoulder.

"No, I owe these scars to an occupational hazard." Charlie shivered slightly and rubbed her arm and shoulder.

"Twelve-gauge?"

"Sixteen. Yes, I was lucky."

"We need your luck. I've heard that you won't stop. We just don't have that type of energy here. We're good cops, but we've got our own way of doing things, and it's not always right. We go at a much slower pace—an island pace."

Don't do it. Stop yourself. You're on vacation.

"What did you have in mind?" Charlie stood up, pushed the chair out, and started pacing. Pepper, sensing the adrenaline, followed her.

"You'd be an adviser or consultant to me and the task force. We—" Tanaka pointed his index finger at Charlie and then at himself. "You and I can decide what's the best way to go about this. And if you help us nail this guy, how could the university turn you away? Every politician in the state would be on them like white on rice to bring you on full-time." Tanaka sat back in his chair, showing relief and just a trace of confidence.

"I'd have to see all the files—complete access to all the information. I'd want to talk with the victims' family members, friends, and associates. I'd have to basically relive the events, trace their footsteps, to get a feel. I need context to understand what was going on so I can start thinking like the killer. I'll start to see what he's seeing and why he's picking out these women specifically."

"We can make that happen."

"Additionally, I know the island, but I'm not a local. I don't have the connections and insight into the people, so I'd want someone to accompany me," Charlie said, running her fingers through her hair, the other hand on her hip.

"Sure, we can assign a detective to accompany you."

"A woman?"

"Probably not. A while back, we had Ruthy Bautista, but she's retired. Ruthy was instrumental in changing the force. She fought back on the height standard—sued and won. Thanks to her, we have a lot more women on the force, but none currently in homicide."

"That won't work. I want a woman that knows the island, is hungry, and will be a good partner. I've worked with enough men in this profession to know that most of them have a really tough time taking orders from a woman, especially a hapa who isn't from around here, and I'm sure HPD is no different."

"This isn't going to go over well." Tanaka could already hear the backlash.

"I bet there are already some who objected to bringing me on, so I'll just be meeting their expectations." Charlie smiled confidently.

"There have been a few."

"Women are more likely to open up to other women, and men are thrown off when they're questioned by two women. Their perceived superiority leads them to be overconfident, which leads to mistakes. They let their guard down."

Tanaka stood up. "We have some competent detectives. Do you have something else in mind?"

"I do," Charlie said.

"Time for dessert and coffee?" Barbara asked, poking her head out from the kitchen.

Honolulu
Friday, February 7, 1986

At the end of the hallway hung a plastic sign with the word *Homicide* above a set of double doors. Charlie looked down the crowded, noisy hallway and tried to determine the best way to navigate it. A few of the officers, some in uniform and some in plainclothes, glanced at her and then turned back to their conversations.

She could feel the hostility as she wove around the officers; few made room for her. Snide remarks and catcalls reached her ears as she passed. *Ignore them, they'll get used to you and even grow to love you, just like the rest. Maybe love is too strong of a word—respect.*

Charlie entered the homicide detectives' room. A group of five men were circled together, dressed in a variety of short-sleeved shirts with either ties or opened collars. Some wore Hawaiian or golf shirts. One detective tapped Tanaka on the shoulder. Soon the whole room went quiet, and everyone stared. Charlie, unfazed by the chilly reception, walked confidently toward Tanaka.

"Detective Tanaka." She extended her hand.

"Doctor, thank you very much for coming. Let me introduce you to the team." As Tanaka and Charlie approached the group, the circle of men opened up. Tanaka did quick introductions. "And last but not least, my partner, Detective Williams."

"Ya, he's Mac," someone said.

"Mac?" asked Charlie.

"Ya, as in macaroni salad. Tanaka is Rice, as in rice ball, and Williams is Macaroni Salad, part of the lunch plate," said a detective wearing a lime-green golf shirt with a little penguin on it.

"Don't waste your breath explaining the joke. The good doctor is not a local. She wouldn't appreciate our humor or how we do our work around here," Williams said.

The other detectives chuckled lightly and looked at Charlie with disapproval.

"You're right, Detective. My mother was from here, I was born here, and we visited often, but 'ya,' I'm not a local." Charlie stared at Williams and extended her hand. Williams turned away and resumed his conversation with the other detectives. Not deterred, Charlie nodded at the others. "Nice meeting all of you gentlemen. I look forward to working with you."

The detectives nodded reluctantly. Tanaka, annoyed, recommended they move over to his desk so they could continue their conversation. He offered Charlie the seat alongside his battered wooden desk. Charlie looked at the floor and saw a small pile of dust. She wondered how many victims and perpetrators had sat there.

"Do you know that you have termites?"

Tanaka looked under his desk. "Ya, it's probably the only way I'll ever get a new desk." He pushed a thick folder toward Charlie. "This is what we've collected so far."

She opened the file and began to flip through the contents.

"We're used to robberies gone bad or a family tragedy that ended with someone getting stabbed. Despite what those assholes may think, we do need your assistance. So please don't let them get to you."

"They don't. I've dealt with much worse. Can I take this with me?"

"I'll make a copy."

"Have Officer Urada bring it by my auntie's house on Monday. I'm going to enjoy my weekend."

"Ya, about that . . . I've spoken with the chief, and he's not crazy about the idea of having Urada jump over more senior officers."

Charlie handed the file back to Tanaka. "Well, then, it's settled. Everyone can be happy. I can go back to my vacation, the chief won't have to worry about troop morale, and the others can rest easy that I won't be getting into their business."

Tanaka watched Charlie walk out of the room. He looked back down at the file.

Williams walked up to the desk and slapped Tanaka on the back. "Her Highness was expecting a royal welcome? Then screw her if we didn't roll out the red carpet for the—"

"Mac," Tanaka said, raising his voice.

The office became uncharacteristically quiet.

"Sensitive, are we? Well, she and you can go—"

"Mac, shut up and get some work done for once." Tanaka shoved the file folder into Williams's chest.

Waikiki
Monday, February 10, 1986

The sun started to rise as Charlie ran along Kalakaua Avenue. She had the road to herself—it was too early for the tourists, and only a few surfers, homeless, and late partiers were out. She passed the high-end retail storefronts, the Moana Surfrider—the oldest hotel on the island—and along Kuhio Beach Park. She looked through the palm trees and took in the ocean. She watched the waves crash over the seawall and fought the temptation to jump in. She could start to feel the warmth of the sun on her shoulders.

She ran past the Waikiki Aquarium and the War Memorial Natatorium and onto Diamond Head Road. She pushed herself to another gear as she began the slow, steady climb. Soon other runners of all ages started to appear, offering each other greetings and words of encouragement. A slight breeze coming from the ocean helped. She was tempted to stop and take in the beautiful scenery, but she wouldn't let herself. Leahi Beach Park, Diamond

Head Lighthouse, Amelia Earhart's marker, and then Diamond Head Lookout.

Charlie made the turn around Diamond Head, past the Hawaii Department of Defense, the Diamond Head Memorial Park, and then the park entrance. The breeze had disappeared, and the sun was beating down on her. Sweat formed on her brow and trickled into her eyes, but Charlie ignored the pain. Her legs started to tire, but she ignored that too. *Getting old sucks. I don't have the stamina that I once had.* She kept running—pushing. She let her mind wander until it found a happy place. She imagined Annie in front of her.

"You're like a cat, so smooth and powerful! I can barely keep up with you on my bicycle." Annie laughed as she rode alongside.

Charlie smiled. "You don't mind if I don't respond? It's hard to keep this pace and hold a conversation."

"Do you love me?" Annie asked.

"I don't believe that question requires a response."

"You don't? Maybe you require a little more motivation." Annie pedaled harder. Charlie laughed and ran faster, trying to catch her best friend.

She arrived at Barbara's house soaking wet, opened the door, and let the dogs out. They swarmed her as she sat on the porch, eagerly licking the salt from her skin. She pushed herself up before she got too stiff and went inside. She pulled a bottle of orange juice out of the fridge and drank from the container.

"Ghastly!"

"Sorry, I should have gotten a glass."

"That too. Look at you. I've never understood the enjoyment of exercise, especially running. What's the interest? The value?"

Barbara, still dressed in her nightgown, took the bottle away from Charlie and poured her a glass.

"Thanks, auntie. It's a healthier way of coping than alcohol or drugs. The burnout factor for law enforcement is pretty devastating." Charlie lifted the bottom of her shirt and wiped the sweat from her eyes.

"You look much better than when you first arrived, but there's still something nagging at you. I can see the lines on your forehead."

"Its hard for me to errarse my bad memories."

"I worry about you." Barbara made her way to the coffee maker.

"I'm doing well. I'll take care of that." Charlie bumped Barbara out of the way with her hip.

"You sure?" Barbara looked out the kitchen window.

"I'm sorry. My mind never shuts off, so I need ways to cope. Most days, it's running; sometimes it's music or a book."

"A man?"

"I don't need a man in my life when I've got you, Salt, and Pepper." Charlie gave her a hug.

"I love you, but you're gross! I need a shower, and now this nightgown has to go into the wash." Barbara pushed Charlie away.

"I'll be fine. I somehow seem to manage."

"You sure?"

Both women turned their heads at the sound of a knock. Salt and Pepper ran to the door and started barking excitedly.

"Be quiet, you two!" Barbara yelled as she opened the front door.

"Excuse me, auntie. I'm here to see Dr. Taylor. Is she in?"

Barbara opened the door, and Officer Urada walked through. Salt and Pepper ran around her, sniffing at her legs. "Let the poor girl in, you two," Barbara said, picking up Salt.

"Thank you, auntie." Lani laughed.

"Well, I've got to get cleaned up." Barbara shot Charlie a look and pointed to her nightgown. "Officer, it's good to see you again." She walked into her bedroom with Salt in her arms, closing the door behind them.

"What do I owe this visit to?"

"You can't repeat a word of this, but I heard there was a knock-down, drag-out fight in the homicide office this weekend. A friend of mine said he's never seen Detective Tanaka so angry. He was even yelling at Detective Williams. I guess it got so bad the chief had to intervene." Lani rocked on her heels and clutched the strap of her large canvas tote bag with both hands.

"Come on in. I take it as a good sign that you're here and wearing plainclothes." Charlie examined Lani's upward-styled bangs, big gold earrings, Jordache jeans, and turquoise blouse with puffy sleeves. "You realize that we're working and not going to a club, don't you?" Charlie teased.

"I'm sorry, did I overdo it? I can go home and change." Lani's knuckles turned white.

"No, you look great. You'll come to find that I've got a wicked sense of humor with a strong dash of sarcasm. You've probably witnessed the alcohol, drugs, and affairs that others use to survive in this profession. I've seen what happens, and I prefer running and humor." Charlie walked into the living room area.

Lani started to relax. "Thank you, auntie. I appreciate your confidence in me."

Charlie smiled. "Did Tanaka give you a copy of the files?"

"I have them here." Lani patted her tote bag.

"Did you look at the photos? Read the reports?"

"I skimmed through them as I made copies this morning at headquarters and again when I was waiting for you outside your house. Did I screw that up too?" Lani asked as she moved toward Charlie to hand her the file. "I really don't know what I'm looking for."

"It'll be a crash course—I'll coach, teach, and make demands of you, but for now, just become familiar with the material. Eventually you'll need to know it backward and forward. So have a seat at the kitchen table and make yourself comfortable. Can I get you a glass of water or juice?"

"I'm fine, auntie." Lani sat down and opened the file.

"Okay, then. I look terrible and smell much worse, so I'm going to jump in the shower, and I'll be with you shortly. Oh, and that's Pepper. Watch out for him—he has an eye for the ladies," Charlie added on her way to the bathroom.

She returned soon afterward, bucking the current fashion trend of big and bold with an understated outfit of navy-blue linen slacks, a white cotton blouse, and a large gold bangle. Her makeup was subtle, and her short hair was still damp. "Had any breakfast?"

"No, I was so busy this morning that I didn't have time to eat."

"Bagels and coffee okay?"

"Ya, ya, sounds good. Your auntie just left a couple of minutes ago. She told me to tell you that she loves you."

"Thanks." Charlie started pulling items from the cabinets and refrigerator.

"You two seem to be pretty close." Lani said, her right knee furiously pumping up and down.

Charlie paused for a moment. "My auntie and halmeoni, my Korean grandmother, are my two favorite people in the whole world—both have always been there for me. Unfortunately for you, you'll come to learn that I'm complicated, controversial, and a major pain in the ass. So accept my apology up front. But they got me. They always seemed to understand." She flipped on the Mr. Coffee and pushed down the toaster lever simultaneously.

"How can I help?"

"I've got this." Charlie went about the kitchen, muttering to herself.

"What was that, auntie?"

"Nothing important, just talking to myself. Another sign of old age."

"You're not old. What are you, thirty-two?"

"I could kiss you for saying that, but I'm forty. You've got to stop calling me auntie, though—it makes me feel really old. Charlie works."

Lani smiled. "All right, Charlie."

"Cream, sugar?" Charlie held up a coffee mug.

"Both, heavy on the cream," Lani said. She got up, pulled the bagel from the toaster, and placed the next one in.

"What stood out the most to you when you looked at the pictures?"

"I guess several things: They were all young women, the areas that the bodies were found—all in or near water, sort of remote—and they were Caucasian. But that's what the papers are saying. Not very insightful, I'm sorry—I'm not very good at this."

"You're not expected to be. You're doing fine. It's the next part that everyone misses. So what is the significance of those facts? That's where we come in." Charlie brought over a tray with coffee, juice, bagels, and jars of jam.

"Mahalo," Lani said as she reached for a cup of coffee.

Charlie passed Lani a bagel. "Don't discount fiction. Poe, Doyle, and Christie had terrific insights into human character."

"I read all of Christie's books as a teenager." Lani sipped her coffee.

"Apologies for the history lesson, but consider it part of your training; it provides you with some context."

"Please, I find this fascinating."

"In the 1940s and 1950s, there were a series of bombings in New York City. The perpetrator had been given the moniker 'Mad Bomber' because for sixteen years, he had been placing bombs in various locations throughout the city. The police were stymied, so they engaged a local psychiatrist by the name of Dr. James A. Brussel to see if he could assist."

Lani put down her cup and stared intently at Charlie.

"The press labeled him 'Sherlock Holmes of the couch,' but Brussel was quick to dismiss the claim. He reviewed all the facts surrounding the case, from where the bombs were placed and how they were constructed to evaluating the bomber's handwritten notes. Based on his experience and knowledge, he developed a profile.

"The profile did a couple of things: It helped focus the investigation on where to look for the bomber using type of employment, skills that he possessed, his upbringing, and physical and mental characteristics. On January 21, 1957, George Metesky was arrested and eventually convicted of the crimes."

"What tremendous insight he had to be able to figure that all out."

"For me the next evolution began with FBI Special Agent Howard Teten. He had been a San Leandro police officer and studied criminology at UC Berkeley when he joined the FBI in 1962. Teten could see the parallels between what he saw at work and what he was learning in the classroom. He became fascinated, and even Brussel believed that a psychiatrist's most important characteristic has to be curiosity.

"In 1969 Teten was asked to join the training division as an instructor. He took his fascination to the next level and convinced his supervisor to let him give a four-hour seminar on what he had learned and how to apply those principles. The first seminar that he gave was to the New York City Police Department, and it was received incredibly well."

"We could use something like that around here," Lani said, spreading the jam on her bagel.

"Don't let Tanaka or Williams hear you say that or they'll burry you in administration."

"I know, I know," Lani said exasperatedly.

"So, Teten then created a four-day course, which he taught at a Texas police academy. Students began approaching him with facts surrounding unsolved crimes, and with his help, they were able to bring some cases to successful conclusions. The seminar became so popular that Teten requested that Special Agent Patrick Mullany, who had a master's degree in educational psychology, join him. Teten and Mullany were a good team. Teten would lay out the facts, and Mullany would demonstrate how aspects of the crime scene revealed the perpetrator's psychosis."

Charlie paused to take a bite of bagel and wash it down with her coffee. She took a deep breath, lightly exhaled, and began to rapid fire again.

"Then, from 1972 to 1976, two other agents of the Behavioral Science Unit continued the evolution when they started to interview serial killers. Although it seemed groundbreaking—and it was—really, it was the next logical step to increasing our understanding and awareness. Their interviews allowed them to get into the minds of these killers. I even interviewed killers myself"

"Wait, what was that like?"

"I didn't interview some of the more nationwide notorious killers, but I did speak with some of Michigan's most famous killers," Charlie said. "I was methodical in my preparation. I took the time to find out everything that I could about them personally, the case, police reports, psychological profiles. We then had a conversation."

"That is why you want me to know everything about the case? But, a conversation? I don't get that." Lani sat on the edge of her chair.

"Yes and yes. I wasn't there to interrogate them, but have a conversation. I had to win their trust."

"How did you keep your composure?"

"It's about discipline and not losing sight of what you are trying to achieve. But before you think this is the end-all-be-all solution, it's not. None of this absolves shoddy detective work. Leads still need to be tracked and followed up on, evidence still needs to be found, and witnesses interviewed. We are enablers, not replacers. So both Tanaka and Williams can be right at the same time for different reasons."

"How did you get into all of this?"

Charlie paused. "I hate to see injustices, and something happened to me personally that I'll explain later."

"Auntie, I'm sorry. I didn't mean to intrude."

"You're fine—it's me—it's always me." Charlie sipped her coffee and looked into the cup. "Sorry, let's start with your observations. You said the women were young, but what were their ages?"

Lani shuffled through the papers. "Pam Adair was twenty-five, Rebecca Saito was age seventeen, and Debra Harris was twenty-one."

"So, statistically speaking, we are looking for someone in their late teens to late twenties." Charlie studied the victims' photos. "Okay, now tell me about the locations where the bodies were found."

Lani paused. "Like I said before, they were found in water. Pam's and Rebecca's bodies were found in the Keʻehi Lagoon, and Debra's body was found in a drainage canal near Moanalua Stream."

"A couple of aspects strike me about the locations, but let's just address where the bodies were placed. The fact that they were found in or near water statistically implies that it was an older man, so our age scale starts to slide from late teens to midtwenties to midthirties." Charlie watched Lani's response. "What about their race?"

"They all were or looked Caucasian. Rebecca's last name gives you the impression that maybe she's of Japanese descent, but that's the name of her stepfather." Lani sounded more confident.

"Take it to the next logical step?" Charlie sipped her coffee and crossed her legs.

"We're looking for someone that looks like them?"

"Although there are instances of serial killers moving across race lines, it's more the exception than the rule. Hawaii is interesting because we have a lot more interracial relationships than you might in some other areas."

"So we're not looking for some white guy?"

"Great question. I'd say at this point, we are still looking for a Caucausion male, but we've got to make sure that we're not blinded by a particular bias or let an assumption cloud a fact." Charlie got up and went over and picked up the coffee pot.

"The profile is in its infantile stage—pretty ambiguous and, frankly, not helpful. So we have to keep going. I'm sure the detectives are getting inundated with calls, and it takes a lot of time and energy to check out each one. Eventually they're going to get a list of suspects that show tremendous potential; however, by using the profile, we can help qualify some suspects and eliminate the others, thus making their investigation more efficient and effective."

Lani looked a little overwhelmed. "What comes next?"

Charlie sensed her uneasiness. "Let's finish our breakfast, then we'll continue to review the file and look at other commonalities. Everything starts with the body—that is the one constant. Like dropping a pebble into a pond, we begin following the concentric circles out from the body. We'll need to develop a plan to speak with the victims' friends and relatives. Can you arrange that?"

Lani took her notepad and wrote down the requirement. "Sure."

"We need to understand the victims—their habits, personality, behavior. It's essential for us to get into their mind as much as the killer's mind. Christie wrote about how everyone focuses on the perpetrator; however, it's the victim that should garner the attention. She was brilliant, ahead of her time. Bottom line, we need to see what led up to the event from their perspective—what did the victim see—and then comes what did the killer see in them."

Charlie spread cream cheese and raspberry preserves on her bagel and took a bite. "Sorry, I didn't realize how famished I was."

"I don't blame you. I saw you running up the hill—you're in incredible shape." Lani reached for her coffee.

"Another occupational requirement." Charlie half smiled. She wiped off her fingers and mouth and reached for the folder. "Take a look at the drop areas. Besides water, what else do they say to you?"

"They are reasonably accessible," Lani said half-heartedly.

"Exactly, but what does that mean?"

"That he knew the area?"

"So most likely a local and not a tourist, but not only does he know the area, but he's confident there at night. I also believe that the killer most likely lives or works nearby. He feels comfortable moving around the area with a dead body. He doesn't look out of place, so no one would be suspicious of him. And look at the immediate area."

"Rocky, uneven," Lani responded.

"Let's, for a moment, take it from the killer's perspective. It's night; he has a dead body in his vehicle—we'll assume the body is in the trunk. For Pam and Rebecca, he had to lift up and in, lift up and out, possibly up and over a guardrail, and the terrain was either rocky or scrub and sand on the way to the water."

Lani watched Charlie closely as she moved around the kitchen replicating the killer's movements.

"You need to understand that the killer is learning and applying lessons. He's watching the news and reading the papers. It seems to him that HPD and the press haven't put together two and two, that these killings are related, but he doesn't want to get caught putting Debra's body in the same location, so he picks a new one. The new site is relatively close to the first two, so the killer's staying in his territory, his comfort zone."

"Doesn't he have to be strong to lift that dead weight?" Lani asked.

"Exactly." Charlie pointed at Lani. "He also starts to think that Rebecca was tiny, Pam was of average height and weight, and now Debra is slightly above average. The killer has to use a lot of strength, energy, and time. Maybe he feels more vulnerable about getting caught. So he wraps Debra's body in a tarp so he can drag it to the drainage ditch."

Lani shivered slightly. "The hair on the back of my neck is standing up. I'm sorry to ask again, but how did you get into all this?"

"When we met on the beach and the reason that I asked, demanded, that we partner, was because I felt like I could trust you. So, was I right? Can I trust you?"

"Ya, auntie, you can trust me," Lani responded excitedly.

"I have tremendous empathy for victims. I want to make sure they have an advocate. I know what it's like to be a victim and have no where to go. I was gang- raped at a party in college. I went with a family friend that set me up with his fraternity brothers. They drugged my drink . . . the rest is history." Charlie sat back in her chair, holding her coffee cup close to her chest.

"I'm so, so sorry. Is that why your so motivated?"

"Ya, I'm sure that's part of it, probably a big part of it."

"I overheard Detectives Tanaka and Williams speaking. After their big blowup, the chief told them to call Michigan, and if they said you were as good as Crawford said, then you were in, and if not, then they would let you enjoy the rest of your vacation."

"I can only imagine what they might have said."

"I'm sorry, I'm just repeating what they said, auntie," Lani said.

"It's okay, nothing that I probably haven't heard in the past."

"They said you were a real bitch—hard to work with, opininated, and a major pain in the ass. They said that you were from the *Twilight Zone*, you had this vision or insight. You could crawl into people's minds. They said you scared the shit out of them, but were fearless. They also said you were amazing with the victims' families and friends. They told Tanaka and Williams to give you whatever you asked for. Let you go on your own. Don't get in your away. They said that Tanaka and Williams would be fools not to have you help. They also wanted to know when you're coming back."

"Pretty fair assessment. Does any of that bother you?"

"Not a bit."

"Good, because before we're through, you'll think of me as a bitch too. Yourself?"

"Nothing compared to you. I just wanted to help people. My grandmother and grandfather were being taken advantage of by punks. I was upset, but I couldn't do anything about it, and the police were being unresponsive, so I joined the force." Lani conscientiously wiped the crumbs off the table and onto her plate with her napkin.

Charlie nodded as she got up. "Need a refill?"

"No, no, I'm good."

"Okay, back to the school lesson. Our next step, we classify the killers into two groups. The first group is called organized. The organized killer, as the name implies, has thought about and planned the murders, so he's not leaving any evidence behind. Most likely these killers are in some type of relationship—"

"Wait, you mean these guys have girlfriends or wives? Can you imagine that conversation? 'Honey, I'm home.' 'Oh, hello, dear. How did your day go?'"

Charlie laughed. "Exactly. This group of killers has some education; they're accomplished, astute, and measured. They're relatively good-looking and appealing. They have a way of seducing the victims. Think about Ted Bundy—he was attractive and charming. From our earliest days, we're raised to believe we can spot the bogeyman, but when that bogeyman is a relative, neighbor, teacher, or clergy, our whole reality is thrown out of whack. What do we know about the sequence of events with the victim?"

Lani fingered her necklace. "Well, we know that they were picked up in one area. We didn't find any evidence at either scene, so they were most likely killed in another location."

"Well done. These killers have knowledge of how police operate, so they make sure that we don't find any incriminating evidence. Additionally, they will follow the investigation in the press both for the thrill and to see if they've made any mistakes. So if the first group is organized, who do you think belongs in the second group?"

Lani shrugged. "The opposite of organized?"

"No stretch of the imagination—'disorganized' is the technical term. These crimes are not planned. Everything is left right there for us to find. In that same vein, it's not surprising to see that most times, the perpetrators have often been abused themselves. They are younger, sometimes under the influence of drugs or alcohol, have average or below intelligence, and are from a dysfunctional family. They live alone, usually without transportation, so they kill close to home. Most times, they will blitz their victims—that is, use sudden and overwhelming force. So, given what we know and don't know, what type of killer do we have?"

"It seems pretty apparent that the killer is organized," Lani replied comfortably.

"Yes, but we need to remember that these are two ends of a continuum, so it's not surprising to see that some killers will have a foot in each camp, or there may be more than one killer."

Lani sat up excitedly. "Two killers! You said about how difficult it would be for one man to lift the bodies and move them to the drop-off points."

"Yes, the thought had crossed my mind. Let's take a break. I need to walk the dogs, and it helps clear my head."

At the mention of a walk, the dogs jumped up from under the table.

"It looks like a unanimous decision," Charlie said.

"I believe so." Lani slapped her hands on the table and nodded in agreement.

The women made their way through the peaceful campus, watching the students on their way to and from class. "When you look at them, what do you see?" Charlie asked.

"They look so young, sweet, and smart. I know these girls aren't much younger than me, but they look so young, happy . . . innocent, I guess. I'm jealous."

"Well, it's not all a bed of roses, but your observations are well taken and not far from how serial killers see them. This is a prime hunting ground for them. We've talked about Bundy at the UW, and in my neck of the woods, there was John Norman Collins, the 'Co-Ed Killer,' at the U of M and Eastern Michigan University. So we look at four basic types."

Lani looked closely at Charlie and then took a closer look at the female students.

"The first is the hunters. They search for a specific victim in their home territory. Like animal hunters, they're after a particular type of prey. For example, a deer hunter isn't going to shoot a rabbit. He's looking for a deer, probably a buck, and if that buck has a large rack, all the better. So the hunter will track and wait patiently until he gets the right deer in his sights, exhale, and slowly pull the trigger. Like picking out a piece of art—they know it when they see it."

Charlie paused and surveyed the campus. She appreciated the architecture and serenity of the campus. She looked at Lani and then started walking again.

"Next, you have the poachers, who'll travel anywhere to hunt game and most times don't have a specific prey in mind. Most poachers will set different types of traps and either entice or drive the game to their traps. These types of killers thrive on the adrenaline of the hunt and kill. They're not afraid of getting caught. They're used to high-risk situations, like former military or police."

"Did you meet any former law enforcement types? That were actual killers?"

"There was a sheriff's deputy in Florida in the late forties and early fifties that was caught. Berkowitz, 'Son of Sam,' that did a short stint in the army. Most killers are aircraft machinists, auto mechanics, or upholsterers."

Lani grabbed Charlie's arm. "The area where all three women were dropped is surrounded by maintenance repair shops."

Charlie studied Lani's face. "That is why I need you, so don't ever second-guess yourself or think that you don't have something to contribute."

"I don't know . . . ," Lani said.

Charlie and Lani walked past the Kennedy Theater.

"The third is the trollers, who are looking for opportunistic encounters. Like fishermen, they move slowly through an area, trying to catch prey. The trollers will use a lot of lines and bait to see what they can snag."

Pepper broke the atmosphere as he pulled hard against his leash at the sight of a mongoose. Lani pulled him in tighter. "Relax, Pepper. Relax."

Charlie shook her head. "That boy."

"Finally, we have the trappers, who create a situation to draw a victim to them. They may use a variety of methods. Sometimes a killer will make use of a situation that already exists, preying on a woman's knowledge. For example, the killer may pose as a police officer, knowing that women are already cautious. The killer flashes a phony badge. 'Don't you know it's not safe to be out here? Haven't you been reading about the women who've been murdered by some psycho? You're in luck! Get in the car, and I'll get you where you need to go.' The offender lies in wait for his victim and then quickly subdues her. The killer will blitz the victim, overcome her defenses, and use force to gain control."

"I know you said they weren't intelligent, but they sound smarter than our local boys."

"Where I come from, most hunters aren't exactly oozing with intelligence. They're usually overweight and dressed in orange gear, and they sit in their blinds for hours on end, drinking beer and waiting for some unsuspecting deer to come by. Most times, they don't shoot a damn thing, and sometimes they shoot themselves or a friend. Maybe it's just men in general." Charlie smiled.

"That's for sure!" Lani laughed.

"What they are most times is lucky, but they do have strong social skills to overcome any objections that these women might have. Let's head back to the house, grab some lunch. I want to cover a couple more things, then we'll call it a day."

Charlie and Lani continued their conversation as they retraced their steps through the campus and back to the house. Charlie and Lani both felt the cool air as they opened and walked through the front door. The exhauster dogs drank from their water dishes and found a comfortable place to nap.

"Do you mind washing the breakfast dishes while I prepare lunch?"

"Not at all," Lani said as she made her way to the kitchen sink rolling up her sleeves. Charlie grabbed plates from the cupboard. "Salad okay?" she asked.

"Salad sounds great." Lani smiled. "When I'm your age, I want to look as good as you."

"Thank you, but getting old sucks."

"You're not old."

"Tell that to my body. I barely can make it out of my bed in the morning, and it takes forever to loosen up."

Over salad and iced tea, Charlie began laying the pictures on the table in sequential order. "We need to understand the killer's specific MO, knowing that the MO is what the killer must do. For example, we can see from the pictures that the killer used the same type of rope to control his victims." Charlie pointed to different areas on the photos. "Now, what I don't see is staging. Sometimes a killer will stage the victim to elicit a response from law enforcement and the public. However, we know that as time progresses, the killer's MO will evolve based on his experience with the victims and possibly to throw law enforcement off his trail."

"Is that why all the murders aren't identical? I see some similarities, but how do we know it's the same person?"

"The changing MO is certainly part of it. If we were to examine the different guys you've dated, would we start to see similarities?"

"Regrettably, ya."

"That's part of the explanation. The other is that to the killer, this is like making love. He wants to have the same experience, but the circumstances are different. Even when you make love to the same person, each experience is a little different—no two are the same."

"Ya, ya, that makes sense. I've got to change up my pattern. I only seem to go after losers."

"Do you have a signature?"

"Sure," Lani said.

"Let's see it," Charlie said, handing her a pen and pushing a yellow pad in her direction. She watched Lani sign. "Good. Now, here's mine."

"I like yours better."

"My mom made us sit for hours to practice our penmanship." Charlie admired the two signatures. "But the other thing is they're different. Most killers have a signature too. It's what they need to satisfy themselves. It's their fantasy coming alive; however, the reality doesn't satisfy the fantasy, so they're driven to kill more."

"So he's not going to stop?"

"Stop? Oh no. A killer might take a pause or hibernate for a while, but no, he won't stop. In fact, this one seems to be picking up speed."

"What do you mean?"

"The first murder took place when?"

"Pam Adair, May 1985."

"The second murder?"

"Rebecca Saito, January 1986."

"And?"

"Debra Hughes, two weeks later. So you're saying he could strike again."

"Yes, that's exactly what I'm saying. Maybe as soon as in the next couple of weeks."

"Shit," Lani said, pausing to take a bite of her salad. "My God, we've got to stop him. What do we do next?"

"We just don't stop, ever. We've got to run faster and harder than the killer and pray to God he makes a mistake." Charlie pulled the yellow pad in front of her and paused. "Let's draft our first profile from what we know."

"Oh, auntie, I don't know if I could draft a profile! My head is swimming with thoughts."

"Perfect. And don't worry, this is part of your training. Just take all those thoughts that are swimming around in your head and put them down on paper. Don't worry about whether they make sense. Just write it all down like this." Charlie began to write words and draw circles around them. "I want you to mind map."

They reviewed the evidence, going back and forth between the file and the pad of paper. They formulated ideas, wrote them down, and discussed their merits. Some ideas withstood scrutiny, while others were scratched out. Soon the page was covered with coherent thoughts.

"Now I want you to go do a couple of things later today. I want you to lay out a plan to visit all the scenes, and then we need to see each victim's family and friends." Charlie stood and stretched.

"All right, auntie. I've got to stop and see Detective Tanaka. He wants me to report to him every day on our progress." Lani got up and grabbed her bag from the back of the chair. "Do you want me to leave the file here? Can I show him this?"

"I'll take the file, and as long as he understands it's a preliminary draft." She walked Lani to the front door, Salt and Pepper trailing them. "Just remember one thing."

"After all that you told me, I only have to remember one thing?" Lani looked bewildered.

"Yep. It's all about Mom. Mother, Momma. They all have mommy issues. Lani, it was a good day. Try to get some rest, because we'll be at it again tomorrow, the next day, and the day after. Take care." Charlie closed the door.

Honolulu
Wednesday, February 12, 1986

"Well, look who's here! Honoring us with her presence," Williams said. The detectives turned to look at Lani as she walked in. "If I'd known you looked so fine out of uniform, then I would have made you a detective sooner," he added, drawing laughter across the office.

Lani tried to ignore the catcalls and whistles and made her way to Tanaka's desk.

"Ya, ya . . . We have no leads. We are getting hundreds of calls every day. My detectives are chasing down every one of them, but it takes time to weed through them." Tanaka hung up the heavy black receiver. He looked at Lani standing in front of him in a relaxed parade rest.

"If it's not the mayor's office, then it's the DA, and if it's not one of them, then it's the press. I'm just waiting for the governor's office to start offering suggestions," Tanaka said. "Officer, please have a seat. You're making me nervous standing there."

Lani sat down and pulled a folder from her bag. She handed it to Tanaka.

"What's this?"

"Hopefully, a start. It's our first draft profile." Lani moved to the edge of her seat. She could feel Williams hovering nearby.

"So, this is the answer we've all been waiting around for?" Williams asked, trying to maneuver closer so he could read the profile. "In less than eight hours, you and the good doctor have solved this, and my life can get back to normal."

When Tanaka finished reading, he looked up at Lani. "How are we supposed to use this?"

"And why isn't she here?" Williams asked.

"I didn't realize she was supposed to be," Lani answered.

"Officer, don't get patronizing with me—this isn't going to last forever. Someday you'll be back on patrol, and I'll make sure that you get every lousy detail possible," Williams fired back, his hands clenched and the veins on his neck starting to bulge.

"All right, all right. So, Officer Urada, what am I supposed to do with this profile?" Tanaka asked.

"Dr. Taylor believes that the profile helps eliminate all the wild-goose chases that you and your detectives are going through."

"Meaning?"

"The way Dr. Taylor described it to me, when a call comes in, if the tip doesn't match someone who fits this profile, you can make that tip a lower priority. If a tip does match this profile, then that tip should be made a higher priority."

"It still takes good police work," Williams chimed in.

"Ya, ya, Detective. Dr. Taylor made sure that I understood completely that our work—I mean, her work—is to be an enabler and not a replacer. I think I got that right."

"You've learned this just by watching her?" Tanaka asked.

"Charlie has been tutoring me."

"So now it's Charlie?" Williams's tone matched his acid expression.

"Dr. Taylor—Charlie—has been providing me instructions. It's like having a private tutor."

"Just remember, she's from the mainland, and when this is over, your ass is going back into a patrol car, and you'll get your detective shield like everyone else. As Smith Barney says, the old-fashioned way—you'll earn it."

"Yes, Detective Williams."

Tanaka handed Williams the draft profile.

"What's this about?" Williams asked.

Lani looked where Williams was pointing. "Dr. Taylor believes there could be two killers. Not copycats, but two killers working together."

"That's nonsense. Your doctor friend needs to stay on vacation, and you need to get your ass back in a patrol car and leave the detective work to the professionals—us." Williams tossed the piece of paper at Lani.

"All right, all right. Thank you, Officer Urada. Mac, their recommendations and rationale aren't without merit."

"Please, partner, don't get soft on me now," Williams said as he walked away.

Honolulu, Wheeler Force Air Base, Wahiawa, and Pearl City
Friday, February 14, 1986

Charlie shifted the gears of the rented silver convertible Mustang GT 5.0 as the women made their way west on H-1. They passed the signs for the airport, Pearl Harbor and the Hickam Air Force Base, and the USS *Arizona* Memorial exits. Charlie pushed the car harder. She exhaled slowly as she shifted again and passed the cars in the lane next to them.

"Charlie, what's on your mind? You seemed stressed."

"I rented this car because I thought I would get more power than my auntie's old Honda has, but it isn't much better," she said, frustrated by the Mustang's lack of responsiveness.

"This is a nice car. I like it."

"This car can't hold a candle to my '68." She pushed the car harder.

"Really?"

"I grew up in Detroit in its heyday, when cars were king. Cars back in the sixties had everything: style and power. Now they're just crappy pieces of plastic—no power, no style. Nada, zip. Sad commentary."

Charlie's mind began to wander.

"Where are we heading?" Annie smiled and rested her back against the passenger-side door.

Charlie returned the smile as she glanced at Annie. Her red hair was whipped by the air rushing in the open window. "A surprise."

"A road trip leading to a surprise." Annie grinned. "I'm all in."

"Then sit back and enjoy the ride."

"I've always enjoyed the ride." Annie pressed back into her seat as Charlie shifted, and the Mustang leaped forward in response.

"We've gotta stay to the right and head north on H-2." Lani pointed to the two lanes bearing right.

Charlie came back to the present and followed the signs to make the climb north along H-2. She noticed immediately that they had left the city and were entering a rural area.

"The first victim's husband works at either Schofield Barracks or Wheeler Air Force Base. I don't know the military units, so I wasn't sure what I was looking for."

"Does he know we're coming?"

"He knows, ya." Lani nodded.

"Those fighter jocks are going to love you."

"Did I screw up my clothes again?"

"No, you look great." Charlie smiled. "Pilot testosterone is in overdrive."

"Nice. Are you married?"

"No, I've never married."

"Really? You're a good-looking woman. Smart, professional. I'd think you'd be a great catch for some guy."

Charlie smiled. *Why is it that everyone wants to know if you're married? I've seen so many miserable people in lousy marriages— why would they wish that on anyone? Maybe they want to see you as sad as the rest.* "No, I'm just too committed to my work. Yourself?"

"No, I'm not married. I have a little one, Leinani. She's four."

"I bet she's beautiful."

"She is, and she knows it. She's so mischievous, ya? What am I going to do when she becomes a teenager? She already has so much attitude."

"Like mother, like daughter?"

"That's what my mama says. It's payback for all the gray hair my sisters and I gave her—and I was the good one. My older sister, she was the one that caused my mama holy hell. You kind of remind me of her. The two of you might get along."

Charlie laughed and shrugged. "Maybe it's all part of being the oldest. Do you have a picture of your daughter?"

"Ya." Lani rummaged through her bag and pulled out a wallet stuffed with receipts and other items. She flipped it open to show a beautiful child with a big grin on her face.

Charlie glanced over at it. "Aw, she is so beautiful! She has a great spirit."

"Mahalo. She's filled with something, and the energy! She just never stops going."

"Dad?"

"Useless, a local boy. He's never once come to see her. He doesn't want anything to do with her. He has a decent job. He's a mechanic at one of the dealerships, but he's never helped one bit. He's married and has his own family now."

"How'd all that happen?"

"Brought my mama's car to the dealership to get fixed. We met there, and he kept pursuing me. I wasn't really interested, but I finally gave in, and we started dating. You know how it goes—one thing led to another. Now I have Leinani to show for it."

"Well, then it wasn't all bad."

Lani nodded as she opened her bag and put the wallet back in. "We're having a family cookout next Sunday. Why don't you come?"

Charlie glanced at Lani. "Sounds good. What can I bring?"

"Nothing."

Charlie gave her a skeptical look.

"Really, nothing. Between my mama, aunties, and tutu, they've got it covered. There will be enough food there to feed the neighborhood. This is embarrassing, but you're like a celebrity around the house. Everyone can't wait to meet you. If you showed up with food, my mama would roast me like a stuffed pig," Lani said emphatically while twisting in her seat to look at Charlie. "We're almost here. We're going to get off at Schofield, next exit."

Charlie maneuvered and pushed the car harder to pass a loaded-down truck, receiving a loud honk in protest as she guided the vehicle into the next lane and just made the exit.

Lani turned back around after watching the truck speed by. "That was close."

"I've got to be more careful and remember where I'm at." Charlie slowed. "What are we trying to learn from her husband?"

"What his wife was really like."

"Exactly. We want to know if there was something about her that might've attracted the killer. For example, in Seattle, they're looking for the Green River Killer. He's responsible for at least forty-two murdered women."

"Forty-two! I thought three was bad."

"Yes, they still haven't caught him yet. He preys on prostitutes and runaways, knowing they won't be missed. What else does it tell you?"

"That he knows the area and feels comfortable there."

"Look at you! Somebody is catching on fast. We'll make a profiler out of you yet." Charlie followed the ramp down to the main street.

"We need to make a left turn at the light."

She slowed further as they approached the traffic light and took in the scenery. "Where are we?"

"We're on Kamehameha Highway. Straight ahead over the bridge is the small town of Wahiawa; this road leads out to the North Shore. Have you been there yet?"

"Not on this trip, but at some point, I do want to get around to see the rest of the island."

"What are you smiling about?"

"I think that I was conceived around here."

"You're a local! The more I get to know you, the more I like."

"I wouldn't exactly say a local, but I was born here. Ya, ya."

Lani laughed. "You're even starting to sound like one of us."

As Charlie made the left, she noticed the small storefronts along the side of the road: the used car dealers, the tailors, the Pizza Hut, Miss Lee's barbershop. All of them geared for one thing—to get the soldiers' and airmen's money. On the other side of the street was a high fence with barbed wire at the top, and beyond that was housing. She moved into the left lane as she approached the next light. She saw the signs for North Shore straight ahead. Past the turn she could see military facilities on both sides of the road.

"I believe the gate is just up ahead on the right-hand side," Lani said, pointing.

Charlie flipped on her turn signal. She was greeted by a soldier in a crisp camouflage uniform and polished helmet. He raised his white-gloved hand.

"Welcome to Schofield Barracks. ID, please."

"Sure," Charlie said as she reached into her purse and grabbed her wallet. She pulled out her driver's license.

"Where are you heading to?" the military police or MP asked.

Charlie looked at Lani. Lani looked at her notepad and leaned toward Charlie and the open window. "We are going to the First Battalion, Twenty-fifth Aviation Regiment."

"You would have been heading to the right location, but they moved across the street to Wheeler Air Force Base a couple of weeks ago." The MP pointed across the street. Charlie looked over her shoulder. "Yes, ma'am. Just drive forward and turn around. Make a right turn, and the gate is on the left, less than a quarter of a mile away." He handed Charlie's ID back.

"Thank you," Charlie called as she turned the car around and headed for the air force base. "Nice guy."

"So professional and so polite."

Charlie drove down Kunia Road till she reached the next gate. She turned in to the entrance and was greeted by an airman in a pressed blue uniform.

"Welcome to Wheeler Air Force Base. ID, please."

"First Battalion, Twenty-fifth Aviation Regiment, please." Charlie handed her license to the airman.

"Yes, ma'am. It's hangar number five." He pointed. "You can park across the street over there in that parking lot next to the warehouse."

"Thank you." Charlie took back her license.

"Another polite and cute military guy. Maybe I should date one of them. I could see myself as a military wife. They certainly seem to have a lot more to offer than anything HPD has going on. Traveling and living in different countries sounds great. I could do that."

"It does have its appeal."

"I really thought I was going to go off the island to college after graduation, get a job, and live there. Eventually come back here to raise a family. All my friends are doing that exact same thing, and probably our children will too."

"The circle of life," Charlie said as she and Lani got out of the car. On the way to the hangar, Charlie noticed how well manicured and neat the lawns were. A pair of boots hung from a telephone wire. Everyone the women saw greeted them pleasantly and assisted them in finding Hangar 5. They noticed different sizes of olive-drab helicopters separated from the planes on the airfield and in the other hangars.

Charlie stopped a soldier in a solid-green jumpsuit and cam-ouflage cap. She noticed a single silver bar in the center of his cap and a black cloth bar on each shoulder. "Hi, excuse me, we're look-ing for Mr. Adair."

The young man looked around and then pointed to a group of men talking and laughing in a circle. "There he is. He's the one with his cap tilted back and the black hair, next to the heavyset guy in civilian clothing on his right."

"Thank you. Can I ask what rank you are?"

"Sure, ma'am. I'm First Lieutenant Powell." He pointed to his name tag. He looked at Charlie and then turned and smiled at Lani. "I can tell that you ladies are not from around here. What brings you to our quaint base?"

"I'm Dr. Charlie Taylor, and this is my associate, Officer Urada." Lani handed her business card to Powell.

"You're investigating Mr. Adair's wife's murder?"

"It's more like research, but thank you for assisting us, First Lieutenant Powell."

"Ma'am, you're welcome, but you only have to address me as lieutenant or Powell. Have a great day." Powell nodded slightly to-ward both Charlie and Lani, who smiled brightly back.

"Do you have a first name?" Lani asked.

"Lieutenant."

"Apologies, one more question. What's up with the boots hanging from the telephone wire?" Charlie asked.

Powell laughed. "No problem. The boots are left there by a short-timer, a soldier or airman who's going to retire soon, either leaving the military or PCSing to another location. The thought is that the boots are no longer needed because their time is short."

"PCSing?" Lani asked.

"Sorry, ma'am. The military is never short on acronyms. Permanent change of station," Powell said. He saw the confusion on their faces. "Next duty location." He smiled and started to walk away.

Charlie felt the chemistry between Powell and Lani. She watched him steal a look back at Lani, and he threw his head back and laughed, knowing he'd been busted. She looked at Lani in her purple-flowered dress and had to agree. The dress showed off her light brown skin, dark brown hair, and athletic body. Charlie nudged Lani and smiled. "We haven't been here five minutes, and they're already koo-koo for Cocoa Puffs."

"What?"

As they approached the group of men, Charlie sensed they were entering an area where women were mostly desired and not always admired, like a boy's treehouse with *No girls allowed* signs posted. She watched as soldiers sucked on their cigarettes, swigged from soda cans, or gnawed on candy bars. They came in all shapes, sizes, and colors.

The man standing in the center of the circle clearly held everyone's attention. Short reddish-blond hair, tall and thin, but well built—he exuded power. One of the young men asked, "Hey, Chief. I heard you got orders for Korea. You going to bring your old lady?"

The chief looked over at Charlie and Lani as they approached and waited till they were within hearing. "Oh, hell no. That's like bringing hamburgers to McDonald's. Why would I do that? Hey, Al, do you know what a taint is?" The eyes of the group were on Al in anticipation of him being used as the butt of a joke.

Al, a stocky man wearing civilian overalls, nervously grinned and shrugged. "No?"

"Damn, Al, don't you know anything? Do I have to teach you everything? Taint is the inch-long piece of flesh between a woman's asshole and her pussy—taint pussy, t'ain't asshole."

Everyone roared with laughter, and some slapped Al on the back or punched him in the shoulder. The group continued their grabass conversation and joking until they all noticed Charlie and Lani. "Break time's over, gents. Ladies are present," the chief said, like a predator that had just detected prey. The men dispersed in twos and threes.

"Mr. Adair," Charlie said as she held out her hand. "I'm Dr. Charlie Taylor, and this is Officer Lani Urada." Lani handed the man her business card.

"Who's the civvies?" The chief strode up.

"Dempsey, I know it's hard for you to believe that women might not actually be here to see you," Adair said, annoyed.

"Impossible," Dempsey declared, sizing up Charlie and Lani. "Anything I can do for you, ladies? Like a tour of the facilities?"

"This is a private matter and doesn't concern you," Charlie said abruptly.

"Well, I—"

"We have everything taken care of, and now, if you'll please leave us."

"Okay, okay," Dempsey said, unsure of how to handle a confident woman.

"Thank you." Charlie turned back to Adair. "Is there someplace we can go to have a quiet conversation?"

"Sure, inside the hangar. We can use my office." Adair led them inside. The floor was smooth concrete, and a large American flag was pinned to the far wall. "We park the helicopters here when we're maintaining them."

"My father was army aviation and then air force during World War II, and he'd occassionally share some stories with me. If these walls could talk?" Charlie said.

"That's for sure. We also hold our unit parties in here. They can get pretty crazy, and before the evening's over, sure as shit, someone is tied up and being lifted to the ceiling by the crane."

"I noticed your rank is slightly different than Lieutenant Powell's. You both have silver bars, but you have some black squares inside of yours."

"Yes, he's a commissioned officer: gold bars for second lieutenants, silver bars for first lieutenants, two silver bars or railroad tracks for captains, bronze oak leaf for a major, silver oak leaf for a lieutenant colonel, silver eagles for colonels, and silver stars for the general officers. Dempsey and I are warrant officers; we're kinda sandwiched between the commissioned officers and the enlisted. We're addressed as 'mister,' where commissioned officers are addressed as 'sir,'" Adair explained as they continued their walk toward his office.

"Stupid question, but is it hard to fly helicopters?" Lani asked.

"Ma'am, it's not a dumb question. I'm a maintenance warrant offficer, so I only fix 'em and don't fly 'em, but it does take a lot of manual dexterity. You have to be able to use both hands and feet to operate a helicopter. Us army aviators think it's harder to fly a helicopter than a plane, but don't say that around flyboys, because they'll lose their shit," Adair responded matter-of-factly.

"What's the difference between the helicopters?" Charlie asked.

"The smaller one, the more rounded, is an OH-58 Kiowa."

"OH-58?" Charlie asked.

"The military is big on names and nomenclatures. It's how they identify all of their equipment."

"Acronyms too," Charlie added.

"Yes, those too."

"Why not just one helicopter? Why do you need so many different ones?" Lani asked.

"Different birds for different missions. The Kiowa basically goes and finds the enemy like a scout. Then it either radios other helicopters that are equipped to kill the enemy or calls for artillery fire on the enemy location."

"Sounds scary and kind of cool at the same time," Lani said.

Adair nodded and pointed to the other aircraft. "The longer ones over there are UH-60 Black Hawks. They're a medium transportation lift. They can carry about nine soldiers."

He continued to point out other items of interest as they moved farther inside the hangar. Charlie noticed a large bulletin board with a sign that said *Knighthawk Safety Board*. On it were pinned *Command Safety Philosophies* in plastic document protectors, various manila folders holding safety notices, and the latest Playmate centerfold to the far right of the board. They walked past a group of eight-by-ten photos with the picture of the president at the top and a sign that read *Chain of Command*.

Adair's office was in the back corner of the hangar. He opened the door and held it for them. Charlie looked around the dirty office with a greasy tan couch sitting in the middle of it.

"Welcome to my world." Adair pointed to a thick piece of plexiglass with dates and numbers in boxes. "On this wall, our master calendar. The numbers represent the vehicles that are in maintenance, and the colors represent the different type of maintenance being conducted. The clipboards hanging over there have all the 2404s and the status of each item and parts orders." Adair pulled out two metal folding chairs. "You better use these. Granted, they're more uncomfortable, but I'd rather have you uncomfortable than sit on that thing and ruin your beautiful clothes. No telling what's living in it."

"Twenty-four-oh-fours?" Charlie asked as she sat.

"Sorry. It's a document that we use to identify what parts are either broken or malfunctioning and need to get ordered." Adair sat back in a padded gray office chair.

Charlie reached over and picked up a magazine with a large *P* and *S* in the upper left corner and the title *The Preventive Maintenance Monthly*. Two voluptuous cartoon characters, Connie and Bonnie, were working on a piece of equipment. She began to flip through the pages. "What's this?"

"The army must think we aren't intellectually capable of reading a regular publication or regulation on how to maintain our equipment, so they put the information in a comic book."

"You must like what you do, and clearly, you're good at it." Charlie looked around the room.

"I don't know about that. I just try to do the right thing. If we screw something up, then somebody could die. It seems pretty straightforward."

"I can appreciate that. Please accept our heartfelt condolences about your wife."

Adair nodded his head. His eyes started to fill with tears. "I hate this place. I'm scheduled to leave soon, and I'm never coming back until they find out who did this to Pam. Paradise? We both thought it was going to be this great thing coming here, but it turned into a living hell."

Charlie was about to say something else but thought better of it. "That's why we're here. I'm a psychiatrist specializing in criminal behavior. Specifically, I help law enforcement with identifying the type of perpetrator that they're looking for."

"What kind of sick mother . . . does this to a woman?"

"You're right, he is sick, and we need to catch him. What helps me in our investigation is to better understand your wife, the type of person she was and the lifestyle she led."

"You're not going to tell me she was asking for this? I've already heard that. Some people around here and in Wahiawa are saying because she worked at that video store that sold pornography and we had an adventurous marriage that she had this coming to her. Backward-thinking assholes."

"I would never think or imply that. I try to know the victims as well as possible, which gives me a better understanding of who the killer might be. You say your wife worked in town at a video store?"

"Yeah, the one that the two women were murdered at just a couple of months ago."

"I'm not familiar with that case. I'm from off island."

"I wish I was off island. Can't wait to leave this rock. The store is part of the strip just before you get to the post. The usual crappy stores, just before you go into Wahiawa."

Charlie nodded. "Thank you. That's helpful. Video stores have a large volume of customers, and most are transient, but we can start looking at the receipts around the time that your wife was murdered. We'll see if we can pick up on a pattern, or maybe a name will appear in another part of the investigation, and then we'll have more substantial information to go on.

"Did she ever mention a particular customer who might have scared her or seemed creepy?"

"Scared? No. She didn't look intimidating, but Pam could hold her own—just ask anyone. Pam wasn't to be messed with. One time, I got out of line, and she made me pay. She's the reason I became an officer."

"So whoever attacked her had to have the advantage, take her by surprise? I want to make sure that I understand that you thought your wife was capable of defending herself?" Charlie reiterated.

"I just can't imagine some guy getting the jump on her like that. I think it would've taken two guys—she was that tough."

Lani threw Charlie a glance.

"Although she was from the country, she was streetwise." Adair got up and started walking around the room. "We'd been married for about five years and had gone through a rough time, but she kept us together. She was the backbone of our family, and I love her with all my heart. It's hard to imagine what life will be like without her."

"Did she like it here? Did she have friends? What did she do when she wasn't working?" Charlie asked.

"At first she was really excited. We were both excited about coming here, but as time progressed, she became more disappointed. The island just didn't live up to our expectations." Adair pulled out his desk chair and sat back down.

"Was it something that happened?" Charlie continued with her questions.

"Not anything specific. In the military there's supposed to be a clear line of delineation between officers and enlisted, both in work and play. Pam wasn't like that. She thought the officers' wives and girlfriends were too uptight, pretentious, and always wearing their husband's or boyfriend's rank."

"So who did she go out with?"

"She'd go out with some of the lower enlisted ranks' girlfriends and wives, but I wasn't too crazy about that group myself."

"My understanding is your wife had gone downtown to meet with some friends. Were these the friends you were referring to, and was this part of her routine?"

"We had an adventurous relationship, so let's say it wasn't un-common for her to head downtown and meet up with friends. I wasn't too thrilled with the girls that she liked to hang with. Some of them weren't bad, just had bad intentions. Sometimes we'd take turns going downtown and partying. Sometimes we'd go together. Just depended on how we were feeling." Adair picked up a photo of his wife from the desk.

"Did your wife have a favorite place to go to?" Lani asked.

"Sometimes she'd go to Hickam—all the fighter jocks, hard-core infantry types, and Navy SEALs would go to the officers' club on Tuesday nights for Hog Night. Real meat market. Women—single, married, young, or old—came. It didn't matter—they all wanted a piece of the action. Occasionally we'd come across the cast and crew from *Magnum, P.I.* I think there was a part of her that hoped she'd get discovered. She was a dreamer." Adair looked off into the distance.

"Could she have been going downtown to meet someone? Is that why she didn't meet up with her friends in the first place?" Charlie asked.

"You mean, was she having an affair?"

"Not necessarily, just maybe someone else besides her girl-friends."

"No, no . . . I don't think so. Pam liked to have fun, but I trusted her. We respected each other's privacy. Most nights, she'd get home at a decent hour, around nine. But when she didn't on the night that she disappeared, I started to become worried. Really worried. I wasn't her first husband. She had been married once before, and she was never happy with her own family's lifestyle. So I don't think she'd do the exact same thing that she wasn't happy with."

"I've never been married myself, so could you explain what an adventurous relationship means?" Charlie asked.

"Let's say we were allowed to have intimate relationships with others, but we weren't allowed to date or develop a relationship."

"Like a series of one-night stands?"

"More or less. I know it sounds seedy and against social norms, but we enjoyed meeting new people, and it kept our relationship exciting."

"Could you provide us with a list of names and numbers for her friends?" Lani asked.

"I think we have a list at the house someplace."

"Is there anything that you would like us to know?" Lani continued with her questions.

"Let me ask you this: Are you good at what you do?" Adair asked.

"She's the best," Lani said, looking at Charlie.

"Like you, if I screw something up, then somebody could die, and that's a hard thing to live with. I'm passionate about what I do. I take this very seriously." Charlie looked Adair in the eye.

"Good, then catch the mother who did this." Adair planted his fist on the desk.

"Thank you for your time, Mr. Adair," Lani said.

"Just find him, please. I did love her, and I miss her." Adair got out from around his desk. "Dempsey was right. Let me give you a quick tour of the rest of the facility on our way to your car."

Dempsey was outside the office door. "Ladies, did you find everything that you need?" he asked. "Paul's my buddy, and I want to make sure that he's all right. If you need any assistance, don't hesitate to ask."

"Dempsey is not as bad as he seems," Adair said. "A bit of a legend in his own mind, but he's actually been a pretty good friend. He's been trying to cheer me up." Adair, Charlie, and Lani continued to walk past him.

Charlie turned suddenly, her intuition kicking in. "Excuse me, I'll catch up." She walked quickly. "Mr. Dempsey, how well did you know Pam Adair? Mr. Dempsey?"

He smiled and looked around to see if anyone could overhear the conversation. "We have a saying in the army, 'What happens on deployment, stays on deployment.' So I'll leave it there."

"You're quite the player?"

"A lot of women, especially married women, are looking for a little excitement in their lives. The whole dutiful-wife-and-mom routine gets old when the old man is going to exciting places like Thailand or the Philippines and she's stuck at home taking care of the kids. They have needs, wants, and desires too. They're looking for something harder and faster to ride, if you understand my meaning. A lot of these guys are just good guys but too damn monotonous, too by the book. They want some excitement."

"Do they like your ride?"

"It ain't bragging if it's true, and let's just say that I've had more than one woman in my cockpit, and no one has ever complained about how I handle my stick."

"I'm sure that you're every woman's dream come true."

Dempsey eyed Charlie up and down. "You're really not my type, a little old, not completely white—Hispanic?—but I'm willing to make exceptions."

"Don't give it a second thought. You're not my type, either, and I'm not willing to make exceptions."

Charlie stepped out of the hangar and looked left and right. She saw Lani and Adair to her left about ten yards away, staring across the tarmac.

"Mr. Adair was going to show us some bullet holes in the tarmac from when the Japanese attacked on the way to Pearl Harbor," Lani said when Charlie reached them.

After observing the bullet holes, they walked toward the long row of hangars and office buildings and the flight tower.

"Why is that hangar pink?" Lani asked.

"That's where Amelia Earhart parked her plane, the *Vega*, while she was staying here in 1935. She was the first pilot to fly from Hawaii to California."

"I'm always amazed by the courage of pioners in any industry, especially women. It seems so commonplace now that we fly all over the world, but it took someone to actually be the first," Charlie observed.

"This is so cool. I've lived here all my life, and I didn't even realize this place existed," Lani added.

The tour continued until they arrived at Charlie's rental car. She extended her hand. "Thank you, Mr. Adair, and our thoughts and prayers are with you. If you happen to remember anything that may assist us, please don't hesitate to contact us. Please, if you could send Officer Urada the list of your wife's friends' names and their phone numbers, it would be beneficial to the investigation."

"Yes, ma'am," Adair said as he stepped back from the car.

The women buckled themselves in. Charlie started the engine and began to pull out of the parking spot when she stopped and rolled down the window. "Is there another way out of here?"

"I'm not sure which gate you came through, but there's one just over there on Kunia Road." Adair pointed in the direction of the gate that Charlie and Lani had come through. "And there's the main gate at the opposite end of the base. Instead of making a left, make a right on Santos Dumont Avenue, the main road. It runs parallel to the airfield, and it will lead you to the main gate. You'll come out onto Kam Highway."

"Thank you. We won't get in trouble if we take a peek around?"

"No, you'll be fine." Adair smiled for the first time.

Charlie maneuvered the car onto the main road and drove slowly along it. "A completely different way of life."

"That's for sure. It's like its own little village. It has housing, a grocery store, a bowling alley, a library, and a pool. Hawaii used to be the same way," Lani said, admiring the homes and facilities.

"Before we interview Rebecca's stepfather, I'd like to stop by the video store where Pam worked and those two women were murdered."

"Sounds good to me."

"What do you think about the interview?"

"I was just about to ask you the same thing. I got the impression that Mr. Adair genuinely loved his wife."

"It definitely seems like it. We have to be careful because when suspects, witnesses, or victims know they're going to be interviewed ahead of time, they rehearse what they're going to say."

"Like an acting performance?"

"Exactly like an acting performance. I'm not saying this is the case here, but we need to understand that for whatever reason, we may not always be receiving all the information. What stood out to me was Adair's comment about their 'adventurous' marriage. I blew it! I should have followed up with more questions," Charlie said, shaking her head in disbelief. "Maybe she did meet someone and what was intended as a quickie with no strings attached got ugly real fast. What does that mean to you?"

"I got the impression that they were willing to try new things. They weren't afraid to push things to the limit, but at the same time, they must have had some boundaries established because he expected Pam home at a specific time."

"I think those are pretty safe assumptions. The other thing is Pam's death garnered so little attention on the island. Why was that?"

"The island is pretty conservative, especially when it comes to families—everything on the island is about the family. So you have a military couple that wasn't from here. She worked in a slimy adult video store, and they had an adventurous life. Her murder just didn't generate much sympathy. What are you thinking?"

"Like I told him, she didn't deserve this, but when anyone starts living life on the fringe, they're more vulnerable."

As they passed through the gate, Charlie caught Lani looking back to catch a glimpse of the soldier on duty. Charlie laughed.

"What?"

"Ooh, you're going to pay for it when Leinani becomes a teenager."

"Shit, she already talks about her boyfriend. Where does she get it from? Don't answer that! I get enough grief from my mom."

Five minutes later, Charlie had driven the short distance to the video store and parked the car. They got out and looked around. Above the door of the tan building was a square brown sign nailed to the wood slats. In large, black, block letters were the words *Wahiawa Adult Bookstore.*

"I don't need to spend a lot of time here, but I do want to get a feel for where Pam worked." Charlie watched the traffic in front of them—a mix of mostly civilians and a few military vehicles. She stepped off the curb and looked in both directions.

"This isn't a secluded place, this wasn't random, the killer knew the location and that he might be seen. Yet he still risked it." Charlie continued to survey the surrounding area.

"Yesterday afternoon and last night, I've made a few calls before we came. Supposedly, the owner was being harassed before her murder," Lani said, studying Charlie.

Charlie nodded as she registered the information. "Good work. Ask the detective if they know when the harassment began. I'm interested in if it started while Pam worked here too. It's a stretch, but she might have known or seen something and then became a target. While you're doing that, I'm going to visit with our two favorite detectives. I want to know if they've started to look at cold cases to see if there are any similar incidents. Let's go inside."

They entered the store and looked around.

"We don't get too many like you in here," the clerk said.

"Like what?" Charlie asked.

"You know, professional and attractive."

"What kind of clientele do you get?" Charlie began to browse through the merchandise.

"Ya, ya. You know, mostly military types and some locals. Older guys who work or live around here."

"Regulars?" Charlie put down a book and looked over at the clerk.

"A few."

"The regulars, what types of guys are they?"

"Like I said, the older types. The military guys are always coming and going."

"The regular guys, are they into sadomasochism? Like to see women being tied up, abused. Bondage."

"A few."

"I'd like to see a list of their names."

"We don't keep that shit around here; this isn't exactly a lending library. Hey, are you cops?"

"Officer Urada is with the HPD, and I'm just here to help. What's your name?"

"Darren."

"Darren, thank you. What I'd like you to do is the next time a regular comes in and buys sadomasochism material, notify Officer Urada."

"Can I do that? Is that legal?"

"Sure is. You're aiding in an investigation." Charlie stopped flipping through a magazine, placed it back on the stand, and made her way to the door.

"Cool." The clerk seemed more relieved as Lani handed him her business card.

Charlie waited at the car for Lani to catch up. "Not only is there a mommy thing going on, but they're into hard-core pornography too."

She made the quick left onto the bridge and headed north on State Route 80 through downtown Wahiawa. "Quaint places like this seem to get lost in all of it. We've got Honolulu and Waikiki at one end, and Haleiwa and North Shore at the other, with Wahiawa stuck in the middle. I like the colorful little storefronts, local restaurants, and small boutiques—'quaint' and 'boutique' may be a stretch, but they're authentic. But I could see this town becoming run-down very quickly too," Charlie said as she looked around.

"We don't come here. If we have off-island guests, then we might take them to the Dole pineapple plantation, but there's nothing here that we can't find someplace else that's safer and nicer. Slow down, turn right here on California Avenue. It's just a couple more blocks up the street, then a couple of side streets."

Charlie stopped the car in front of a depressing apartment complex. Lani checked her notes; this was the place. When they finally found the apartment and rang the doorbell, a small Asian man opened the faded green door.

"Mr. Saito, I'm Dr. Charlie Taylor, and this is my associate, Officer Lani Urada. We are here to investigate the abduction and murder of Rebecca. May we come in?"

Saito opened the door wider and allowed Charlie and Lani to enter.

Charlie looked around the room. Unlike the run-down complex, the apartment was neat and tidy. A small living room contained a nondescript couch in a slightly faded green-and-pink floral pattern with two matching chairs. One chair's cushion was well worn and had a small depression, leaving Charlie to assume this was Saito's chair. Across from it was a small color TV. Slightly off to the right was a wooden kitchen table with four matching orange-cushioned chairs. The plain tan walls were covered with family photos.

Saito directed Charlie and Lani to the couch. "I apologize, but I don't have any faith in you finding Rebecca's killer. As far as I am concerned, you and everybody else down there are controlled by the rich and powerful. You're all pretty weak and stupid." Saito sat back in his chair and looked out the window.

Lani sat back and clenched her hands tightly, but Charlie didn't flinch at the verbal barrage. She knew she had to tread slowly— one wrong word might set Saito off. She'd seen it before.

"Mr. Saito, please accept our condolences, and thank you for your willingness to talk with us. We tried reaching out to the school and her mother, but everyone refuses to talk."

"They're all losers down there."

"What do you mean, Mr. Saito?"

"I was dead set against her mom, my ex-wife, moving to Waipahu. Sure, we've got our share of transients around here, but they have real losers down there. Cars up on blocks, they don't respect anything. Nothing but a bunch of crooks and thieves. That's why she went to high school up here."

"I'm not from the island, so could you please explain more?"

"Rebecca was white—she looked white. The Samoans hate the Filipinos, the Filipinos hate the Samoans, and they both share a hatred for whites. She was a tiny, sweet person, and white. The Samoan girls would chase her down, trying to beat her up."

"Thank you. Can you tell us about Rebecca?" Charlie asked, settling back into the uncomfortable couch.

"Rebecca was not my biological daughter. She was five when I met her and her mother on the mainland when I was in the service. My ex-wife and Rebecca's father had divorced, and she was working on the post. I raised her like she was my own. That's why she has my last name."

"What type of girl was Rebecca? What type of friends did she have?"

"Rebecca was naturally shy, but she was friendly and would do anything for anyone. She was sweet, smiling. I don't know anything about her girlfriends, but I couldn't stand her boyfriends. I was the one that put my foot down. My ex-wife gave her too much freedom. She needed more discipline. The trouble was my ex-wife and Rebecca were more like sisters than mother and daughter."

"How often did you see her?" Lani asked.

"I hadn't seen her since she and her mom moved away. Even though she went to high school here, I never saw her."

"Why was that?" Lani followed up.

"Like I said, she and her mom were very close, and once we got a divorce, that was it. My ex forbade Rebecca to see me."

Charlie could see the anguish and disappointment in him. Family and friends tormenting themselves with what-ifs. She could see that he was starting to drift off to another place in his mind, physically present but not mentally. She squatted in front of him. "Thank you for your time, Mr. Saito. We'll let ourselves out."

Charlie took one last look at Rebecca's stepfather. Tears were welling up in his eyes and slowly falling down his cheeks.

Neither woman said a word as they got in the car. "Now you really know why I run. This job will eat you up. You'll see the best and worst of humanity. Most times, it's the worst, then it becomes just a matter of degree."

Lani nodded and wiped a tear from the corner of her eye.

"Crying is allowed, and I encourage it—a healthy coping mechanism."

"Rebecca's high school is nearby. Do you want to see it?"

"No, I don't think that'll be necessary. Any luck reaching Debra's husband?"

"No, I haven't been able to reach him. The navy doesn't seem to be as accessible as the army."

"All right, then, from an efficiency standpoint, let's make our way to Waipahu. I want to see the bus stop Rebecca disappeared from, and then let's head east toward the city and see the drop-off points. How do we get there?" As Charlie started the car, two helicopters flew overhead, making their way to Wheeler.

They drove along Kamehameha Highway, past the main entrance to the air base. The highway was soon enveloped by vegetation on both sides as it sloped downward. "Sorry if I'm not very talkative. I'm not used to working with anyone. I have a bad habit of getting lost in my thoughts."

"I don't mind. I like being with you. I've learned so much just watching you interact with the victims' families and look at everything so closely. Nothing gets past your attention. I've been telling my family about you, and they can't wait to meet you—my mama, tutu, Leinani, and even my older sister. They'll disown me if you don't show up. Okay, let's take Farrington Highway."

"Thank you, I've also enjoyed the company."

"Slow down," Lani raised her voice.

"What is it?" Charlie asked, somewhat startled.

"There's a bus stop just around here where Debra Harris was last seen. Just over there."

Charlie parked the car in the vicinity of the bus stop, and the women got out and began to look around.

"Her apartment complex must be nearby," Charlie noted.

The women made their way up the path and could see an apartment complex just in front of them. To the right was an entrance to Pearl Harbor.

"Well, the geography makes sense. Debra had dinner with her husband. A relatively short walk from his ship back to the apartment complex. She probably follows her same routine, gets ready for bed, goes to sleep, and wakes up in the morning and goes about her business, getting ready for work. She leaves the apartment like she does every morning and comes on down to the bus stop. But something is different this morning. Was she running late? Did she miss the bus? Why did she get in the car with him? What compelled her to get in the car? We know that Rebecca was running late, and that's why she was probably susceptible." Charlie put her sunglasses on.

"So it would make sense that Debra did the same thing," Lani added.

Charlie looked all around her. She listened to the sounds and took in the sights. "It would be helpful if we came back one morning to replicate the morning she disappeared. How far are we from Rebecca's house and bus stop?"

"Maybe five or ten minutes away. Creepy."

"What is it?" Charlie asked.

"It's hot outside, but I just had a cold shiver that ran through my whole body. Like I could feel the evil presence just talking about it and being in the same area that these women disappeared from."

"Don't discount your feelings and intuition. Sometimes we forget to use all our senses and rely too heavily on our eyes and what our mind registers when there's a lot more information being presented. Let's go."

Charlie and Lani got back into the car and made the short drive into the heart of Waipahu to Awanai Street. As they drove through Rebecca's neighborhood, Charlie looked at the street and the driveways filled with cars—some nice, some worn and beaten, and some on blocks. The houses came in all shapes and sizes, the paint often faded. Each home was surrounded by a chain-link fence; most had *Beware of Dog* signs attached to them. Dogs ran up to the fences barking and snarling as they drove by. It was a blue-collar neighborhood; residents likely worked the night shift at the airport or hospital or spent the day cleaning up hotel rooms.

"Welcome to Waipahu."

"Looks like the American dream, Hawaiian style: a house, chicken in the pot, and five cars in the drive."

"Ya, everyone wants their own car. Pretty soon, the traffic is going to get so bad around here. This is her mama's address. She took Rebecca's younger brother and moved away."

"Okay, which way to the bus stop?"

"It should be just down the street a little ways over there."

Charlie looked around the surrounding area as she and Lani arrived at a bus stop on a busy street across from a diner. She spotted a phone booth a short distance away. "What do you think?"

"It's like you said, he must be really confident and charming to be able to approach the women in public, in daylight, and convince them to get into his car."

Charlie nodded in agreement.

"What are you thinking? You seem lost in thought," said Lani.

"Let's go to where the bodies were dropped off," Charlie said.

"Pam and Rebecca were dropped off very close to one another at Ke'ehi Lagoon, not far from here. Debra was a little farther away, but not by much," said Lani. "It's quicker if we go by H-1."

"Is there an alternative?" Charlie asked.

"We could go by Farrington," said Lani

"Which way would our killer want to go? He doesn't want to run into a cop. He'd want to use roads less traveled," Charlie said.

"Then he's going to use Farrington and then pick up Kam."

The women drove in silence. Lani had adapted to Charlie's retrospective moods and stopped trying to make nervous small talk.

"We'll need to make a right turn onto Lagoon Drive."

Charlie watched the surroundings closely as they drove down Lagoon Drive. On the right side were various warehouse buildings for aviation and maintenance companies and aviation schools. They made a left turn onto Palekona Street and eventually ran out of road and parked the car.

"Did you ever want to learn how to fly?" Lani asked.

"It's funny, my parents encouraged my sister and me to try everything: music, dance, horseback riding, shooting, and swimming, but never flying. I think my dad was so scared by his war experience that he didn't want to get into another airplane unless it was absolutely necessary."

"I think it'd be really neat to be like a bird and look at everyone down below you."

"Then you ought to give it a shot. Who knows, maybe you can get one of those cute aviators to teach you how to fly."

"Don't I wish."

Charlie walked over to the water's edge and opened the folder containing the photos of Rebecca's dumping spot. "Okay, this is where Rebecca was left. Farther back up Lagoon Drive is where Pam's body was left. What are your initial impressions?"

Lani hesitated.

"Think about it this way. What type of vehicle would go unnoticed in this area?" Charlie asked as she looked across Ke'ehi Lagoon. The water and sky were tranquil, disrupted only by the jet airplanes flying overhead. *Two violent crimes are associated with this area.*

"A truck?"

"Exactly. We're looking for vans, pickup trucks, or older cars. Nothing fancy or out of the ordinary. The vehicle has to fit in so the killer can come and go—unnoticed, unseen. The other thing is that he wants the bodies to be discovered. He's got something to prove."

"I'm sorry, I'm not holding my weight."

"You're not expected to. This is all brand new. Hell, this whole field is brand new, and we're discovering it's a lot more art than science. Hey, we're losing daylight. Let's head to Debra's dump site."

Charlie and Lani jumped into the vehicle and drove back the way they had come along Lagoon Drive. "After we finish here, you up for some dinner?" Charlie asked.

"I'd love to."

They stopped at the busy intersection of Lagoon Drive and Nimitz Highway. As the light turned green, Charlie crossed Nimitz under the H-1 overpass. "I'm still wrestling with a couple of things in my mind."

"Such as?"

"First, the killer must be out all the time driving around, looking for opportunities."

"What do you mean?"

Charlie flipped on her signal and made a quick right turn. "We know that Pam was abducted sometime late at night in downtown Honolulu—Waikiki. Next, both Rebecca and Debra are abducted around eight in the morning at bus stops."

"Ya, you can pull the car over there," Lani said.

Charlie parked the car, cut the ignition, and faced Lani. "Another thing, we know that the drop sites are not the murder locations, so where is he taking them? I've assumed that the killer is raping and murdering them in a third location. So what type of work allows him to travel like he does at all hours of the day? He can move the bodies in and out of the vehicle on four separate occasions without drawing suspicion—the abduction, one; out of the vehicle to rape and murder them, two; back into the vehicle to drive to the drop site, three; and the drop site, four. That's a lot of moving pieces and very risky."

"Maybe he's a delivery guy and takes them back to where he lives," Lani said, picking up on Charlie's thoughts.

"I like the idea of a delivery guy that has a specific territory—that's why we see all the killings associated with the central part of the island. The three drop-off locations are in very industrial areas. My intuition is telling me that he delivers aviation or car parts, which allows him the freedom to maneuver around.

"He can come and go as he pleases because nobody is watching him. If he gets behind schedule, he can either blame it on traffic or make it up some other way. Nobody is tracking his movements, and as long as no customers complain, he's free and clear. He has to be living relatively close by in a single-family home that is remote—no nosy neighbors that can see or hear anything—or maybe he's using an old, abandoned warehouse."

"Shit, where did that all come from?" Lani unbuckled her seat belt and opened her door.

"My brain never stops," Charlie said. She locked the car and walked toward the canal.

"It was approximately over here where the body was discovered."

"None of the locations are impossible for one man to drop off a body, but there's a degree of difficulty too."

"So are we dropping our theory that it may be more than one?"

"Not yet, but now I like this guy being in his late thirties or early forties. There's a level of maturity and sophistication associated with these crimes that a young man just doesn't possess. I was going through the files again and looked closely at the medical examiner's reports, which state semen was present but no sperm, so it looks like the perpetrator may have had a vasectomy."

"There's a couple of guys I'd like to give a vasectomy. You're right, guys my age wouldn't dream of getting the procedure. It's always on us to make sure we're protected."

The women watched the fiery sun start to go down. "Let's call it a day. Tomorrow I'd like for you to start thinking about areas that the killer could live in and see if there are any abandoned or unused warehouses on either side of Nimitz. Now, where do we go to eat?"

Haleiwa
Saturday, February 22, 1986

Charlie thought spending some time at the easygoing North Shore would provide her some relief, a chance to clear her mind. She dodged the cars and tourists as she ran slowly past the art dealers, surf shops, and swimsuit stores. She left Haleiwa and made her way back, running on the shoulder of Kam Highway. Tourists and locals alike parked their cars along the narrow right shoulder. They'd scurry across the street between the breaks in traffic. Despite the number of people there, only a few were going into the water. Only the experienced surfers braved the high waves on North Shore.

Charlie finally arrived at Waimea Beach Park, where she had left her car. She unlocked it and pulled out her towel and beach bag. In the women's changing room, she stripped out of her wet running gear, tossed it into the bag, and changed into a one-piece black swimsuit.

She left the changing room and stood on the edge of the concrete pad, waiting her turn. The pad was covered in sand except for the places where the shower water had displaced it. Beachgoers stood next to an aluminum pole with showerheads at different heights and pushed a button to let the cold water spray down on them, washing the sand off. Charlie was amused by the little ones with their bright smiles, tan bodies, and small white butts. They squealed and squirmed under the cold water, and then their mothers bundled them up in large, brightly colored towels.

Charlie pushed the button and was immediately hit with a blast of cold water. She tried not to squeal like a toddler. When the shower stopped, she swiped her hair out of her eyes, picked up her bag, and walked to the beach. She found a comfortable place and laid her towel on the sand.

Black Wayfarers on, she spread Hawaiian Tropic on her arms, legs, and face. Her skin had transitioned from white to pink to a lovely light tan. She pulled out her latest mystery novel and stretched out on her side, trying and failing to absorb the words. She tossed the book aside and sat up.

In front were men, women, and kids bodysurfing. To her left, about twenty young men with farmer tans were playing touch football; their tan lines and short hair spelled military. There were plenty of young women watching, laughing, and cheering them on. Farther off to the left were a couple of young men who had climbed the high lava formation that rose out of the ocean. They timed their jumps with the waves, leaping out and plunging into the water below.

To the right were sunbathers like her, enjoying a beautiful day. Far right, in the distance, Charlie could see the white tower and orange roof of the Mission of Saints Peter and Paul rising up out of the palm trees against the deep blue sky. *Do people really find peace with their faith? Does God know? Why doesn't he answer? Am I a sinner?*

"Stop saying that! You're not going to die. The doctors can give you something. Daddy's gone, and he's not coming back. Now you're telling us the same thing is happening to you. Stop it,

you're going to get better. You've got to get better! Aunt Charlie, you're a doctor—do something!" Melissa pleaded.

"Honey, I know this is hard on you and Josh, but we need to have this conversation. I must know that you're well taken care of. Aunt Charlie will take good care of both of you—she loves you."

"Is it true what Dad said about you and Aunt Charlie? Is it true?" Josh asked, determined.

"Josh, I love you and Melissa, maybe more than you'll ever know," Annie said.

"Is it true? Just answer the question," Josh demanded.

"Honey, I cared for your father, but . . ."

"That's gross. You're both gross, and I hate you. I hate you!" Josh stormed out of the room. Melissa followed her brother in tears.

"I'm sorry. They love you. They're having to come to grips with their father's death, and now they've realized they're losing their mother—it's a lot to comprehend for anyone." Charlie put her arm around Annie's bony shoulders.

"At night I go to their bedrooms and look at them sleeping peacefully. I worry about who will take care of them after I'm gone. I pray for them. I wonder if my judgment day has arrived, and God's punishing me for all that I've done wrong. I ask for forgiveness." Annie shuffled over to the big armchair and collapsed.

Manoa
Sunday, February 23, 1986

"How's she doing?" Kim asked.

"Who?" Tanaka asked.

"Barbara's niece. Who else do you think I'd be talking about? Someone's distracted." Kim joined her husband at the kitchen table and started to gather the plates.

"She's fine, I guess. I really haven't seen much of her. Urada reports to me daily, so I know that she's actively involved, and she's already given us a helpful draft profile, but that's about it." Tanaka looked at his empty coffee mug to see if it was worthwhile to try and get another sip out of it.

"That all sounds good." Kim got up and retrieved the coffeepot.

"She's the least of my concerns." Tanaka held out his cup, and Kim poured hot coffee into it. "Thanks."

"What is it now?"

"It's the way we're structured. We've violated every rule in leadership. The chief appointed two lieutenants in charge of the investigation with equal command and authority over the investigators. So we're getting conflicting orders. Mac runs to the opposite lieutenant that I'm associated with. All the other detectives are under a lot of pressure to succeed. Do you remember what my biggest nightmare was?"

"That you'd screw this case up like the last one," Kim said, pouring coffee into her own mug.

"It has come to fruition."

Waikiki
Sunday, February 23, 1986

Williams walked over to the mirror and looked at his blood-shot eyes, stuck out his tongue, and scratched his groin. In the mirror he saw the reflection of a body lying on the crumpled and stained bedsheets. He vaguely remembered meeting her at one of his favorite bars, and after numerous kamikaze shots, it seemed like a good idea to both of them to hook up for the night. His brain was in a fog, and he could barely remember their conversation, let alone her name.

His eyes swept the cheap hotel room with its gaudy wallpaper, plastic furniture, plastic cups wrapped in plastic, and photographs of various Oahu beaches screwed to the wall. He tried to recall his actions, but his brain was unable to shake the effects of his powerful and painful hangover.

He walked into the dingy white bathroom and turned on the light. He felt a stabbing pain in his brain like someone had stuck a shiv into his right eye. He swiped at the light switch and had barely lifted the toilet lid when his stomach started to make hard, painful convulsions.

Driven to his knees, he stuck his head inside the toilet bowl and wrapped his arms around it. He was wracked with pain; his stomach ached, his throat burned, and there were no words to describe the vile taste in his mouth. Even when there seemed like there was nothing left in him, his body tried once more to rid itself of the poison. *Haven't driven the truck this bad in years.*

He pushed himself up, a cold sweat breaking out all over his body. He cupped cold water from the faucet and greedily gulped it down. His stomach reacted immediately, and he vomited again. He collapsed to the floor as everything spun. Eventually there was nothing left in him. *Just let me die and let the pain stop.*

He regained enough equilibrium to make it out of the bathroom. He almost fell over flat on his face when he tried to pick his underwear out of a pile of her clothes. He stood over her and looked down at her body. She was curvy, her breasts and butt round and full. Her stomach had a small paunch to it.

Her body was tan except for the small white triangles on her breasts and the larger one that highlighted her black, bushy pubic hair. Mac was used to Asian women's straight pubic hair. Her body type was foreign to him. She didn't seem to be moving—he poked at her to see if she was still alive.

"Dude, you have issues." She rolled over onto her back and covered her eyes with her forearm.

"That's what they all say," Williams replied, trying his best to pull on his pants without falling over.

Manoa
Sunday, February 23, 1986

Charlie capped her pen and reviewed her notes. She closed her notebook and rubbed her tired eyes. *I'm going to need to get my eyes checked.* She rubbed the dogs' bellies with her feet, and Salt and Pepper were happy to have her attention.

"The dogs miss you so much," Barbara said as she walked into the room.

"I'm sorry I haven't been a very good guest. I've neglected you and the dogs—it seems to be a personality flaw that I'm inflicted with."

"Don't blame yourself. It's my selfishness that got you into this in the first place. I've watched you working all the time, and this is supposed to be your vacation—you're out at all hours of the night. Every now and then, I'll check your bedroom, and you're not there, and then I'll go back in the morning, and your bed hasn't been slept in. You're going to have to head back soon, and none the better than when you arrived here."

"Auntie, I'm fine." Charlie pulled a long manila envelope out of the desk drawer and handed it to Barbara.

"What's this?"

"I wrote a letter to my supervisor asking for a sabbatical. I just received their response."

"Am I going to like this?" Barbara asked as she removed the typewritten letter from the envelope and carefully read the letter. She grabbed Charlie and pulled her into her arms. "Chanting really does pay off."

"I can't attest to the chanting, but you were right. I needed some more time to get myself whole again. It's not as long as I'd like, but it's definitely better than nothing. But the best part is that it gives me a chance to spend more time with you."

"Oh my, that's wonderful news, but when this dreadful thing is over, promise me you'll take some real time off. Now I'll start to work on the dean and provost." Barbara held Charlie tight against her body. Salt and Pepper sensed the change in emotions and started to bark.

"Be quiet, you two. You can ruin the nicest moment. I'm thrilled to have you stay longer. Please stay as long as you like, but I have a feeling your sabbatical is not just about the cases."

"No, it's not just the cases."

"Broken heart?"

"That's part of it too."

"You'll find love again, trust me. I thought that I would never find love again, but your uncle appeared one day. Chant for love. Chant for the best possible outcome. You'll find love again."

"Thank you, but right now, I don't have much faith, and I don't know if I want to find love again. As much as I hate to admit it, the case is a great distraction."

"Charlie Taylor, you're a strange one. Who says that searching for some psychopath is a great distraction from love?"

"I do, and you're right, I am a strange one. I think I got it from my mother."

"You're probably right about that." Barbara laughed. "Now, what are your plans for today?"

"I'm going to hang here for a while, and then Lani has invited me to her family's picnic for Sunday evening dinner."

"Great, then the dogs and I have you as a captive audience for a while. I know this isn't the idea that either of us had in mind for spending quality time together, but do you mind going grocery shopping with me? I'd like to drive down to Chinatown and pick up a few items and then hit the Safeway on the way back."

"Sounds great, plus I should bring something to the picnic." Charlie picked up Salt and petted her. Pepper pawed at Charlie's leg out of jealousy.

Later that day, Charlie looked in the mirror at the fourth outfit she had tried on. *So resolute when making decisions—why doesn't this apply to all areas of my life?* Charlie blamed it on her mother for always questioning her fashion sense. *Today's fashion has a lot less to be desired: big hair, shirts and jackets with shoulder pads, leather and chains, and overpowering perfume. I've survived the sixties and seventies. Can I survive another decade of feeling out of place?* She stripped out of the peasant dress and tossed it toward the bed.

Pepper watched and ran after the dress as it flew over his head. He jumped up, trying to pull the dress off the bed. "Pepper, behave." He stopped immediately and looked back at Charlie like a boy who had been caught with his hand in the cookie jar. "You're a naughty boy. The clothes by themselves are bad enough without you tearing holes in them. On second thought, go ahead and rip everything to shreds."

Charlie looked in her closet. She glanced at the package sitting on the shelf. She pulled a denim skirt and white blouse off their hangers. *Annie, I could have used your eye for this evening. You always knew what fit well.* "Pepper, I think this will work. Besides, I've run out of outfits to choose from." She slipped on the new outfit and adjusted the collar and skirt. "Voilà! I think this is it." She grabbed her purse, shooed Pepper out of the room, and closed the door behind her.

"Bye, auntie!"

"Bye, honey. Have fun." Barbara came out from the kitchen, drying her hands on a kitchen towel.

"Mahalo, auntie. I shouldn't be too late, and you, mister, behave yourself," she said, pointing her finger at Pepper.

Charlie meandered her way through the side streets until she was able to jump on H-1. Sunday's traffic was relatively light. Squinting, ducking, and flipping the visor down, Charlie tried to avoid being punched by the light of the setting sun. She fumbled for her sunglasses and pulled them on.

She checked the directions and the map occasionally to make sure she was traveling in the right location, trying to avoid rear-ending the car in front of her. She eventually made her way to Aiea and started the climb. *Damn it.* She pulled into a driveway and turned around when she realized she had missed a turn.

When she turned onto the correct street and saw all the cars parked to the side, she knew she was close. She drove slowly past the address and saw people in the garage and driveway talking and laughing. Kids were running around in the yard, and smoke drifted from several barbecues. She drove to the end of the long line of cars and parked the Mustang.

She could smell the delicious scent of barbecued meat as she walked toward the house. Her stomach started to rumble, and she realized she hadn't eaten much all day. As she stepped onto the driveway, everyone turned toward her. An attractive older woman yelled out, "Lani, your guest has arrived." A young girl burst from the crowd, ran toward Charlie, and gave her a hug.

"You must be Leinani!" Charlie wrapped her arms around the child.

"How did you know?"

"Your mom has told me all about you. She's very proud of you."

"Really?"

"Really."

"Leinani, girl, give Dr. Taylor a break. You're smothering her and wrinkling her clothes," Lani yelled as she made her way down the driveway.

"Aloha, Lani. Here's a little something for Leinani, your mom, and you." Charlie smiled as she handed her a bag.

"Mahalo—I told you not to bring anything." Lani smiled and hugged her.

"Mom, let me see, let me see!" Leinani pulled at the bag in her mom's hands.

"Stop it, I'll show you later. We've got guests here."

"Charlie's a funny name for a girl," Leinani remarked as she held Charlie's hand and smiled up at her.

"You are so right—it's definitely not as beautiful as yours, but it's the one my parents gave to me."

"Child, where are your manners? It's 'Dr. Taylor,' and if you don't behave, she'll give you a shot."

Leinani immediately pulled her hand from Charlie's. "You're going to give me a shot?"

Charlie smiled. "No, I won't ever give you a shot, but you better listen to your mother."

Relieved, Leinani smiled back at Charlie, stuck her tongue out at her mom, and then ran toward the group to announce the arrival of 'Dr. Taylor.' She told the other children that if they didn't listen to her, she was going to tell Charlie—Dr. Taylor—to give them a shot.

"Leinani!" several aunties yelled in unison.

Charlie laughed, "she is gorgeous, and she has lived up to the billing, but I've changed my assessment. You're going to have to start worrying about her when she's thirteen."

"Ya, ya, I know. Karma can be such a bitch, and that's just Leinani—wait till you meet the rest of the family. My mom and tutu are huge fans of *Murder, She Wrote*. They're going to pester you for information on the case and want to know how soon you're going to solve it."

"It's understandable. Everyone wants some type of reassurance that the bogeyman or monsters don't exist in our closets or under our beds at night. Everyone wants resolution right away so they can get back to their normal routines. As we've discussed, these cases take time—and, unfortunately, sometimes luck."

"Ya, ya. I've told them a thousand times that I can't talk specifics about the case, but it's like they're deaf. My mom is thankful that you've given me this opportunity. She now thinks I should get my medical degree."

"Lani, you wonder where Leinani gets her bad manners from? She gets them from you. Introduce your guest to our family and friends," said a lovely older woman in a bright purple flowered muumuu.

"Charlie, this is my mama."

"Mrs. Urada, it's a pleasure to meet you. Lani has told me so many wonderful things about you," Charlie said, smiling.

"Mahalo. Please call me Carolyn. She'd better have, considering how long I was in labor delivering her and that older tita of hers." Carolyn placed a double plumeria lei with green orchids around Charlie's neck.

"Mahalo. This is so beautiful and fragrant." Charlie smiled.

Lani blushed from embarrassment. "Now you know why I've waited so long to bring you here."

"Hush, child. Make sure she meets your tutu. Watch out, she's a big fan of *Murder, She Wrote*, so she's going to ask you lots of questions. Speaking of which, who do you think the murderer is?"

"Mama, she isn't going to tell you. She can't. How many times have I explained this to you?" Lani said, exasperated.

"Carolyn, Lani's right. I understand and share the concern, but we can't provide any information. But what we can share is that women need to be safe. They shouldn't be so trusting, taking rides from strangers. Clearly, the women were all in very public areas, and you'd think that they'd be safe, but this hasn't deterred the killer at all."

"Kamalu! Kamalu is Hawaiian—it means to do evil to others in secret. What is this island coming to? We're getting as bad as the mainland." Carolyn took Charlie by the arm and started to escort her up the driveway.

Charlie nodded in agreement.

"I'm as rude as my daughter and granddaughter. You must be hungry. We have a lot of food. Please help yourself and make yourself at home."

"Mahalo for the wonderful hospitality, and the flowers are so beautiful. You should be very proud of Lani—she's a real natural. Frankly, I usually prefer to work alone, but she's been a real blessing and very helpful in the investigation."

Lani wrestled Charlie away from her mama and started to introduce her to all her immediate and extended family, along with her friends. Charlie paid close attention to all the names and tried to remember them and who was related, but somewhere lost the ability to do so. They finally made their way to two large picnic tables filled with all sorts of food.

"I'm famished, and everything looks so delicious," Charlie said as she picked up a paper plate and plastic utensils. She made her way down the line with Lani, who explained all the different types of food.

"You should try some poke if you haven't had it already. You absolutely have to have some kalua pork. My uncle started cooking the pig early this morning. This over here is pork lau lau, which is pork wrapped in taro leaves—it's really delicious. Then you have to have some Huli Huli chicken." Lani placed a leg and thigh on Charlie's plate.

"Wait, wait. I don't think my plate or my stomach can hold all of this food." Charlie laughed, trying to manage the paper plate as it sagged under the weight of the food.

"Shit."

"What is it?" Charlie asked, surprised by the change in Lani's tone and attitude.

"It's my oldest sister. She's coming this way. I was hoping she'd left or we'd at least get finished with dinner in peace."

"She can't be that bad."

"I'll take that bet. I've come across a lot of mean and tough men in my time, but she's worse. In a fight I'd put my money on her," Lani said.

"Lani, really?" Charlie asked.

Lani leaned closer to Charlie and whispered softly, "We think she's a lesbian. Just look at her."

Charlie watched a striking, confident woman approach them. Her face was untouched by makeup, and she wore her long black hair pulled back in a ponytail, the sides shaved close to her head, exposing multiple piercings in her ears. She was wearing a black tank top that showed off her muscular shoulders and arms.

She looked strong. She looked powerful. Her left shoulder and the top of her left breast were covered in a Japanese-style tattoo: a shiny black background with intricate flowers in shades of pink, red, orange, and turquoise. She was wearing faded cutoffs, and her legs were tan and lean. Peeking out of her shorts on her right thigh was the end of the same tattoo.

"Charlie, this is my sister, Kailani. Everyone calls her Kai."

"Hey, Punk," Kai said. She stood in front of Charlie, hands on hips, eyeballing her. "Punk tells me that you're a pretty good runner—tough. I was going to ask you if you'd like to join me for a run tonight. We've got a great trail right up to the road, but I see you're not dressed for it, and you're still eating. How about surfing? Do you surf?"

"I haven't been up on a board in years. I used to as a kid and did some competitive swimming, but nothing special. It looks like you'd be a pretty good surfer."

"I can hold my own." Kai looked at her flexed arms and smiled.

"I'm sure you can."

"Kai, can you give it a break?" Lani asked, annoyed.

"Punk, take it easy—don't get your undies in a bundle. I'm leaving. I just wanted to meet the famous Dr. Taylor that I've heard so much about."

"Likewise. I've heard a lot about you too."

"I'm sure you have. I'm sure Punk has told you plenty." Kai smirked and walked away.

"See what I mean?" Lani asked. She walked over to one of the coolers near the picnic tables, opened it up, and plunged her hand deep into the icy water, eventually pulling out a can of beer. She switched the beer to her other hand and shook the first one, sending water flying everywhere.

"I can be pretty tough on my baby sister too." Charlie smiled and took a bite of kalua pork. "Wow, this is good. This is really good."

Honolulu
Wednesday, March 12, 1986

"Detective, how may I be of assistance?" Charlie inquired as she sat down in the chair alongside Tanaka's desk.

Tanaka sat back in his chair and threw his pencil on top of the paperwork covering his desk. "We're swamped with tips, even with your recommendations and observations. We can't keep up. I read your last report, and do you really think he's going to strike again?"

Charlie looked at Tanaka critically. *He seems to have aged.* "Yes, I do, and soon."

"I read your rationale, but can you be more explicit?" Tanaka picked up the can from his desk and spit into it.

Charlie leaned forward. "He's successful; he sees the interest that's being generated in the press and the fear he's causing. He's running on adrenaline. He's a star in his own movie and getting great reviews."

"Shit. What do we do?"

"For starters, do you have anyone hanging around or even coming in volunteering to assist?"

"Not that I know of."

"Keep your eyes out for someone. For example, at bars that are frequented by HPD—is there someone that seems to be pumping them for information? Or the dump areas? Killers will return to relive the experience. They might volunteer here to assist with taking reports. It adds to the thrill to be alongside and watching law enforcement.

"Focus on the central part of the island. I believe he works in or around the greater airport area. I realize Pam Adair was attacked in Honolulu, but everything else is centered around this area." Charlie walked over to a map tacked to the wall, picked up a marker, and drew a large square. "Specifically here." She drew another box inside the first one.

Tanaka pushed himself away from his desk and out of his chair. "Why?"

"He lives and works in this area. He knows it. He's comfortable in his surroundings. Look at where the women were picked up and where they were dropped off. He's out driving every day, looking for the right opportunity. He's not going to stop."

Everything went silent in the homicide office. All heads turned toward Tanaka and Charlie. Charlie exhaled and began to speak again, quieter. "Sorry. As far as I can tell, these women had a sense of independence. They were not intimidated or scared to grab a ride with a smiling stranger. Set up decoys, have female police officers at bus stops to see if they can lure him in, especially around these bus stops."

Tanaka nodded in agreement.

"Do you have anyone looking at cold cases with similar circumstances or clues?"

"Yes, we've got a team scouring them now."

"I'd like to have a look myself. The killer may have had another murder in his younger, more critical years that defined him."

Aiea
Sunday, March 16, 1986

Kai looked at Charlie's hiking attire of tan shorts, navy-blue tank top, athletic socks, and heavy-tread walking shoes. "Nice. After seeing you at the picnic, you looked like a prissy type, but Lani said you were a hard-core runner, so I wasn't sure what to expect this morning."

Charlie laughed. "Don't worry, I can handle myself. I come well prepared for all occasions. Besides, with your in-your-face attitude, I knew what I was up against."

"Fair."

"With all this rain, it wasn't hard to imagine the trails being muddy."

"Ya, the trails are a mess, but the waterfalls are awesome. Go when it's nice, no falls. Go when it's messy, and the falls are breathtaking. Hey, I do appreciate you taking time out of your insane schedule to go with me. Punk tells me that you're in and out of the office at all hours."

"This work matters to me, but I'm really looking forward to this." Charlie adjusted her small backpack. "Let's go."

They entered the Aiea trail, navigating small streams and making their way along the muddy path. "We're going to take a small detour to show you the wreckage of a World War II plane. It crashed in '44, and there are still parts of the plane there."

They slipped and slid down the muddy trail until they began to see the plane: a wing, parts of an engine, and landing gear strewn through the dense vegetation. Charlie made her way to each piece and touched it.

"Story goes the plane was some type of bomber on its way to Australia, but it missed a turn and crashed into Pu'u. All the crew died, but they were able to recover the bodies. This is everything that hasn't been taken by scavengers."

Charlie walked over to a piece of the wreckage and laid her hand on it. She made a sign of the cross and said an Our Father.

"Religious?"

"Not really. I was born and raised Roman Catholic. Catholic elementary, high schools, and college. Just seemed appropriate. My auntie has encouraged me to do a Nichiren Buddhist chant. I'm not sure what I am really—lost my faith and don't see it returning anytime soon."

Kai nodded. "I know how that goes."

"I was just thinking about the crew. How they were someone's son, husband, or father. I thought about my dad and how this easily could have been him. He was stationed here during the war. Sorry, I'm spoiling our day."

"Forget it. I've got something better in store for us. Let's go."

They began the climb back up and across the trails. By the time they had finished, they were wet and covered in mud. They paralleled the river, water rushing over rocks. Eventually the path ended, and they hiked down closer to the river and began to climb over large, slippery boulders. Up ahead they could hear children laughing and screaming with joy.

Charlie watched Kai slightly ahead of her and picked up her pace to make up the last few yards. Below them, water dropped off the rocks and into a large pool where kids were swimming and playing.

"You did bring your swimsuit underneath your clothes?"

"As instructed."

Charlie watched Kai smiling at her as she pulled off her tank top and jean shorts and threw them in several directions. She kicked off her shoes, not caring where they landed.

"Better than I expected." Charlie smiled. She was mesmerized by the brilliant tattoo that flowed diagonally down Kai's chest, belly, and leg, set off by her white bikini and light brown skin. It was like a well-framed and matted piece of art. Kai smiled devilishly. Without taking her eyes off Charlie, she stepped backward off the edge of the rock and vanished.

Charlie ran up and looked over the edge as Kai disappeared into the water far below. She broke the surface and shook her head, spraying water as she whipped her ponytail from side to side. She looked up at Charlie. "Come on in."

Charlie, not to be outdone, pulled off her top, kicked off her shoes, and removed her shorts. She folded her clothes neatly on top of her backpack and placed her walking boots alongside. She stood at the edge of the rock in her metallic-blue bikini with her hands on her hips and smiled at Kai.

"Better than I expected," Kai said.

Charlie smiled and stepped off the edge of the rocks, falling ten feet into the pool below. The displaced water shot a funnel high over her head. The water was cool and refreshing. She pushed off the bottom and shot back up.

"This is incredible!" she said. The water cleansed her—it felt so invigorating, like nothing she had ever experienced swimming in a pool or lake.

"I thought you'd like it." Kai waded over to Charlie and drew close. She touched Charlie's hips and pulled her closer, her hands sliding along Charlie's body. Charlie felt a conflict between her loyalty to Annie and her body's craving to be touched. Not knowing how to respond or what to do, she defensively put her arms up across her breasts.

Charlie stared into Kai's eyes as Kai wrapped one leg around hers and pulled Charlie closer while Kai's hands slid along Charlie's arms. Kai grasped Charlie's wrists and slowly guided Charlie's hands onto Kai's hips.

Charlie caught a trace of Kai's scent. "Patchouli?"

"Yes."

"Suits you well." Charlie leaned into Kai and sniffed her neck.

Kai leaned in close and whispered, "It's probably nothing they haven't seen already, but we don't want to shock the kids." Her hands stroked Charlie's breasts as she took hold of Charlie's bikini top and pulled it back into place over her breasts.

"Tease, a little nip slip." Charlie pushed Kai away.

"More like two dials on a radio, but it could have been worse—a significant wedgie or showing your lulu." Kai smiled and jumped backward, kicking water in Charlie's direction.

"My what?"

"You know, your lulu." Kai kicked a little more water, spraying Charlie in the face.

"I don't believe that I'm familiar with that anatomical term."

"Ooh, excuse me, I forgot that I was talking with a medical expert." Kai kicked a massive amount of water at Charlie.

"Be careful what you ask for, because you may regret it."

"What is the badass doctor going to do about it?" She kicked a little more water at Charlie as she floated on her back.

"You know, Lani was right—you're a pain in the ass. Game on!" Charlie spread her arms wide and slammed them together, creating a big splash that doused Kai.

The kids didn't know what to make of two grown women splashing each other and laughing hysterically. Charlie and Kai soon noticed that they had an audience. They looked at each other and began to turn their sights on the kids. The kids laughed as they retaliated. The sounds of the waterfall were drowned out by the happy screams and laughter of all the participants.

Charlie and Kai climbed back up to the upper level and sunned themselves on the warm rocks, their heads next to each other and their bodies pointing in opposite directions. Sunshine broke through the broad leaves.

"Thanks—I haven't laughed that hard in a long time," Charlie said as she looked at the perfect sky above them.

"It felt good to me too."

"Kai's a pretty name. Does it have a meaning?"

"'From the sea.'"

"Very appropriate. I can see you're a natural in the water." Charlie adjusted her folded towel underneath her head.

"Charlie's unusual. I like it."

"Growing up, I paid hell for it. Wasn't till I was older that I came to appreciate its uniqueness."

"How did your parents come up with the name?"

"I was named after one of my father's crewmen who died during the war."

"I can see why you were so moved by the wreckage." Kai adjusted her ponytail.

"When did you suspect?" Charlie reached over to her back-pack and pulled out her sunglasses.

"I really didn't. It was more just wishful thinking on my part. The way my sister described you physically, your work ethic, and the way you responded to my questions made me hopeful."

"That's a lot of assumptions."

"Ya, ya, just hopeful thinking."

"To find someone, that feeling of invisibility—the struggle is real. At my age just getting laid is a significant accomplishment." Charlie put on her sunglasses.

"How old are you?"

"I turn forty this year."

"I would have never guessed."

"Disappointed?"

"No way. I would have said thirty-five at the most."

"I like the way you Urada women think of me. You? Any luck in the relationship department?"

"Not really. Let's just say I've kissed a lot of frogs, and most of them turned out to be just that—frogs and a couple of toads, but no princesses among them. There are a few clubs downtown, if you know where to look, but that scene gets tiresome—same lonely and desperate women. Most times I hook up with the occasional tourist or softball or volleyball player. It seems to make things easier."

"Are you trying to avoid something?"

"Disappointment! I enjoy being active, constantly in motion. I haven't found a woman who enjoys being outdoors as much as me. Most women are self-conscious about their bodies, so instead of getting in shape and taking care of themselves, they handle their depression by gorging on Hostess Twinkies and CupCakes."

"At least it's not Little Debbies."

"Doctor, that was pathetic."

"My weakness is for homemade chocolate chip cookies with walnuts, so I'm as guilty as the rest."

"I love my chocolate-covered macadamia nut candy," Kai said. "How about yourself? Are you seeing anyone now?"

"I've had a few—some awful ones that almost killed me—but then I met someone special. Annie was that one."

"Are you still seeing her? Where is she now?"

"I can't believe how much weight I've lost. I eat like I usually do, but nothing seems to stick. I feel like the Wicked Witch of the West—I'm melting. Even Garrett is down to next to nothing. He looks like he's just skin and bones," Annie said.

"No," Charlie said.

"Your family? Do they know?"

"I think they've figured it out by this time—they've stopped trying to fix me up on blind dates and asking if I'm bringing anyone special to the holiday dinners. Yours?"

"Hawaiians used to be pretty cool and accepting—there's a term, 'moe aikāne'—but then you uptight white Christians showed up and started to impose your values on us. Ya, so my family, I think they're conflicted and still trying to figure me out. I think they've got some pretty strong suspicions. Punk, the poor kid, she's always trying to figure me out."

"You shouldn't call her that! She's fabulous—she's got great potential in law enforcement."

"Her actual name is Leilani, but when everyone started to say, 'What a pretty little Lei,' my parents realized their error. They didn't want a bunch of horny teenage boys coming to the house and asking for a 'lay.' They couldn't change her name, so we just started to call her Lani."

"It's beautiful. I enjoy working and collaborating with her. Still, you need to cut her some slack. You can carry a joke too far, and then it just becomes mean."

"She was a pepe li'ili'i, or 'tiny baby'—so everyone would say. When I was little, I would point at Lani, and my two-year-old gibberish sounded more like 'Punk' to everyone than anything else, so it stuck. I would go around telling my parents, 'Punk wants this' and 'Punk needs that.' My mom was worried that Lani would never learn how to talk because I would do all the talking for her. But I'm not surprised to hear that she's doing well. I give her a lot of shit, but I love her. She's a great mom, sister, and daughter."

"Your poor mother has her hands full."

"She does. My dad is a good guy and all, but he isn't much help."

"Speaking of help, I could use yours."

"Sure, name it," Kai said, rolling onto her side and propping up her head with her hand.

"You seem to know a lot about the island. Would you be willing to show me around? I'm not talking about the tourist spots— show me from a local perspective. I need to get an insight from an islander's perspective."

"Sure, but isn't that Punk's job?"

"Lani has been terrific, but she doesn't see things or people like we do. We have to be inherently more careful and cautious." Charlie sat up and looked at Kai. She suppressed the desire that rose up in her.

"Anytime. I'd be glad to show you around."

"I need to get a better feeling of how this killer can move among us and go undetected."

"This isn't a date, then. This has to do with the murders. Punk was right about you. You are driven." Kai sat up.

"Occupational hazard and part of the baggage that comes with me." Charlie shrugged her shoulders.

"So is this." Kai leaned into Charlie and kissed her softly on the lips.

Haleiwa
Sunday, March 16, 1986

Lani sat cross-legged with Leinani in her lap. She rubbed suntan lotion on her shoulders and arms. "Go." She slapped her on the butt, and Leinani jumped up and ran toward the ocean. "How did you get my number?"

Dempsey was lying next to her on the blanket with his aviator shades and a smile on his face. "After you left, I went snooping around the office. Adair had left your business card on his desk, and I took it."

"I had mixed emotions when you called. I wasn't sure if I wanted to go out with you."

"Why?" Dempsey removed his sunglasses and held his hand over his eyes to protect them from the sun's glare.

"Don't get me wrong, you're a good-looking guy."

"Thank you."

"You're cocky as hell too."

"Whatever."

"But I'm a mom now, and I've got to take Leinani into consideration. I shouldn't have brought her here. For all her tough exterior, she's a romantic at heart. She wants to see me happy and for us to be a family. I can't be playing with her emotions. Hey, how did you know that I had a daughter?"

"I made some calls, impersonated people. It's amazing how gullible people can be. I found out as much information as I could, and I even followed you around."

"You followed me around? I'm trying to decide if I should be flattered or scared—that's creepy."

"Consider it a form of flattery. I've never done anything like that before, but there was something about you that motivated me to find out more."

"I'm telling you, I don't want any games or lies. I've been through that with Leinani's dad. I'm not going to tolerate lies anymore."

"Slow down, slow down. I'm trying to give you a compliment. I've never done this before for a woman, especially one with a rug rat."

"Rug rat!? You think Leinani's a rug rat? Keep it up, mister, you're setting a new world record for digging your own grave."

"Shit, I can't believe how hard this is, and I'm trying to be on my best behavior. I'm trying to show you that I actually care. I'm trying to do the right thing. Can you give me a little credit?"

"Nope! You're going to have to crawl through broken glass to show me that you really care."

"That might be less painful! Can we start over?"

"I'll think about it."

"True confession: I'm getting tired of living life in the fast lane. I'd come home from a deployment, and it'd be depressing as hell to see all the families with their signs welcoming their men home. The wives and kids were so happy to see them. Sure, I'd have an occasional girlfriend show up, but that wasn't really the same thing. The idea of coming home to a clean house, a hot meal, and companionship sounds perfect."

"It sounds more like you want a maid and a dog."

"Stabbed to the heart!" Dempsey mimed removing a knife from his chest. He sat up and placed his hands around Lani's neck. "You're killing me."

"Hey, knock that shit off. That's how these women are dying."

"Sorry. How's the investigation going?"

"Slow. I can't speak with you about it."

"Okay. Then what's up with your boss?"

"Charlie? She's amazing."

"She seems wired a little too tight. I just got different vibes from her."

"Why, because she didn't melt at your feet? She's going to find out whoever's doing this—she's going to nail this guy's ass!"

Ke'ehi Lagoon Beach Park
Monday, March 24, 1986

Charlie stretched to alleviate the back pain from sitting in the Mustang for hours. The hardest part of any stakeout was the sheer tedium of just sitting, waiting, and watching, followed closely by mosquitoes and bathroom breaks. She checked her watch; it was almost two in the morning. It had been almost midnight when she parked her car in an out-of-sight location at the beach park as she had done so many other nights. She knew killers returned to their pickup and drop-off locations to relive the thrill until their next kill.

"Charlie, I'm sorry to tell you this, but Annie's blood test results came back positive. She has acquired immunodeficiency syndrome," Susan said.

"AIDS?" Charlie was trying to reconcile the fact with her beliefs and the denial racing through her mind. "Of course, I've read all the literature and how it's affecting the homosexual community, but Annie?"

"We're starting to see more and more cases in the heterosexual community, especially with prostitutes. Sharing of needles and unprotected sexual intercourse are some of the reasons why, but it's spreading."

"But that's not Annie—she's apple pie, wholesome, and a mother. She doesn't do any of those things."

"It's quite possible she was exposed through her husband based on his risky lifestyle. Charlie, I know that you and Annie are close, so you need to get yourself tested."

"You mean I may have HIV?"

"Charlie, I love you with all my heart. You are my sister, fabulous aunt to my children, and brilliant at what you do, but you may have been exposed too. You aren't immune—none of us are."

"How can that be?" Charlie felt faint—she might lose her best friend and lover, and now her own life was at risk.

"Because you may have had unprotected sex with Annie. Let's say that you performed cunnilingus, and if Annie was discharging any type of bodily fluids, then you're at risk. Mom and Dad have suspected but have a tough time accepting your sexual proclivities, but I've known for a long time that you're a lesbian. We're not blind, and we couldn't care less. We just want to make sure that you're safe and healthy."

"Of course I'll get tested right away, but what can I do for Annie?"

"Unfortunately, there isn't much of anything. We have no effective treatment—none of the drugs we've experimented with have had an effect. We're trying different cocktails of drugs to see if those work, but nothing has been shown to combat the virus. This is the plague of our time. See how the religious right is telling homosexuals that this is God's way of punishing them for their abhorrent behavior? It's a terrifying time. The best you can do is to make sure that she's loved and as comfortable as possible."

Charlie watched the occasional vehicle drive down Lagoon Drive. She wasn't sure what she'd expected to see, but she'd know it when she saw it. She reached over to the passenger seat and grabbed a thermos of green tea. She opened it and tilted it over the cup, but only a few drops came out. *Damn.* Charlie tossed the empty thermos back on the seat and rolled down the window.

A soft trade wind rustled the trees, and she smelled the delicate fragrance of plumeria. She inhaled the scent and felt an odd sense of peace despite the uncomfortable sitting position. She allowed herself to close her eyes momentarily and lost the fight to exhaustion. She dreamed.

She felt like she was at a party. She could sense others around her; it seemed like they were in a living room, and the host was speaking to her. He lifted up a blanket, and on an ottoman were two big snakes that started to slither away. "The goal is to kill the snakes before they attack you," the host said.

Charlie sat up, trying to shake off the image, and rolled down the window farther to let more breeze in. She wondered what the dream meant. She still felt zoned out when she heard the noise. She listened carefully, but she could only hear the rustling of leaves in the wind.

Charlie tried to shake off the feeling, attributing it to her dream and exhaustion. She heard the noise again. Her eyes continued to scan her rearview and side mirrors to detect any movement, but it was too dark. *Has the killer seen me? Is he now after me? This isn't like him, but who knows?*

Her heart was pounding from the adrenaline flowing through her. *Stop being a wuss. You're overreacting.* She turned to look out the rear window when she felt the presence next to her. She turned quickly to see the face staring at her and a hand rising up.

"Boo!"

"You shit, I could've shot you. I probably should shoot you for scaring the shit out of me like that," Charlie said. She opened the door, got out, and stretched.

"Punk told me what you've been up to at night, so I thought I'd trail you and see if you'd like some company. Plus, I thought you might need some food." Kai held up a bag.

"Thanks, but you could've made yourself known."

"I didn't want to ruin your stakeout, so I thought it would be better if I came here quietly. You're so easy to follow—you're so self-absorbed in your thoughts. You're lucky I wasn't the killer, because you wouldn't have seen me coming."

"Thanks again. Come on in."

"Pretty good, huh?" Kai opened the door and slid into the passenger seat.

"Yes, pretty damn good. So, what do you have there? I am hungry, thirsty, and bored. Your timing was excellent." Charlie climbed back into the car.

Kai reached into her bag and pulled out a water bottle and a package of Spam musubi. "Only the very best."

"Thanks, this is great."

"I saw how you enjoyed the kalua pig, so I thought you wouldn't be too sensitive to eat Spam."

"Well, you thought right. I love this stuff." Charlie begun to unwrap the cellophane-covered package.

"I know you're working, working all the time, but I had a good time on the hike, and I thought that the only way I might get to see you again was if I came to your work. Hope you don't mind. I can leave if you'd like me to."

"You mean under all that Billy Badass routine is a sensitive and caring person?"

"*Shh*, it's our secret, and don't let Punk know. I've got an image and reputation to uphold."

"Your secret is safe with me, and this is great. I'd like to see you more, but you're going to have to be patient until the case is over."

"I understand, and I can be patient. Do you really spend every night out here looking for him?"

"Not every night. I also spend a lot of time driving around to different bus stops and other areas."

"Why?"

"He's out hunting every day for young women, and I have to hunt him."

"So you just sit here and watch." Kai took a bite of Spam musubi.

"Pretty much so."

"But why here?"

"Because he's left two bodies over there and a third very close by, so there's a chance that he might return to this location."

"Gives me the creeps thinking about it," Kai said.

Juliana Garcia's Story

Kauai
Wednesday, March 26, 1986

"Honey, why don't you spend one more night with us and fly out tomorrow morning?"

"Sis, I appreciate it, but I need to get back to my babies. I miss them so much. I've got this one too," I say, rubbing my belly.

"Ya, ya, but I worry about you. There's some crazy shit happening on the island."

"I know, I know. I'll be careful."

"Listen to me. Look at me. You're making good progress. You're getting your shit together. You have three babies to take care of and one on the way. Promise me that you won't take the bus home. You got to promise me," she says, grabbing my arms.

"Hey, be careful—this is my favorite blouse!" I gently smooth the white fabric with its cheerful red flower print.

"Hey, promise me." She squeezes harder.

"Okay, okay. Sis, I promise that I'll be careful. I'll run away if anyone comes near me. You know I'm quick. I was one of the fastest girls on the island. I have the ribbons to prove it."

"All right, we'll drop you off at the airport."

I look at my family—six sisters and three brothers and their families. I've had fun being with them. I hadn't been home in such a long time. Sis is right—I need to get my shit together. Take care of my boys, get my little girl out of foster care, and take care of the little one inside me. I make my goodbyes short and sweet, with plenty of kisses and hugs all around. I wave and enter the airport.

The flight is short and smooth. I look out the window as the plane touches down, bouncing slightly and swaying. The plane slows down, and it begins to taxi to the gate. I grab my few belongings when the seat belt light goes off, feeling anxious.

The airport is quiet—it's empty. I have such mixed feelings. I feel sad about leaving my family, but I'm excited about seeing my kids. I can't wait to hug my boys. My mind immediately goes to my little one stuck in foster care. I think about different ways of trying to get her out and back home with me.

I make my way toward the exit sign, and the sliding doors open as I approach. The fresh evening air feels good. I walk along the sidewalk under the overpass until I get to the crosswalk and wait for the light to change.

It's dark and late, and I'm tired. When I get to the bus stop, I feel drained. I light up a cigarette and wish I could have something stronger—just a little something to calm my nerves. I squeeze my hands together. I just want to get home and be with the kids. I wonder what time it is and how long before the next bus comes along. I turn when I hear a car horn.

"Hey, it's late. You need a ride somewhere?"

"No, I'm okay. Thanks."

"Hey, haven't you heard what's been going on around here?"

I laugh. "Ya, ya, my sister was all over my case about being safe."

"Then you know you shouldn't be out here alone. I'm heading away from town, toward Waipahu and Ewa, but I can drop you anywhere. I'd feel terrible if something happened to you and I could have done something to prevent it."

"You're heading to Waipahu?"

"Yep."

"Really, you're heading to Waipahu?" I ask. I'm getting excited about the idea of getting home faster.

"Yep, again." He smiles encouragingly. He leans over and opens the passenger door.

"Wait, how do I know that you're not the killer?"

"Do I look like a killer? Is this the face of a killer?"

"No, no. You've got a nice smile." As I walk closer to the car, I look around to see if anyone is watching.

"Your chariot awaits you," he says as he gestures toward the car.

"Thank you. I appreciate this so much."

"Hop on in, and I'll get you to wherever you need to go."

I run back and grab my backpack off the bench. He opens the door wider. I jump in and smile at the driver, shutting the door behind me.

He smiles back. "Are you ready?"

We pull away from the curb. "You look like a party girl."

"I used to party with the best of them, but I'm trying to put those days behind me."

"You seem a little anxious. We could have a drink and take the edge off."

"No, no, I just want to get back home."

"I understand, princess."

I nod my head in agreement and look at him out of the corner of my eye. *What is it? Something seems out of place—sincerity.* His eyes are black, not like the color black, but dead. The hair on the back of my neck starts to rise.

He looks over at me and smiles again. I hear the door lock behind me.

Waipahu
Wednesday, April 2, 1986

"Hey, Mac, we may have another one," a detective yelled from across the room.

"Another what?" Williams asked. He looked up from a pile of tip sheets. The room grew quiet.

"Some sugar workers on an overpass saw the body of a nude woman down below them. At first they thought it was a little girl."

"Shit. Where's Rice?"

"He's down the hall. He should be back in a minute," another detective said.

When Tanaka entered the homicide room, he felt all eyes on him and instantly knew, "when and where?"

Tanaka grabbed his hat and strode out of the homicide room with Williams in close pursuit. Williams in one smooth motion; started his car, turned on the siren, and swiftly pulled the car out of the stall. They made their way to the drop off point. It wasn't long before, Tanaka and Williams pulled up behind all the other emergency vehicles and made their way to the group of officers.

They looked down at a woman's partially undressed and decomposing white body. Her tattered white blouse with red flowers made a sharp contrast to the high grass. Her hands were tied behind her back.

"She looks like a child. She's so small and thin," Williams said.

Tanaka watched as the officers parted to make room for Charlie and Lani.

"Doctor, what do we have?" Tanaka asked.

The medical examiner looked up from the body. "Caucasian woman, twenty-two to thirty-two. Pregnant, won't know how old the fetus is until I get back to the lab and run more tests. From the look of her hands and feet, she's had a hard life. Based on the bruising around her throat, she was most likely strangled."

"Any identification?" Williams asked. Everyone murmured no or shook their heads.

"I'll take her fingerprints, and maybe we can identify her that way," the medical examiner responded.

"May I?" Charlie asked.

The ME looked at Tanaka for assurance. Tanaka nodded.

Charlie moved up alongside the ME and began to methodically examine the body. "Given the weather and level of decomposition, she's been out here for about a week."

The ME looked at Charlie more closely. "Yes, I'd agree, but I want to confirm before I make a definitive response."

"Detectives Tanaka and Williams, take a look at her hands."

They moved closer. "Looks like the same parachute cord as all the rest," Williams remarked.

"You're right, the cord is the same, but her hands are bound differently than the first three. The killer has wrapped it around her wrists more." Charlie pointed out the differences as her audience closed in tighter. "She's wearing her blouse, but her pants or skirt and panties are missing."

"Do you think this could be someone else?" Tanaka asked.

"Maybe our phantom partner?" Williams asked.

"No two killings are ever the same, so I don't want to rush to judgment, but it's a mental note that we should take into consideration. Body of water?" Charlie asked as she stood up and moved away.

"Waikele Stream." Williams pointed.

Charlie moved through the patrol officers and looked around the area with Lani in tow. She looked up at H-1, where cars were racing along.

"Do you think he could have dropped her body from the highway above?" Lani asked.

"Possibility," Charlie acknowledged. "I'll grant you this guy is pretty cocky, but to unload a body from a highway overpass seems extreme."

"What are you thinking?"

"I'm getting closer—I can feel it, but there's something that's missing, and I can't seem to put my finger on it."

Honolulu
Friday, April 4, 1986

"Detective, do you think these murders could have been committed by more than one person? Do you think there is the original and a copycat killer?" The attractive KITV reporter was sitting in the front row. The constant clicking sounds from cameras rippled through the crowded room.

Tanaka shifted in his seat and looked down at the microphone. He wished he were anywhere else. He thought about what Charlie had told him previously. "It's possible, but we do not believe that to be the case. The copycat killer would have to be extremely familiar with the facts of the cases."

"It's been a year since an FBI agent warned local law enforcement about the potential of a serial killer operating in Hawaii. In that period what have you done to prepare for such potentiality?" This was the seasoned beat writer for the *Honolulu Star-Bulletin* in his faded aloha shirt.

I used to like him—no more easy access for him. "We continue to study and follow major cases and try to learn from them."

"What are you doing now that you wouldn't have considered in the past?" the TV reporter from KHON2 asked as she looked up from her notepad.

Just keep your composure. "We've brought on Dr. Charlie Taylor as a consultant and to create a psychological profile of the killer." *Thank God they didn't know she was here on vacation and it was only by a sheer stroke of luck that she was available.* "Dr. Taylor is on sabbatical from the Michigan State Police and has agreed to assist us. She has an excellent reputation with both the MSP and FBI."

"What are some of the recommendations that you have taken into consideration?" The question came from the back of the room.

"I am not at liberty to discuss those at this time."

"Will Dr. Taylor be available at future press conferences?" The question came from a reporter from the *Honolulu Advertiser*.

"I'll have to check with Dr. Taylor before I commit to her availability."

"What would you like the public to know?" asked the KGMB reporter.

"We understand their concerns and fears. We are working very hard to apprehend this killer. We also need for the public to use good judgment. Just as we tell our children, do not accept rides from strangers. That is all I have for you today. Our public affairs office will inform you of our next press conference."

Honolulu
Friday, April 4, 1986

"You handled yourself well in there," Charlie said.

"I'm known for saying a lot but not providing any real information. Besides, the press get what they deserve, but they're the least of our concerns. We've got the governor, mayor, and DA breathing down our necks," Tanaka said.

"Have they identified the body yet?"

"Juliana Garcia, age twenty-five, mother of three, and three months pregnant. Never married, but she was living with her boyfriend, a construction worker, and her two sons. Her address is listed as on Hana Street in Makaha, but she currently resides in Waipahu."

"I'd like to speak with the boyfriend, if that's okay."

"Absolutely. Speaking of family, Debra Harris's mom has arrived. I'd really appreciate it if you'd meet her. As you can see, we're swamped, and you seem to have a better bedside manner than any of us. Plus, you're from off island and can relate better."

"Sure. Do you know where she's staying?"

Tanaka pushed the papers around on his desk until he found his notepad. He ripped a sheet from it and handed it to Charlie.

Waikiki
Saturday, April 5, 1986

Charlie walked along Kuhio Avenue, admiring the flowers and watching the people. How different Honolulu was from Detroit! She allowed her mind to rest. She watched a woman in front of her pull a sheet of paper from her purse and tape it to a telephone pole. She looked weary but so resolute in her actions. Charlie watched with continued interest.

She must have lost a pet. Out of curiosity, Charlie walked over and took a look. A letter-sized white sheet of paper with a handwritten note and a picture in the center. She watched the woman enter a hotel and looked at the poster more closely. The woman had lost so much more. *REWARD $7,000.00 Offered for Information leading to the Conviction of persons who murdered Debra Harris. Reported missing Jan. 30, 1986 and found Feb. 1, near Salt Lake, Honolulu, Hawaii.* A phone number followed.

Charlie entered the lobby of the hotel and looked around. To the left of the front counter was the woman sitting on a couch, looking absently out the window. Charlie could see the dark rings around the woman's eyes, her fist clenched around a handkerchief. She walked up to introduce herself.

"Mrs. Howe?"

The woman jumped a little as she was pulled back to reality.

"Yes."

"I'm Dr. Charlie Taylor, and I'm assisting the Honolulu Police Department with their investigation. My thoughts and prayers are with you and your family. May I sit with you?"

"Thank you and please." Mrs. Howe dabbed the corners of her eyes. "Sorry, I'm Leslie."

"Leslie, in piecing together the information, it's important for me to understand what Debra was like. Would you be willing to share with me your daughter's behavior and personality?"

Leslie pulled one of the posters from her bag and handed it to Charlie. "I made these posters. I'm going to plaster them all over the city. I want everyone to know that Debra was unique, she was a special person. You know that we raised the amount of money to seven thousand dollars?" She pointed to the dollar amount on the poster. "I know that doesn't sound like much, but it's all that my husband and I could scrape together. I don't want this bastard getting away with it."

"It's not the amount that matters. You want to catch your daughter's killer. We all want to catch her killer," Charlie said reassuringly.

"See how beautiful she looks? Debra had a smile that could wash away all your troubles. I only have a few pictures of her. I'd only just arrived on the island for a short time when my purse was stolen, and all my money and most of my pictures of Debra were in it. She had this way about her. Everyone loved her."

"My God, I'm sorry. Did you report this to the police?"

"Yes, but they weren't to optimistic in finding my things. I just want to know what happened to Debra."

"I understand. How are you holding up?" Charlie figured Leslie was about the same age as she was, but she looked so much older.

"I'm so tired, empty, so full of anger I could scream. I had a nightmare the night she was taken. I can see this man chasing her. I still have that dream every night."

Charlie looked at Leslie and extended her hand. Leslie took it and squeezed tight.

"She had only been working for about three months. She worked at the phone company and was so excited about her job. She finally thought life was taking a turn for the better. We had some difficult times, and now she was going to get past it all."

Charlie watched Leslie closely. "Are you getting any rest?"

"No, no, I haven't slept much in a long time . . . since the night she disappeared. It's the same every night. Can you take me to where her apartment was and where her body was dropped? I'll be going home soon, and for some strange reason, I think it will give me some small sense of relief having been closer to her."

Honolulu
Monday, April 7, 1986

"Gregg Peters and I met during the Ted Bundy investigations and have kept in touch over the years, and we meet at the odd conference now and then. I thought it might be helpful if we speak to him. First, to see if there were any correlations between Green River and our killer. Second, lessons learned that we could apply to our own investigation," Charlie explained and dialed the number. "Hi, Gregg, this is Charlie."

"Hi, Charlie, where are you now?"

"I'm here in Honolulu."

"Shit, paradise. I'd rather be there than here. You know how crappy springs are here in the Northwest. What can I do for you?"

"I want you to know that I have you on speakerphone, and I'm here with Detectives Tanaka and Williams and Officer Urada. I'm assisting the HPD with their investigation of four murdered women that we believe are the work of one man. What we're trying to confirm is if there's any relationship or correlation with the Green River Killer."

"Sure. Please describe your victims."

"They're all Caucasian, seventeen to twenty-five years of age, attractive—"

"Apologies, but let me stop you right there. Our victims cross all racial boundaries—most are of mixed race. They were either prostitutes or runaways, and this will sound cruel, but most of them were unattractive."

"Aloha, Gregg, this is Frank Tanaka. I just want to confirm that you think there is no correlation between the murders there and here."

"Frank, so-called serial killers prey on a certain type of victim and use a similar method to slay them. Based on how Charlie started to identify the victims, I knew we didn't have a match."

"Thanks, Gregg, it was worth a try. How's the investigation going there?" Tanaka asked.

"Slow."

"This is all very new to us—any lessons learned that may be of assistance?" Tanaka asked.

"Sure, it's the sharing of information. We continue to find out that someone may hold a clue or key but is none the wiser because they don't know what they're holding on to or looking at."

"Appreciate it, Gregg. I recommend that you look closer to where the women disappeared from. He knows the area and feels very comfortable there," Charlie said.

"Charlie, always a blessing. Gentlemen, it was good talking with you. Best of luck and happy hunting."

Charlie hung up the phone. Everyone was quiet.

"So that turned out to be a big fat zero and a waste of time. What's next?" Williams asked.

"We had to eliminate the possibility," Tanaka said. "What bright ideas do you have?"

"To start with, we put her back on patrol where she belongs, and she goes back on vacation and leaves us to do our work," Williams snapped.

"What police work have we stopped you from doing? Please tell me how Officer Urada and I have in any way interfered with your investigation," Charlie fired back.

"First, your profile only matches about eight thousand males on the island, and the bullshit theory that there might be two of them is lame."

"Mac, knock it off. Attention, I need the rest of you out of the room. Give me ten minutes. This is a private conversation."

The homicide room cleared immediately.

"Nobody is going anywhere. I'll make the decision on when Urada returns to her regular duties, but until that happens, she is part of this team. Dr. Taylor, I appreciate all the time and effort that you have put into this case. You've been more conscientious than most of us—regardless of where you're from. You haven't asked for a dime, which the department is thankful for. We asked you—correction, *I* asked you—to assist and take time away from your much-deserved vacation. So if you decide to return to your vacation and tell the rest of us"—he looked at Williams—"to go to hell, I'd completely understand, but I'd appreciate it if you stayed on in your capacity as a consultant."

Charlie cleared her throat. "Taking Detective Tanaka's recommendation, I'd like to suggest that we bring the team back in and review all the information that we know."

Tanaka looked at his partner.

"What the hell do I know?" Williams, still miffed, got up and walked over to the coffee machine to pour himself a cup.

Tanaka called everyone back into the office, and they gathered around the large cork bulletin board at the end of the room. The board contained a link chart with pictures, a map with pins, articles, and notes handwritten on pieces of paper.

"I want to get something cleared up and make sure there are no misperceptions," Tanaka said. "Dr. Taylor and Officer Urada are as much a part of this team as any of you. Is that clear? Any comments to the contrary are not accepted. Do we understand each other?"

Most of the detectives nodded, while a few looked at Williams for validation. He shook his head in disbelief and pointed at the board.

"What do we know about our latest victim? What are the similarities?" Tanaka asked.

"She didn't look much like the other women, so I just don't see the connection," said one detective.

"She was waiting for a bus," another detective added.

"She was from Waipahu, so there is the central Oahu connection," said another.

"Her family last saw her on March 26, so it puts her actual murder closer to the others."

"She was pregnant, which is something different," said a detective.

Charlie spoke up. "Killer probably didn't know she was pregnant, but we do know that this killer is opportunistic; what I mean by this is he's taking advantage of women at bus stops versus stalking his victims. He knows the area; he's comfortable in it. Yes, Pam Adair and Juliana Garcia were abducted from Waikiki and near the airport, but he returns to central Oahu.

"We need to identify women police officers who meet the description and start using them as decoys. He's enjoying this, and we haven't given him any reason to stop. Next, we need to do a better job of informing the public, not just through the press but by conducting a series of town halls. Most likely, he's never been in trouble before, so he won't come up in any of our searches.

"I know that I sound like a broken record, but he's a Caucasian male, age thirty to forty-five, living or working in central Oahu, most likely at some type of delivery job, and don't be surprised if he's married or living with a girlfriend. What I keep asking myself is, Where does he take the victims? We know the actual rape and murder haven't happened in either the pickup or drop sites. So where? His home? It's most likely a single-family unit with no neighbors nearby. Potentially an abandoned warehouse? We need to check these areas to try and flush him out."

"All right, everyone, get back to your jobs, and listen to what the doctor is telling you. She's trying to make our jobs easier," Tanaka said.

The detectives returned to their desks and started to go through their notepads of tips.

"Mac and Officer Urada, could you give Dr. Taylor and I a couple of minutes?"

Charlie watched Williams and Lani leave the homicide room and turned to face Tanaka.

"Thanks, Doc. I'm sorry for Mac's attitude. Ya, ya, I know he can be a real jerk, but his heart is in the right place—he wants to nail this guy. He's used to being the star and everything coming effortlessly, so this is a first for him. He's under a lot of pressure, and instead of scoring the game-winning touchdown, he finds himself getting stuffed at the line of scrimmage. He's come to the realization that he's not in the same league as you and the killer, and he's having a tough time with it."

Charlie nodded. "Given this is a large and difficult investigation, you might want to consider using different colors of yarn and pins. Men are visual, and this may help them see the connections more clearly," she said as she turned and walked out of the office.

Makiki
Wednesday, April 9, 1986

Lani maneuvered the car through traffic. "At least they listened to you and seem to be taking your suggestions seriously. I've had several female officers come up and get my insight on the case. We don't have a lot of numbers, but everyone wants to help. Beats walking around writing parking citations. It's why we entered the force in the first place."

"I have no clue if it will even work, but we have to try everything. Like I said previously, we'll catch this guy during a routine traffic violation. Most times, this is how it works."

"Hope you don't mind, but I volunteered too."

"No, I don't mind at all, but you don't exactly meet the physical characteristics."

"I thought about that. I was going to lighten up my hair. Kai, for all her issues, is actually pretty good at hairstyling and coloring. Hey, what's up with you and my sister?"

"Nothing that I know of. Why? We had a nice time on the hike, but that was about the extent of it."

"She's usually very tight-lipped about her friends, but she keeps talking about you and how much fun she had on your hike. She almost seemed normal. Ya, if you could make her reasonable, then you'd really be a miracle worker. My mom is already ecstatic about you. She's practically adopted you. If you pull something off with Kai, it will be damn near impossible to live in that house."

Charlie flipped down the sun visor, looked in the mirror, and then flipped the visor back up. "Well, if Kai could do something about my hair, then she'd be the miracle worker."

"We must be getting close. The traffic is crawling, and I can hear sirens. Over there." Lani continued through the traffic, finally making the turn into the apartment complex.

They exited the car and walked past all the emergency vehicles with their lights flashing. A metal staircase led them to the second-floor lanai. As they got to the landing, they were met by an officer. Lani flashed her badge. "When are you coming back to us?" the officer asked.

"Don't know when."

"Miss us?"

"Fat chance." Lani laughed.

The women threaded their way past the officers on the lanai until they arrived at the apartment. Some of the detectives recognized them and allowed them in. Charlie entered the small, cramped apartment, made smaller by all the law enforcement going about their business. She observed the tiny, naked Japanese woman lying on the floor. She seemed to be staring back at Charlie with her lifeless eyes—asking for help. She had been severely beaten, and there were bruises around her neck.

A detective came up behind Charlie and started to report the facts as he knew them. "Mabel Lee—"

Charlie looked skeptically at the officer.

"Ma'am, I swear to you that I didn't make that up," the officer said, executing the three-finger Boy Scout salute.

"All right, I believe you. Who can argue with a Boy Scout?"

"She's age forty-seven, Japanese heritage. It looks like she was beaten to death but possibly strangled, based on the bruises around her throat. A friend of hers found her at eight thirty this morning like this—faceup and naked. He said the apartment looked like it had been ransacked."

"Thank you, Detective. This isn't our killer, but you're looking for a young man, eighteen to twenty-two. He was probably looking for money, jewelry, or some type of other valuables so he could buy drugs. He must have seen her leave and thought she was gone for the day, so he ransacked the apartment, but she came home and surprised him. He freaked out and couldn't control his emotions, so he beat and strangled her and then stripped her of her clothes. He might be going through withdrawal. He most likely lives in this apartment complex."

The detective watched Charlie leave the apartment and then looked at Lani. "How does she do that?"

Honolulu
Friday, April 11, 1986

Charlie leaned forward in her chair as she explained what the task force was trying to accomplish to the two editors from the *Honolulu Advertiser* and the *Star-Bulletin*. "We need your assistance. We understand the public is well aware of these murders, but we want to make sure they know the precautions they need to take."

"Do you speak in an official capacity for the HPD or the mayor or governor?" asked George Tilman of the *Advertiser*.

"No, but you can use my name and say I'm working as a consultant."

"Can we quote you?" asked Margaret Kobayashi of the *Star-Bulletin*,

"Please," Charlie said, sitting back in her chair.

"We're all ears," Kobayashi said skeptically.

"I understand your hesitation. Some of this will seem like stating the obvious, but I believe it's critical that everyone understand what we're up against and that no one is immune. We believe— correction, I think—that the murders are connected to the central part of Oahu. All the victims are Caucasian, but that doesn't mean women of Asian, black, Hispanic, or Pacific Island heritage should believe they are not vulnerable. Three of the victims were waiting at bus stops, so there is a correlation there.

"The killer's driving along, sees a woman standing alone at a bus stop. She intrigues him or piques his interest. He watches her. He watches her closely. He sees that she keeps looking at her watch, she keeps looking for the bus, and she appears anxious. So he drives up, puts on his best smile, and reassuringly promises to get her where she needs to go on time—hassle-free. The woman, relieved, accepts the ride, and we know what happens next.

"Ted Bundy would feign an injury, such as putting his arm in a cast or sling, and then ask for help. He impersonated an off-duty cop. He was preying on their emotions. He took advantage of his good looks, intelligence, and ability to articulate his thoughts. He didn't have a sign hanging from his neck that read *Serial Killer*. They are good at blending in with the rest of us.

"I highly recommend that women travel in pairs. They absolutely shouldn't travel alone. They need to make sure their families and friends know where they are going, when they are leaving, and when they arrive. Women should not take rides from any strangers. The warning not to accept rides from strangers even in broad daylight should go without saying, but it bears repeating.

"Women need to be alert and cautious of their surroundings at all times. They need to understand the danger that surrounds them, and they shouldn't be hitchhiking. Three of them were waiting for buses but somehow were either convinced or coerced to give up the bus and get in a car or van. This killer is a real smooth talker. These killers are smart; they know what they're doing. Stay in well-lit areas. Finally, women shouldn't be overconfident that they can hold their own against a man, but if they find themselves compromised, they need to fight as they've never fought before. No rules—all proprieties go out the window, because their lives depend on it."

Manoa
Tuesday, April 15, 1986

There was a line of women waiting to make their way into the university library. They filed in, and the front seats were filled very quickly. Williams adjusted the microphone, blew into it, and heard feedback. Satisfied, he began his opening remarks.

"We want to assure all of you that we are doing everything we can to solve these murders. Officers in their usual capacity are aware that the bus stops may be target areas. Citizens are remiss in their civic responsibilities when they demand the public release of circumstantial evidence gathered during our investigation. Let's be clear, to do so would jeopardize a successful prosecution.

"I'm sure most of you have read the recommendations given by Dr. Taylor in both newspapers, and we want to reiterate those comments. Don't travel alone. There is safety in numbers. Plan your trip and inform a family member or friends of your plan, especially departure time, means of travel, and arrival time. Know the bus schedule on your route, and avoid long waits at the bus stop. Use bus stops frequented by other people or near populated areas. If a car passes by your bus stop and returns while you're waiting, be wary if a driver of a vehicle or a passenger approaches you for whatever reason. The killer will be smiling, encouraging, and will open the door. Be on guard, and seek help.

"Never accept a ride from, or accompany, a stranger—no matter what the pretense. Note the license plate number, car, and driver descriptions of any suspicious passersby or loiterers. Carry a whistle or noisemaker. If you are attacked, yell 'fire' and not 'help' at the top of your lungs, and don't stop even if they threaten you. Use it to attract attention if you sense danger. If your instinct tells you something is amiss, heed the warning, be on guard, and seek help."

Charlie and Lani stood in the back of the hot, crowded library. Williams allowed a short question-and-answer period, which he stumbled through. As the room began to clear, a dark-haired woman walked up to Charlie and Lani. Charlie could see the tension in her body and the anger in her face.

"From all of this"—she turned and swept her arm across the room—"it seems that you are more concerned with catching the killer than preventing the crime."

"Dr. Taylor, this is Aubrey Atwell. Aubrey, Dr. Taylor," Lani said.

"I know who she is. Dr. Taylor, you should be ashamed of yourself. You should be more concerned about protecting women than trying to catch this killer." Aubrey turned and stormed off before Charlie could respond.

"Who was that? What was that?" Charlie asked.

"Aubrey is a former HPD officer. Let's just say she has many anger issues. She had a reputation of being a real bitch and didn't get along with anyone."

"The anger must come from someplace, justified or not. Interested in grabbing a bite? I'm going to get something to eat before I start my stakeout. Or do you have a date?"

"Not you too! You and Kai are so much alike—teasing, poking, trying to get under my skin. You older sisters never let your foot off your baby sister's neck."

"Me, a tease? The thought never crossed my mind. Just remember, if I didn't like you, then I wouldn't tease you."

"Kai says the same thing, and I don't believe her, and I'm starting to have my doubts about you too. No, I don't have a date—tonight. Yes, I'm up for a bite. I'm going to take you to a special Hawaiian cuisine place."

"Really?"

"Ya, ya. It's called Liliha's. They have delicious baked goods, and the food is a mixture of Asia, States, and Pacific all rolled into terrific comfort food. I love their pancakes, fluffy and light, with some eggs and Portuguese sausage."

"Sounds delicious," said Charlie.

"Do you think we're making progress?" Lani asked as she and Charlie left the library.

"It's hard to tell if we're making progress, but at least we can make it as hard as possible on him. My concern is how many women we aren't reaching."

"You believe there are women out there that don't know what's going on? Gun sales are going through the roof. Everyone seems to be on edge."

"You and I are in this day to day, so we see and feel how dangerous this killer is, but other women, they know that there's a threat and something terrible is going on, but they don't think it will happen to them. That includes you—you need to take the proper precautions. It's like a traffic accident—when we see one, we're sympathetic, but we justify that it will never happen to us. It's a coping mechanism; if it weren't for 'it will never happen to me,' many of us would never leave our homes," Charlie said.

"Makes sense, but how do we break through the barrier to get to them?"

"We just keep plugging away. We have to use a variety of methods to continue the dialogue."

"But if we are successful and women understand the dangers completely, then won't it make it harder for us to catch him?" Lani asked.

"Possibly, but I'd prefer to prevent another killing and take longer to apprehend him."

"I hate to sound defeatist, but do you think it's possible? To catch him?"

"Being discouraged is part of the roller coaster. We're going to have good days, some horrific days, and a lot of days moving sideways. So hang in there. You are doing a tremendous job. Yes, I really believe we're going to catch him. I think we're close, and one of these days, he will slip up, or we'll find one of the missing pieces of the puzzle, but yes, we are going to nail him." Charlie unlocked the car doors and accelerated out of the parking lot and it wasn't long before they'd arrived at the iconic bakery.

A short Filipina waitress with streaks of gray in her hair and dark, wrinkled skin smiled as they entered. "Two?"

"Please," Lani said. Turning to Charlie, she added, "We're in luck—not only is there no line, but there are seats available."

The waitress shuffled a short distance and pointed to two open seats at the counter. As Charlie walked past, she checked out the other customers' plates—the food looked and smelled delicious. Shortly after they sat at the counter, the waitress took their orders and returned shortly with a plate of warm, grilled, golden butter rolls in front of them with two small plastic cups of strawberry-guava jelly and two cups of coffee.

"No coffee for me," Charlie said, but the old woman had already shuffled away.

Lani smiled as she watched Charlie. "What's up with you, Punk? What are you smiling at?"

"I'm just waiting."

"Waiting for what?" Charlie picked up one of the rolls and took a bite. The roll melted in Charlie's mouth with a delicious taste of butter. She stared at Lani. "I think I found a legitimate replacement for sex."

"I knew you'd like it. I just knew it that you'd love these rolls."

"If the rest of the meal is as good as these rolls are, then I'm ecstatic."

"Speaking of sex, I have another date."

A couple of men sitting at the counter overheard Charlie and Lani's conversation and elbowed each other and smirked.

"Good for you! How's it going?" Charlie asked.

"It's good, it's nice. He gets the demands of the job, so he doesn't lose it when I tell him that I'm not available."

"A level of maturity—always a good sign. Has the family met him yet?"

"Well, sort of. He took Leinani and me to the beach, but it's way too soon for him to meet the rest of the family. Leinani asks a lot of questions because we talk on the phone almost every night. She wants to know about the next time we're going to the beach. I've got to be careful—that girl doesn't miss a thing."

"Sounds nice. Having someone show interest in us makes us feel good. Brings some excitement into our lives, which, for most of us, consist of everyday drudgery." Charlie smiled.

"It's nice to have someone to talk with that's not on the force, family, or a kid."

"Well, I apologize for calling him a jerk—that was rude and inconsiderate on my part," Charlie said, taking another bite of a roll and winking at Lani.

"I never said who it was! You've just assumed. Besides, it may not be him, and I'm not going to tell you."

The waitress placed plates in front of them, and Charlie didn't hesitate to fork up a considerable amount of mashed potatoes and gravy.

"I'd have never imagined you as a meatloaf-and-mashed-potatoes type."

"I'm from the Midwest, and sometimes the best thing going is creamy, smooth mashed potatoes with delicious brown gravy. Is brown even a flavor? So, tell me more about Mr. Dempsey."

Kalaheo, Kauai
Saturday, April 19, 1986

"Amen." The Catholic priest completed the sign of the cross and then sprinkled holy water on the casket. Charlie watched family and friends circle around the grave. They were dressed casually, and she felt out of place in her subdued dark gray dress. After the burial, she watched Juliana's friends and family disperse. She made her way to the grave and looked down at the small headstone that read *She fell by the wayside and the angels took her home.*

"Can I help you?"

Charlie turned and recognized Juliana's features on another woman, an older sister, perhaps. "I came to pay my respects."

"Thank you, but you don't look like you're from around here. Whatcha doing here?"

"I apologize, I didn't mean to intrude. My name is Dr. Charlie Taylor." As she spoke, she watched another woman whisper into the older sister's ear.

"You that lady doctor who's investigating those murders?"

"Yes."

"Any closer to catching the killer?"

"No, we're not as close as we'd like to be."

"Well, thank you for coming."

"Could I talk with you about Juliana?"

The sister hesitated. "Ya, sure."

"What was she like?"

"I'd warned her about taking the bus, but she wouldn't listen, which was pretty typical. We wanted her to spend one more night with us and then fly back the next day, but she was too anxious to get back to her kids. We miss her badly, and she had a baby inside of her. Doctor, how can someone do this to another person?"

"I wish I had a good answer for you, but I don't."

"Such a shame. We hadn't seen her home since she left the island seven years ago. We had a nice visit. We're a big family—three brothers and seven sisters, ya? She was excited about her life. She finally thought that she was getting her life straightened out for the first time."

"What kind of problems did she have?"

"She dropped out of high school, took drugs, and was living with beach people for a while at Makaha. She always had these ideas in her head like she could run away if some guy came around. Ya, ya, she'd won some track medals in high school, but she was a tiny thing, not more than five feet four and weighed ninety pounds or so. She could have never fought off an attacker."

"If a stranger approached her, somebody who acted kind?"

"She tried to keep to herself, but she could be too trusting and easygoing."

"We appreciate what you and the police are doing for Juliana and the other women," the second sister broke in, "but can you provide us with some more information?"

"I'd be glad to share with you what I can."

"Follow us—we're about to sit down to some lunch. Be careful where you step. I'd hate to see your nice shoes and dress get ruined."

Honolulu
Saturday, April 26, 1986

Charlie looked at the anxious faces across the hotel restaurant as she and Lani settled into their seats and adjusted the microphones just before the red on-air light went on. "Good morning, and welcome to our show. We are at the beautiful Sheraton Hotel's restaurant. We have two special guests today, and given how crowded the restaurant is, you know all about them," William Stewart announced.

I wished it were under better circumstances, but we're fortunate to have with us Dr. Charlie Taylor, a criminal psychiatrist. Dr. Taylor is a graduate of the University of Michigan and is with the Michigan State Police. She's a consultant to the HPD, trying to solve these terrible killings that have recently plagued our island. We also have our own HPD officer, Lani Urada, who is part of the task force and assisting Dr. Taylor. Ladies, thank you for coming here this morning."

Polite applause came from the audience.

"Thank you very much for hosting us," Charlie said.

"What would you like to say to our audience?" Stewart asked.

"I truly wish we were here under different circumstances, but unfortunately, we're not. What I would like to suggest to the audience, especially young women listening, is this: Before you open that car door, you should ask yourself, 'Do I trust this person with my life?' Because that's precisely what you're doing, and if you're not sure, then you'd better not. Even though I'm a guest here on this magical island, I can feel the ohana. There's a sense of trust that, I'm sorry to say, you're going to have to guard against.

"Women need to stop thinking about Charles Manson when they conjure up an image of the strangler. This person knows what they're doing. People shouldn't automatically trust people wearing uniforms—such as security guards, bus drivers, military personnel, ministers, or police. We've had issues with people impersonating police officers. The killer will see this as a challenge."

"Officer Urada?" Stewart asked.

"For one thing, posters will be placed on every bus in Honolulu within the next two weeks. There will be radio announcements and newsletters. Businesses will be asked to take steps to protect employees in parking lots. Telephone repair crews, meter readers, taxi drivers, and road repair crews will be asked to join the lookout. Second, I'd like to add that we'll continue our efforts to solve these murders."

"Ladies, thank you for stopping by our show today. I think that I can say that we pray to God that no one else is hurt and that you catch this killer as quickly as possible." More polite applause. "When we return from our commercial break . . ."

Laura Ayres's Story

Honolulu
Tuesday, April 29, 1986

"**D**amn it! I can't believe this stupid car." I jump out and run around to the front, clueless as to what I might find or how to do anything about it. I slide my hand under the hood, feeling for the release latch and scratching and pinching my fingers until I find it and pop open the hood. *Shit, now what?*

The honking from impatient drivers behind me is making me a little crazy. "Go around, go around! I hear you, but laying on your horn isn't going to solve the problem. Go back to the mainland." I reach into the dirty engine compartment, trying not to get my suit dirty. I check the battery for any clues.

"Know what you're looking at?"

I glance up at the friendly face of the man standing next to me and laugh. "No clue. You?"

"Let me look." He peers down into the engine, "I'll remove the battery caps to see if there's water, and then I'll go and check the tubes and belts."

"I really appreciate this."

"It's probably the starter, so you're going to have to get it towed."

"Shit."

"Well, I'm on my way back to work. I can drop you off at one of the car dealers, or someplace else, if need be. They should be able to get you a tow back to their maintenance department."

"Sounds pricey. Plus, I'm pressed for time."

"Not as pricey as a new car."

"True." He looks disturbingly familiar. "Where do you work?"

"I'm over by the airport, just a stone's throw away from here. I work for one of the aviation maintenance-and-repair shops."

"That's it! We've met before."

"Nah, I don't think so . . ."

"I sell pagers—I think we talked about getting you one. You're a mechanic, right?"

"You're right, now I remember you coming into our shop. I also deliver parts to different locations around the island."

"You sure it won't be an inconvenience? I don't want to be a bogart," I say anxiously.

"Bogart! I haven't heard that term in a long time. No, you won't be a bogart. I've got my van parked right behind your car."

"I appreciate this so much." I open the passenger door to his white van.

"Are you from here?" he asks as he starts up his van.

"No, I grew up on the mainland. I've been on the island for about fourteen—no, fifteen years. Are you from around here?"

"Nope, just like you. I grew up in the Midwest. What did you do before you were selling pagers?"

"I'm embarrassed to say this, but I did some dancing in clubs, here and on Guam."

"No need to be embarrassed. We all have to make a living some way." I can see his eyes staring at me through his Ray-Ban Aviators. I smile back. "I can see it. You've got killer looks and an attitude about you."

"Attitude?"

"I don't mean that in the wrong way, but I could tell that you take your job seriously, and you weren't afraid of approaching a lot of people to try and sell your pagers. Yeah, you've got an attitude, and that killer look. I bet you made plenty of dinero dancing."

I laugh. "I've heard other words used, but 'attitude'—that has to be a first."

"There are always firsts for everything."

"That's for sure. I guess that I was something of a wild child growing up. In my younger, more carefree days, I hitchhiked across the US. Now, that was a wild summer, but I had a lot of fun."

"Wow, that sounds crazy."

"I wasn't out of control—well, maybe just a little."

"Man, you weren't worried about getting picked up by some whack job?" He slows down as the traffic light changes to yellow, then red. He looks over at me queerly.

"No, not really. I probably should have been." I laugh. "I did meet some squirrely guys, and there was this one guy in particular . . . Never mind, I had a great time, and everyone was cool, but I never thought my life was in danger."

"You must have good radar. I served in the army, and I've met some crazy sons of bitches."

"Ya, I like that. I do have good radar. I feel like I can spot a phony or creep quickly. I've had a lot of life experiences with lots of different men, so yeah, I'm a pretty good judge of character and know enough when not to get into a car." I peek at my watch as we drive along. I start looking for a way to get out of the van.

"I see you keep looking at your watch. You've got that appointment, right?" He looks at me.

"Sorry, I've got an evening meeting scheduled with my boss and team members. This whole car thing has thrown me for a loop. I'm kind of in a hurry, and I don't want to be a burden any longer. I'll just jump out at the next light."

"No need to be in such a rush. Understandably, you're anxious about the car and meeting and all. I'll get you where you need to go."

"Okay, but we seem to be heading in the wrong direction. Aren't the dealerships in the other direction?"

"Ya know, you're not exactly my type. I usually prefer someone younger."

"What?" I look at him, feeling dumbfounded. He removes his sunglasses and smiles.

Ke'ehi Lagoon Beach Park
Thursday, May 1, 1986

From her vantage point, Charlie watched the police cruisers on Lagoon Drive. They would stop, turn their searchlights on, and scan the shore and water. She grew curious and drove over to investigate. She flagged down one of the patrol cars.

"Yes, ma'am. Can I help you?"

"Hi, Officer. I'm Dr. Taylor, assisting Detectives Tanaka and Williams on the Strangler case," Charlie said, opening her wallet to show some identification.

"Hi, Doc. What brings you out here tonight?"

"I was going to ask you the same thing. Most nights, I park over there to watch and see if our guy shows up," Charlie said, pointing to her lookout at the beach park.

"Doctor, that's great. Have you noticed anything, either tonight or last night?"

"No, nothing out of the ordinary. Why?" Charlie's curiosity grew.

"We got a call late Wednesday morning from a woman reporting her roommate missing. She hadn't shown up since Tuesday evening. Not like her; she has a seven-year-old daughter. Pretty responsible."

"Physical characteristics?"

The officer picked up his notepad. "Thirty-six, Caucasian, lives in a house on Ala Mahamoe Street in Moanalua Gardens."

"I apologize, but I'm still pretty new to the island. Where is that located?"

"Near the highway, right next to Fort Shafter."

"Thank you," Charlie said, trying to picture the geography in her head.

"We also have reports of her blue Toyota parked with its hazard lights flashing along Nimitz Highway between Middle Street and Puuloa Road."

"Thank you, Officer, for taking the time to speak with me," Charlie said. The patrol officer rolled up his window and moved on with his search.

Back in her car, Charlie opened the glove box and looked at her map of the island with circles, dots, and stars drawn on it. She found where the woman lived and where her car had been found. *Her vehicle was near the other drop locations, but she's older.*

Manoa
Friday, May 2, 1986

Charlie used to embrace the mornings, but now she slogged her way through her run—the miles just dragged on. She returned to her auntie's house and opened the front door to take the dogs for a walk through campus. The dogs must have picked up on Charlie's moodiness—even Pepper was well behaved and quiet. They wandered through the serene school grounds, ending their walk at the Japanese teahouse—Chashitsu Jakuan, the Cottage of Tranquility. She pulled out her beads and began to chant. She always started slow and tried to focus on an answer to a question that had been bothering her, but most times, her thoughts just returned to Annie.

A dark and wet fall day. Out of sight, Charlie stood in the background. Annie and her kids, Josh and Melissa, Garrett's parents, and a few close friends, all dressed in somber black and gray, watched the casket being lowered into the grave. Annie had her arms around her children. Josh was trying to be stoic, while Melissa buried her face in her mother's chest. Charlie lifted her collar to try to keep out the cold.

She finished her chanting and put her beads away. Salt lifted her head off Charlie's lap, and Pepper looked at her. "All right, all right, we're going." She gathered up the leashes, and she and the dogs made their way off campus as it started to come to life.

Back home, the dogs ran inside and greeted Barbara, barking and scurrying around her.

"Ya, ya. I'm so glad to see you too. Yes, I've missed you." Barbara knelt and petted the dogs. "Your usual routine?"

"Pretty much so, but the campus is so lovely at this time of day, and we always have the place to ourselves. It's a great time to gather my thoughts."

"Hungry?"

"Yes."

"Good, I prepared us a little breakfast, nothing fancy. If you set the table, I'll bring out the food."

"You know you don't have to go through all this trouble for me. You've got work, and I'm used to being on my own and taking care of myself."

"I know, but I enjoy doing it. Routines are important—I always made your uncle's breakfast. Like everyone else, I can get tired of the tedium, but when the routine stops, I find myself a little out of kilter. I make my bed every morning, been doing it since I was five. I know no one will notice or care whether I make it, but at the end of the day, I enjoy pulling back the bedspread and climbing into the sheets."

"That makes sense. Routines have been missing from my life."

"If your work schedule here is any indication of your work schedule in Michigan, then I can see why."

"It may not seem like it, but I've tried to do better here."

"We're all enjoying whatever we can get. The dogs love the early morning walks, and just having you poke your head into my room to say 'good night,' 'good morning,' and 'love you' is a godsend."

Charlie smiled as she placed the forks, knives, and spoons on the table. "It's the first time that I've felt at peace at home. Please don't say anything to my folks, especially my mom. I know how you two like to share everything, especially when it comes to me." Charlie paused. "I've always felt like an outsider in my own family."

"Why do you think that?"

"I don't know. It's never been anything said, more of a feeling."

"Charlie, you need to understand that your mom loves you with all her heart. She may not be the perfect mother, but she always has your best interest at heart." Barbara walked out of the kitchen and handed Charlie a plate.

"No, I get that."

It wasn't long before Pepper waddled over and sat down underneath the table next to Charlie's legs. He reached up and pawed her. She took a small piece of scrambled egg off her plate and held it under the table. Pepper gobbled it up. It wasn't long before he pawed her leg again.

Barbara shook her head. "As tough as you are, you're a softie when it comes to that rascal."

"He's a smoothie," Charlie said as she looked underneath the table and scratched Pepper. "Aren't you?" Pepper, unmoved, pawed her leg. "So that's how it is? You only want one thing. You're no different from all other males, are you? Food and sex. Life must be so simple. On the other hand, we females are so much more complicated. Isn't that so, Salt?" Salt trotted over and joined the group. Charlie took another small piece of egg off her plate and gave it to Salt. Both tails wagged.

"This man who broke your heart—do you mind telling me about him?" Barbara looked at Charlie inquisitively.

Charlie shrugged. "There's nothing much to tell."

Barbara leaned forward and grasped Charlie's hand. "I know that I have no right to ask, but I'm just trying to get to know you better. Make up for all these years."

"I understand and appreciate the concern. It's awkward and still painful to discuss."

"Can you at least describe him? Give your auntie just a little to go on."

"A terrific smile that would light up the room. Ah, a little mischievous, but a heart of gold. Warm, kind, and thoughtful." Charlie stroked the fork with her thumb and index finger as she carefully selected the adjectives that ran through her mind.

"He sounds wonderful," Barbara said as she pushed her breakfast plate aside. "I'm sorry it didn't work out for you, but you'll find someone new and just as special, maybe even more."

Charlie skimmed a spoonful off the top of the bowl of homemade vegetable soup and gently blew on it to cool it. She put the spoon to Annie's lips.

"What is it?"

"Vegetable, your favorite."

Annie slowly nodded her head. "I've always loved your homemade soup."

"Please try to eat just a little. It'll do you good. You need it, honey," Charlie said.

"I'm sorry, I don't have the strength to even sip it. I'm just so tired," Annie said, barely audible.

"Honey, I know, but it would help give you a little strength," Charlie begged.

"How are the kids?"

"From everything I can tell, they're well. I try to visit or call every day, but neither Josh, Melissa, nor your parents are too receptive to me."

"Thank you for not giving up on them—or me. Please look after them after I'm gone. I find peace knowing that you'll be there for

them, especially Josh. Melissa's oblivious to everything, like her father, but Josh is sensitive and picks up on everyone's emotions. The two of you are so much alike."

"You're not going to die, so stop this silly talk."

Annie's lips cracked a little smile. "Thank you for being my Good Samaritan, a good friend, and caring for me. Most people have run and hid because they think I'm contagious—a modern-day leper—I even have the black spots to prove it. Even my own family refuses to see me out of some shame, but not you. Even after you found out that Garrett and I had sex, which caused all of this, you didn't leave me. I could've made you sick, but you didn't leave."

"Shh, I will never leave you," Charlie said as she coaxed Annie to sip the soup.

"I'm not ashamed," Annie said. She put her bony hand on Charlie's.

"Ashamed? You have nothing to be ashamed of. None of this is your fault." She skimmed the next spoonful and blew on it.

"No, I mean of us. I'm happy to have found you. I've cherished the times we spent together—the four of us playing board and card games, going on hikes and bike rides, and just having dinner together. I loved that." Annie started to cough.

"Hey, take it easy," Charlie said. She held a glass of water to Annie's lips and adjusted the cold compress on her forehead.

"Do you think someday women like us will be able to live together without shame or fear? Having our own families and not having to worry about somebody taking our kids away from us or treating us like pariahs?"

"I seriously doubt it. I know one thing for sure—it's not happening anytime soon."

"You're beautiful." Annie smiled.

"Now I know you're really sick." Charlie smiled back.

Annie laughed lightly, coughed, and then whispered, "I've made peace with God. Not many people can say this, but I've had a good life: two beautiful children, a good career, some travel, and you. I met someone who really loved me, and she is with me on my deathbed. Doesn't everyone wish to die in the arms of their lover? This may all seem unfair, but what's the alternative—get run over by a bus?" Annie closed her eyes and started to drift off.

Charlie got off the bed and adjusted the blankets around her. Annie opened her eyes briefly. "I don't want to be alone right now—lie down next to me." Charlie lay down carefully next to her.

"Promise me one thing?"

"Anything!"

"Don't be angry," Annie said as she smiled and drifted off. Charlie held her frail body close. There was nothing left of her—Annie had evaporated.

Charlie looked out the window and watched the brilliant sun sink into the horizon until it vanished. Annie's last breath was small and peaceful. Charlie pushed the red hair off her forehead and softly kissed it and her lips. She gently closed Annie's eyelids. "Sweet dreams."

She stayed next to her, face in her hands—she mourned. The room filled with darkness.

Charlie pulled out of her memories and smiled. "I hope so. I miss the feeling of being loved and wanted." Pepper pawed Charlie another time. "Pepper, that's not exactly what I had in mind." She looked under the table at the mischievous dog.

"What's on your schedule today? Any chance for some time off? You look exhausted," Barbara said with concern.

"Slim. HPD is holding an out-of-the-ordinary press conference. Another woman is missing, and they're asking for the public's help to locate her. Additionally, they want to reinforce safety precautions that every woman should be taking. Oh, you might want to stay away from Nimitz. HPD is setting up roadblocks to ask commuters if they recognize the car or might have seen something."

"Oh my God, another one was taken? This is tragic. Our beautiful island used to be immune to all mainland crime and depravation. Do you think it's him?"

"Pray she's not in any danger and we find her okay. We don't know for sure if it's the same guy—we can't jump to any conclusions until we have more facts," Charlie said, staring into her coffee cup. *Ten years older, taken from town, works for the Telepage Company.*

Charlie, Barbara, and the dogs were startled by the telephone ringing.

Barbara got up and walked across the room to answer it. "Hi, Officer Urada. Yes, she's here. Yes, one moment." Barbara put her hand over the receiver and walked it to Charlie, the twenty-foot cord stretching behind her. Charlie smiled as she took the handset from her.

"Hi, what's up?" Charlie asked.

"Detectives Tanaka and Williams would like for you to come over to the station."

"Sure. Anything I need to prepare for?"

Honolulu
Friday, May 2, 1986

Charlie and Lani pushed open the doors and watched the flurry of activity going on inside—multiple groups having loud and heated conversations, phones ringing from various desks, and testosterone in overdrive. The room was a mix of sweat, Brut cologne, and Mennen Skin Bracer. Charlie observed the perspiration stains under the armpits and just above the waistbands in back. She nudged Lani and nodded in the direction of Tanaka, Williams, and Crawford. They appeared to be strategizing in front of the busy bulletin board, which now had different colors of yarn to represent the connections or links between victims, locations, and cars.

"Gentlemen, how can we be of assistance?"

"Thank you, Doctor and Officer, for coming in," Crawford said.

Tanaka looked at Williams, then handed Charlie a piece of paper. "We've received several reports of a Caucasian male, thirties to early forties, in either a white or beige-colored van near the car the night that our latest victim disappeared."

"Your profile was spot-on," Crawford confirmed.

Lani subtly squeezed Charlie's arm.

Charlie looked at Crawford, Tanaka, and then Williams, who looked away.

"Any idea where you think she could be?" Tanaka asked.

Charlie walked closer to the link chart on the large map of the island, and the men encircled her. She felt somewhat claustrophobic—anxious—in the confined area. "He's already disposed of the body, somewhere close to the others."

"We've scoured the Ke'ehi Lagoon area," Williams said. He pointed to the map.

"I don't think we're the only ones in that effort, either," Tanaka added.

Charlie looked closely at the map and turned to face Lani and the men. "We've stated that this is connected to central Oahu—correct?" Crawford, Tanaka, and Williams nodded. She turned back to the map, and her index finger followed the colored yarn as she spoke. "Pam lived in Mililani, abducted in Waikiki, and found in the Keʻehi Lagoon. Rebecca lived in Waipahu, abducted in Waipahu, and found in the Keʻehi Lagoon too. Debra lived in Pearl City, abducted near the Waipahu interchange, and located in the Moanalua Stream, not more than a mile from Pam and Rebecca. Juliana lived in Waipahu, abducted from a bus stop in Honolulu near the airport, and found beneath the H-1 overpass near the Waikele Stream. Now we have Laura, who lived in Moanalua, was abducted off Nimitz Highway, body location to be determined. From the eyewitnesses' accounts, I believe we're comfortable with the profile, but something is missing from our board that connects all of them together." Charlie looked at them like a high school math teacher explaining a problematic calculus equation to see if they comprehended it.

Crawford looked keenly at the map. He took off his heavy, black-framed glasses. "Do you think someone in uniform is doing this?"

Tanaka and Williams looked closely at the map again. Lani leaned closer to the map to understand what Charlie was trying to get them to see.

"Possibly. The thought has occurred to me, and I'll have more on that later, but that's not where I'm going with this right now," Charlie said. "As it relates to these cases, what do the military and our person of interest have in common?"

"Military wear uniforms, they're spread all over the island, and they come and go frequently," Tanaka said.

"They're all a bunch of uptight assholes and one sick bastard," Williams said. Crawford and Tanaka looked at Williams with disappointment.

"I believe there's an aviation connection with the crimes, thus potentially a military one too," Charlie said. "The killer is most likely working in or near the airport at one of the maintenance or parts shops. His work is most likely parts delivery—hence the van. His route takes him to places like Schofield Barracks, Fort Shafter, Hickam, and Pearl Harbor, so that is why we're seeing where the women have been picked up and where their bodies are being dropped off."

"I'm sorry, Dr. Taylor, but I just don't see the connection," Williams said, trying to trip up Charlie.

"Fair enough. Opportunistic killers stalk in areas they're familiar with, either work or home or both, so when you look at the map, you can start to visualize him driving from someplace in the vicinity of the airport to all these bases, and then you start to see how his route encompasses all the marks on the map." She drew an imaginary boundary around all the colored pins.

"Come on, Dr. Taylor. We live on an island, which means you pretty much can't take a shit around here without running into the military," Williams said, throwing up his hands in frustration.

"Detective Williams, give Dr. Taylor a chance to finish her theory. So far, her profile has rung true," Crawford said, placing his hands on his hips.

"I'm glad that Detective Williams is challenging the thought process—this is actually very healthy," Charlie said. Williams looked at Charlie in disbelief. "Detective Williams, did you play sports in high school or college?" she asked.

"Sure," Williams responded smugly as he crossed his arms across his chest.

"I'm sure that you were an outstanding athlete. Did you receive any trophies?"

"Ya," Williams said. His arms dropped to his sides as he started to wonder where the questions were leading.

"Do you have them still? Maybe in a trophy case?"

"Ya, I keep them with all my other memorabilia in my man cave."

"Is there one particular game, or several games, that you played a significant part in? For example, where you hit a game-winning home run?"

"Ya, ya."

"Was your name in the paper? Did it make you feel proud? Did girls suddenly start to take notice of you?"

"Hey, I've never had a problem with the girls noticing me," Williams boasted.

"Do you ever drive by the playing fields and instantly feel or see yourself back in time, reliving the moments?"

"Well . . ." Williams started to get defensive.

"I should've figured," Tanaka said.

"Hey, at least I played sports."

"Gentlemen, let's keep on track," Crawford said.

"No, this is good. Serial killers behave the same way," Charlie said, as she turned and looked each man in the eye.

"Are you saying that I'm like a serial killer?" Williams asked incredulously.

"How the mighty have fallen," Tanaka quipped.

"Nothing of the sort! What I'm saying is that you, a star athlete that kept your trophies and memorabilia, read and kept the newspaper clippings of your accomplishments, and relived those life-defining moments, and our killer is doing the same. When we find him, we'll see his trophies that he has stored someplace, like pictures, ID cards, panties, shoes, or jewelry.

"He thinks like a big-game hunter, but instead of a trophy head on the wall above the mantel, he keeps the victims' items to touch and smell. Every day, when he's delivering parts or going about his work, he drives past those specific spots where he either picked up or dropped off the women and gets to relive each moment. He cherishes these moments, these memories. Finally, his ego is stroked every day as he reads about himself and how he has us stymied—he relishes the idea that he's outsmarting us," Charlie said pointedly to Williams.

"Okay, I'll give you this for the time being, but you still haven't shown us where Laura Ayres's body was dumped—or the killer," Williams said.

Charlie picked up a piece of yarn and tied one end to a pen. She took the other end of the yarn and held it with her index finger on the eastern edge of Honolulu International Airport, just on the western shore of Ke'ehi Lagoon. She adjusted the length of the yarn to cover the drop sites. She then began to draw a circle.

"Are you trying to tell us that we'll find Laura's body in this area? That's a large area to cover. We don't have that type of manpower," Williams said.

"Yes, this is the general area, and I agree with your assessment that it's much too large to be of any value to you, so let's start disregarding areas by a simple process of elimination." Charlie looked at the group. "Lani, could you give me a hand?"

"Ya, be glad to."

Charlie handed her a piece of chalk. "As we eliminate areas, I want you to draw a large X over them. Does anyone object if we eliminate residential areas?" Charlie asked.

"Seems reasonable," Tanaka said. Lani started to cross out those areas.

"If I may interject, wouldn't we want to eliminate areas that are not near some type of body of water?" Crawford said as he loosened his tie.

"I know you said there was a military connection, but I don't think he would drop off a body on an actual military installation—it would be just too risky," Tanaka said.

Lani watched everyone nod and continued to cross out more areas.

"Well, I think we can eliminate high tourist areas like Chinatown," Williams added.

Everyone stared at the map once Lani had finished.

"We now have a more reasonable area to work with, but I think we can be even more precise," Charlie said as she handed Lani a red piece of chalk. "What do all the areas have in common?" Charlie dusted the chalk from her hands.

"Near water and industrial areas, so he's less conspicuous," Lani said, stepping back from the map and looking at it from a different angle.

"Exactly, so now draw a circle around Sand Island. I believe that's where you will locate Laura Ayres's body."

Lani drew a big red circle around Sand Island.

"Don't be surprised if we get a tip that says the body is located on Sand Island or someone comes in stating they had a dream that told where the body was located. The killer wants to make sure that he's front and center at all times. He desires the attention as much as he craves the killings."

"Thank you, Doctor, that exercise was beneficial. Detectives, let's get some teams out there to start searching the island right away." Crawford adjusted his tie and started to leave.

"Before you go, I wanted to discuss a couple of theories with you," Charlie said.

"Absolutely. What's on your mind?"

"You asked if I thought it might be someone in the military."

The deputy DA nodded, and everyone else started to circle around Charlie.

"No serial killer's victims are exactly alike; however, they do have leanings toward a certain type of victim. In our cases each woman was Caucasian. Three were at bus stops, but Pam and Laura had their own cars. All the women were abducted from within a two- to three-mile radius, apart from Pam—she was taken from downtown. All the women have been abducted within a month of each other—once again, except for Pam, who was taken seven before Rebecca. All the women are in their late teens to early twenties; however, our latest victim, Laura, is at least ten years older than the other women."

"Doctor, where are you going with this?" Williams asked.

"Apologies. What I'm trying to say is that they are all connected; however, Pam's doesn't feel right—that seems more personal in nature. That's why I believe there may be a military connection besides what we previously discussed," Charlie said.

Tanaka glanced at his watch, "I think everyone could use a break, so go get yourselves some lunch."

"Is there any place to get some lunch around here?" Charlie asked Lani as they descended the stairs.

"Nothing in the immediate area. There are some vending machines on the first floor."

"Okay, let's grab some terrible coffee and go outside to enjoy the fresh air."

Coffee in hand, they went out the side entrance to an expansive park dotted with trees and large concrete planters. A sidewalk with lampposts ran through it. Charlie sat down on one of the planters, leaned backward, and looked up at the sky. "I'm envious. Even at police headquarters, you can go outside and be in a park and enjoy the sun and breeze—this is truly paradise."

Lani nodded nonchalantly.

"Admittedly, I've watched the opening to *Hawaii Five-0* a thousand times and thought all this time that the Ali'iolani Hale building, with the statue of King Kamehameha, was headquarters, only to find out that I was wrong." Charlie looked over at Lani when she didn't respond. Charlie sat up and took a sip of her coffee. "What's wrong? You're usually the talkative, lively foil to my quiet, pensive personality."

"Nothing."

"Is everything all right with Leinani?"

"She's great, but soon she'll be out for summer break, and I'm dreading that."

"Don't mean to pry if it's personal and none of my business—just say so."

"Do you really think it could be someone in the military? I mean, all that you said back there about your intuition with Pam?" Lani sounded anxious.

"I can't put my finger on it right now, but yes, I do." Charlie paused, placed her index finger under her nose, and gathered her composure. "Quite a few years ago, early on in my career—I was about the same age as you are now—I was involved in a case similar to this one. Tremendous pressure to get it solved, the community nervous and frightened. In the course of the investigation, I met someone, and we became involved. For some very personal reasons, I let my guard down and shared too much information. Just be careful of what you say and who you say it to."

Lani sighed and exhaled softly. "Shit."

"I'm sure everything is okay. Let's go catch us a killer," Charlie said reassuringly. She stood and offered her hand to Lani to help her up.

Manoa and Sand Island
Saturday, May 3, 1986

Charlie was walking down a gray hallway empty of light and objects. Out of the shadows, a giant snake bared its fangs and struck at Charlie's face. She instinctively raised her left hand to protect herself and let out a shriek.

Pepper whimpered, and Charlie looked down at the cowering dog. "Sorry, buddy. Didn't mean to scare you," She tossed off soaked sheets and put on a silky robe that stuck to her skin. She peeked out of her room to see if anyone could see her through the windows, Pepper between her feet. She dashed out of her room with the dog in hot pursuit and picked up the phone after the fourth ring.

"When? Where?" Charlie wrapped an arm around her waist so her robe wouldn't open and expose her nude body. She watched Pepper as she listened intently. She hung up the phone and saw Barbara standing in the living room with her hand covering her mouth. "Sorry, auntie. I've got to go. We may have found our victim."

"Is this the woman who went missing on Tuesday night?"

"Auntie, I don't know, but it looks like it, maybe."

"When is this senselessness going to end?" Barbara looked defeated.

Charlie groped for a response. "I wish I knew."

She knew her auntie was not alone in her exasperation. She could feel the tension as she left the room. She returned to her bedroom and closed the door. Pepper scurried after her but was too late. He whimpered and scratched at the door until Charlie opened it up. "Get in here." She dressed quickly and slipped out the front door.

Charlie raced along the streets. Her route took her over the canal where Debra Harris's body had been left a mile upstream and past Ke'ehi Lagoon, where Pam Adair's and Rebecca Saito's bodies had been found. She was driving through the industrial area of Honolulu—this was the route of the killer. Charlie made a right turn onto Sand Island Access Road—a four-lane road separated by a median. Small businesses lined each side of the road.

As she drove, the small businesses were replaced by large parking lots for trucks, warehouses, and storage containers. She picked up speed as they flew past the Sand Island wastewater treatment facility and the expansive Matson shipping area. She traveled past the US Coast Guard Base and other shipping and maintenance facilities. Charlie noticed the entrance to Sand Island Beach Park, slowed down, and entered the park.

Charlie traveled along Sand Island Parkway, past numerous parking areas, campsites, and softball fields. Beachgoers stopped what they were doing to watch her fly pass, suspecting something wrong had happened, given all the police and medical vehicles that had driven past in the last ninety minutes. Charlie's car dropped momentarily, and she could hear the undercarriage scrape as they moved off the paved road onto dirt and gravel. She could see the commotion in front of her.

An officer showed her where to park her car, and she made her way quickly to the group. Lani spotted her and met her halfway.

"Hey, thanks for the call. What do we have?" Charlie asked as she strode toward the scene.

"Fairly decomposed body of a female, approximate age twenty-five to thirty-five, but no positive identification. ME is about to take her back and begin an immediate autopsy," Lani said, matching Charlie stride for stride.

Charlie's nostrils flared. The fragrance of the flowering trees and bushes was overcome by the odor coming from the decomposed body as they moved closer to the site. She stood next to Tanaka and looked down at the completely nude body of a woman with her arms tied behind her back with a nylon cord, gold bracelets still on her bony wrists. *Lani was right*, she thought. It was hard to tell if this body belonged to the attractive Laura Ayres.

"Good morning, Doctor. You were right on both accounts: location and we received a call from a man that said he and his wife had been hunting for cans to recycle when they discovered the body."

"Do you have a way to contact this person again? It seems like a pretty isolated location to hunt for recyclables."

"You think it was the killer who led us here."

"The possibility exists."

"You're on a roll! Now, if you can tell us where to be before he murders his next victim, I'd be eternally grateful," Tanaka said.

"I'm working on it day and night."

"We're going straight to the ME's facility, if you care to join us," Tanaka added.

Honolulu
Saturday, May 3, 1986

Charlie watched Dr. Megumi Hiroshima, the tiny Japanese city pathologist with long, nimble fingers, move quickly and respectfully as she concluded her methodical examination. "From the fingerprints and the jewelry, I can positively identify the victim as Laura Ayres; however, I'll need to run further laboratory tests to determine if she was strangled."

"Thank you, Doctor. Before we make a press release, I want the ex-husband and daughter notified," Crawford said. Tanaka and Williams nodded in agreement.

"I'd like to go and visit her roommate. Do you have the address?" Charlie asked Lani as they left the ME's facility.

"Yes. It's not too far away."

"Lead on."

Moanalua Gardens
Saturday, May 3, 1986

Charlie and Lani got out of the parked car on Ala Mahamoe Street and walked up to the front screened door. Lani pushed the doorbell, and they could hear the ring through the quiet house. She was about to push the bell again when they heard a soft voice through the door.

"Who is it?"

Charlie nodded at Lani.

"Ma'am, it's Officer Lani Urada with the HPD and Dr. Charlie Taylor. We'd like to speak with you, if that's okay."

A slender woman with long dark brown hair came to the screened front door. She looked exhausted and confused.

"Can I see some identification?"

"Of course." Lani pulled her police badge out of her purse.

"Sorry, I've been inundated with phone calls and people knocking on the door asking for questions and requesting interviews."

"You're smart," Charlie reassured her.

"After Laura disappeared, I'm afraid the killer might show up here. He may have her keys . . . I'm so scared," the roommate replied, standing behind the locked screen door.

"That's understandable. The extra safety precautions are not without merit. We hate to intrude, but we'd really like to speak with you," Charlie said.

"I'm Marianne, by the way," she said as she unlocked the door.

Charlie and Lani followed her into the clean and orderly house. Charlie sat down on an overstuffed floral-print sofa with a heavy wood frame. Lani followed suit. Marianne sat in the matching armchair. Charlie looked around the room and noticed toys and coloring books mixed in with fashion magazines.

"Any news on Laura?"

Charlie moved forward to the edge of the cushion. "I'm sorry to have to tell you this, but early this morning, we found a body of a woman. We're still awaiting final confirmation from a family member, but we're convinced that it's Laura's body." She watched the roommate closely.

"No . . . no, this is so unbelievable. How can this be? How can this have happened? There's your frequent petty crime, but I can't wrap my head around the idea of someone going around and abducting women and raping and murdering them." Marianne looked out the front window at the kids playing in the street.

"I've been studying these types of killers for over ten years, and they seem to defy logic. They're our coworkers, neighbors, and church members—they've got a way of blending in so no one notices anything." Charlie paused to give Marianne a chance to absorb her words.

"What about Randi, her little girl? How do you tell a seven-year-old that her mom was picked up by some psycho guy and murdered? She'll be scarred for the rest of her life."

"I realize this is little consolation, but she's with her father, and we'll make sure that she gets all the help she needs. I know that still doesn't fill the void of losing a mother," Charlie said.

Marianne picked up a package of Eve 120 cigarettes from the coffee table, tapped the top until one came sliding out, and placed it in her mouth. Like a teeter-totter, the cigarette rapidly bounced up and down as she spoke. "I promised myself I wasn't going to touch another one of these the last time I quit." Hesitantly, she took the cigarette out of her mouth and looked at it. "Bastard has me practically chain-smoking." She picked up a slim, elegant lighter and held the blue flame to the end of her cigarette. She inhaled deeply, slowly blowing the smoke into the air. "I need to get out of here! I need to find someplace else to live—maybe even leave the island. I guess there's just no place safe anymore."

"Do you mind if we ask you a few questions?" Charlie asked gently.

"Go ahead . . . you said you study these guys? What does that mean?" Marianne pointed at Charlie with her cigarette hand.

"Yes. I'm a criminal psychiatrist with the Michigan State Police and here as a consultant to the Honolulu Police Department to assist in their investigation of these crimes. Based on the information that I and others in my field have learned from studying other killers like the Honolulu Strangler, we've started to understand how they think and operate. Based upon our studies of crime scenes, facts surrounding the cases, and studying the victims' lifestyles and behavior, we can develop a profile of the perpetrator, which then will help the detectives narrow the scope of their investigation."

"What a terrible thing to go through all the time. God, it's got to take a toll on you."

"Yes, it can be burdensome." Charlie nodded at Lani.

"Thank you for allowing us to visit with you. How long have you and Laura lived here?" Lani asked.

"We've been here in this house going on about two years. Neither of us is originally from here. Let me see, Laura's been on the island for almost fifteen years, and I just passed my tenth anniversary."

"How did you meet?" Charlie asked.

The roommate smiled. "You could say that we met serendipitously, but actually it was more like plain dumb luck—we met at a bar. She was celebrating her divorce, and I'd just gotten fired from my job—my prick boss expected me to give him head while he was sitting at his desk. I told him to go to hell." Marianne crossed her legs and started to swing one back and forth. "We were both ordering blowjob shots—considering the circumstances, it seemed appropriate. Well, I mistook her order for mine and started to reach for the shot glass when she said, 'Hey, I think you've got my drink.' I replied, 'No, I'm pretty sure that's my shot. It has my name all over it.' She said, 'Okay, whoever has the worst story gets the shot.' By the time we finished telling each other our stories, we each figured that the other had it worse.

"The bartender laughed, shook his head, and placed two shots down. He said, 'I think it's time for both of you to move on to orgasms.' I think we both said, 'Damn right' at the same time. We grabbed our shots, clinked our glasses, and threw them down. We had a lot of commiseration going on—that was a wild night." Marianne exhaled a plume of smoke from her nose.

Lani was about to ask another question when Charlie gently placed her hand on her knee.

"She was a fun girl—beautiful, outgoing. She was smart too. Not just book smart but streetwise. That's why I don't get how this guy could've gotten the jump on her. We'd talk about the other girls being abducted and being murdered. I thought since we were older and smarter that the asshole wouldn't be interested in us. I guess we thought wrong."

"For those very reasons, we've been warning all women, because there's never a one hundred percent correlation between victims," Charlie said.

"What type of work did Laura do?" Lani asked.

Marianne stubbed out her cigarette on top of a Coke can and dropped it inside. She reached for another one. "She was a sales representative for McCaw Telepage over in Kaka'ako."

"As a sales representative, did Laura have a territory she was responsible for?" Charlie asked.

"Ya, I think she had the whole airport area—that's a big area to cover. She worked her butt off," Marianne said reflectively.

"Please, keep going."

"She'd come home exhausted. Every day, she'd go door to door, literally knocking on doors, small and large businesses, asking if anyone wanted a pager. If someone was interested, then she'd set up a follow-up appointment to explain the services, get a check, and issue the pager. We'd have a good laugh because Laura used to say that dancing was a simpler way to make more money and less strenuous."

"Dancing?"

"Ya, before Randi was born, Laura used to dance at different strip joints, here and on Guam. Like I said, Laura was beautiful—not only her physical appearance, but there was this aura about her. Guys would go bonkers. I'm sure she made a killing every night."

"What made her stop?"

"After Randi was born, she changed her life around. She realized that she couldn't be so carefree. You know, that whole 'que sera, sera' thing. She grew up. She was responsible for her daughter, wanted to set a good example."

"Did she ever explain what happened when she met with potential customers?"

"You know what jerks guys can be. She'd go to the appointment thinking the guy was interested in a pager when all they really wanted was to see her again and ask her for a date." The roommate was about to take a sip from the Coke can and realized she'd been using it as a makeshift ashtray.

"Can I interest someone in a Coke?" Marianne walked toward the kitchen.

Charlie and Lani followed her and watched as she opened the refrigerator. It held a few carryout cartons and a six-pack of Coke with three of the two cans missing and the plastic rings still attached. Marianne held the cans with one hand and pulled one free with the other. "That's all I seem to be living on these days—sugar, caffeine, and nicotine." She tore off the pull tab and took a swig of Coke.

"Did Laura mention anyone that may have given her the creeps? I understand guys wanting to hit on her, but someone that stood out from the others?" Charlie asked.

"She came home one night a while back, and there was one guy that she described as a real weirdo."

"Did she describe him? Physical characteristics?"

"No, she never went into specifics."

"How about boyfriends?" Lani asked.

"Laura had plenty of dates. She was popular, but she wasn't seeing anyone in particular." Marianne sipped her Coke.

"The same question—did any of the guys she dated make her feel uncomfortable?" Charlie asked.

"She'd come home after a date and say something like 'another loser.' Then we'd laugh as she'd go into details about the date and why the guy was either a total jerk or just a loser. I think we had more fun talking about them than she actually had on the dates." Marianne went back to the living room to retrieve her cigarettes.

"But did she talk about any one of them in the same way she described the man that she'd met in her business?" Charlie called out the question.

Marianne walked back into the kitchen. She tilted her head as she contemplated the question. "No, I don't think so. Nothing stands out like the one guy. Laura was very confident, and she tried to laugh it off, but I could tell that it affected her. I remember a shiver running down my spine as she told the story."

"What about it made you afraid?"

"It was the slimy way he came on to her. She said he was a real smooth talker and it didn't take long for him to start talking about sex. It was very inappropriate—creepy. I mean, if you're interested in or attracted to a woman, I get it, but it's the way it escalated so fast and went so far into detail."

"Is there anything else that you can tell us?" Lani asked.

Marianne took a long drag on her cigarette and blew the smoke out. "No, no. Just catch this asshole."

Honolulu
Saturday, May 3, 1986

Later that afternoon, Charlie and Lani were huddled over poke bowls from a hole-in-the-wall takeout restaurant. Charlie picked up a cube of raw ahi tuna and a slice of radish with her chopsticks. "This is really good." She surveyed the customers waiting in line to place their orders.

"Glad you like it. This is the best poke around, especially for the price."

"Definitely not paying for the ambiance."

"Be thankful we were lucky enough to get a seat at one of the picnic tables, or we'd be eating in your car."

"Parking is a pain in the ass too."

"Hey, this is the best, real Hawaiian cuisine. You're kind of in a bitchy mood today. What's up?" Lani looked up from her bowl.

"Today was our first substantial lead, along with the eyewitnesses' accounts. I'd like you to do some good, old-fashioned detective work. Get with Tanaka and Williams, tell them what we've learned, and see if you can get Laura's calendar or call sheet to see if you can identify the potential client, the one that gave her the creeps. I'll meet you Monday morning at the station."

"Okay. Can I ask what you're going to be doing?"

Charlie held up a piece of tuna and inspected it. "You know, where I grew up, guys would think this is bait and wouldn't even consider eating raw fish. Here we consider it a meal, almost a delicacy. Well, I'm going fishing, and I'm going to be the bait."

Aiea
Sunday, May 4, 1986

"Thanks for seeing me," Charlie said as she walked into the little salon.

"Anytime." Kai smiled and swung the chair around. "What did you have in mind?"

Charlie sat down, and Kai spun the chair back and looked at Charlie in the mirror. "I was thinking a trim, wash, and I'm trying to decide on coloring."

"I'd keep it soft, nothing bold or audacious, but I love the color. The gray looks good against your skin color. If you have your heart set on coloring, then I'd go silver—embrace the fabulous you."

"Thank you, but I don't know if he'll like it."

Kai stepped back for a moment in shock. "I . . . I got the impression that you were like me. I didn't realize you were a switch-hitter. Shit, I thought there was a chemistry between us—how could I be so clueless?"

"What are you talking about?"

"It's okay if you want to see other people. I got the impression that you were trying to get over your relationship with Annie. I just thought at some point that you and I would hook up—what a stupid shit!"

Charlie grabbed both of Kai's hands and pulled her arms down until Kai's face was next to hers. She looked at her in the mirror. "Did you think that I was getting my hair done for someone else?"

"Well . . . you said you didn't know if he'd like it."

"Yes. And who do you think that 'he' is that I'm referring to?"

"Hell, I don't know. I got this shitty feeling that you were dumping me—are you dumping me? We're not even really a couple, but why do I feel like you're dumping me? Shit, my heart's pounding, my stomach is queasy, my knees are weak." Kai tried to pull away, but Charlie gripped her arms.

"*Shhh*, take a deep breath and gently exhale. Do it again. Again. What do I do, twenty-four seven?"

"You hunt for that psycho killer."

"Good answer. So, who do you think 'he' is?"

"Shit, I don't know . . . I jumped to conclusions, didn't I?"

"I'd say so, but I'm flattered. I'm really flattered. I've got to stop this guy before he kills again. I need to make myself attractive to him."

"I'm worried that something bad is going to happen to you."

"I'll take care of myself. I want you to trust me. Do you trust me?"

"Ya, but . . ."

"*Shh*." Charlie let go of Kai's arms and kissed her softly. "Now help me catch a killer."

Mililani
Sunday, May 4, 1986

"I like this," Lani said, resting her head on Dempsey's abdomen and letting her fingernails caress his inner thigh.

"That was insane."

"What? Us?"

"Hell yeah. I've never—"

"What, experienced a real woman?"

"God, you had me completely fooled."

"I told you that I wasn't looking for one-night stands and I want a commitment. You've just been having sex. This was the first time that you experienced lovemaking."

Dempsey caressed Lani's back. "I've got to cancel our dinner date tonight."

"Why?" She sat up. "You meeting with another one of your girlfriends?"

"No."

"Really?"

"Yes, I mean, no. I'm not meeting with anyone tonight. I've got to go in to work."

"If I find out that you're up to something else, then I'll cut your you-know-what off." Lani grabbed and squeezed hard.

Waikiki
Sunday, May 4, 1986

"Another Bloody Mary?"

Williams looked at his drink and placed his hand over it. "Wait, why not?" From his seat in the bar, Williams watched the tourists make their way up and down Kalakaua Avenue. He loved watching the women—they came in all shapes and sizes. He played the game of "Would I, or Wouldn't I?"

"Here you go." The waitress put down a fresh Bloody Mary and picked up the old glass.

Williams nodded to her and added more Tabasco to his drink. He loved being with women, but he didn't want to live with them or get married. He had tried that once, and it had been a complete and utter disaster. He challenged his thought process; he didn't like women at all. After he had gotten his rocks off, he had little or no use for them. He remembered getting home early from school and hearing a grunting noise coming from his parents' bedroom. He recalled how he'd been intrigued by the animal sounds coming from the other side of the door. How his hand had reached for the doorknob and turned it slowly. How shocked he'd been to see his mother naked on top of their neighbor. Her breasts bouncing up and down. The sweet and sweaty smell that emanated from the room. "Mom, I know Mother's Day isn't for another week, but here's to you." Williams took a sip of his drink.

A couple of minutes later, a woman had caught his attention. He watched her as she made her way leisurely down the avenue, stopping occasionally to look into stores. Other tourists went around her. She eventually passed him, not more than thirty feet away. She had a great body and a butter face. *What a shame!* Williams threw a twenty down on the table and exited the bar.

Manoa
Sunday, May 4, 1986

As Tanaka cut the grass, he let his thoughts go all over the place. He was muttering to himself when Kim called out, "Would you like to have a conversation with a real person?"

"Funny." Tanaka stopped pushing the lawn mower.

"Well, you seemed like you were chewing someone's ass, so I thought that it might be helpful if you got a response. Should I worry?"

"My beautiful wife, it has nothing to do with you. You can start to worry when I hear the voices answering me back. Then I'll be worried too."

"Why don't you wait to cut the grass in the afternoon when it's cooler outside?"

"Part of my therapy, my dear."

"Can I get you something cold to drink?"

"No, I'm almost done. I can wait a couple more minutes."

"Okay. I don't want you getting sunstroke."

Tanaka smiled and resumed his mowing. A few minutes later, he put the mower back in the garage and entered the house through the kitchen. He watched Kim in her pink shorts and a sleeveless white top as she reached up to take a bowl down from the cupboard. He looked at her muscular calves and firm butt and felt a rush of desire.

"Oh, you startled me! I didn't hear you come in. Can I fix you your iced tea now?"

"No, I'm good."

"Then why don't you go shower? You're smelly, and sweat and cut grass are not high on my list of fragrances. What are you looking at? What's gotten into you?"

"Why don't you join me? Like we used to."

"How old are you? We're not college students anymore."

"Why should they have all the fun?" Tanaka grabbed his wife.

"Frank, get away! You're gross. Get away . . . I'll make you a deal. We can do it tonight. I'll take a bath and put something nice on for you." She pushed Tanaka from her.

"I need you now."

"I'm flattered, but . . . Frank, don't kiss my neck . . . oh God, stop nibbling on my ear—that's cheating. You know my weaknesses . . . all right, the last one in the shower is a rotten egg."

Honolulu
Monday, May 5, 1986

Charlie and Lani walked into police headquarters looking like television news reporters, smart and sophisticated. Charlie wore a navy suit with a white blouse, a small string of pearls, and black pumps. Lani was in black slacks and a blue silk blouse. This time when they walked down the hallway, the men moved out of their way, offering greetings and positive comments.

They could hear the noise coming from behind the double doors of the homicide office.

"Thank you, Doctor, Officer, for coming in," Crawford said when they entered. "You look like you're well prepared for this afternoon's press conference—thank you." He was dressed in an unseasonably warm gray suit with a white shirt, navy-blue tie, and white pocket square.

He looked at Tanaka and Williams with disapproval. "I'd like both of you to join the detectives and me as part of the panel on stage." Charlie nodded, and Lani smiled slightly at the professional recognition. "I want to review what we're going to discuss at the press conference and then what you two will talk about at the Waipahu library event."

"Makes sense," said Charlie. "Any progress on identifying a potential suspect from Laura's calendar?"

"We've narrowed the list by cross-referencing the profile, witnesses' descriptions, and tips that we've received," Tanaka said.

"Like I've said, good old-fashioned detective work will win the day. None of this psychology mumbo jumbo," Williams added.

Microphones were placed in front of them. Crawford, Tanaka, and Williams, all in sport coats and ties, hands folded over their notes, were joined by Lani and Charlie.

"Ladies and gentlemen of the press, currently we've got a twenty-seven-member police task force that includes our most experienced detectives working 'round the clock to apprehend this killer. Additionally, we are taking full advantage of FBI resources and have brought in other resources like Dr. Taylor to assist with the investigations." Crawford wanted to reassure the public and city hall that law enforcement were doing everything they could to apprehend the killer.

When he had concluded his comments, Tanaka took over. "The death of the latest victim, Laura Ayres, has yielded the most considerable evidence to date. We've stopped hundreds of cars on Nimitz Highway near where Ms. Ayres's blue Toyota was found last Wednesday. From eyewitness accounts, we believe she may have experienced vehicle problems and was approached by the killer. Eyewitnesses identified the suspect as either Caucasian or mixed race, but not black or Asian, and driving a late-seventies or early-eighties van. Thanks to public assistance and work by the task force, we believe that the killer is a Caucasian male, medium build, in his late thirties to early forties, who drives a light-colored or white cargo van and is probably experiencing marital or personal relationship issues."

"We'll focus our investigation on the airport area, Sand Island, and Waipahu, where the bodies have been dumped," Williams added.

As the conference came to an end and attendees started to gather their personal items, Tanaka quietly said, "All these indicators matched the profile Dr. Taylor developed for us, which has aided us in our search. We believe all five women were killed by the same man. However, the evidence in one of the cases is not as convincing as the others. So there are strong indications that four of the cases are related—possibly all five."

All the attendees and panel members stopped and looked at him.

"Rice, what was that all about?" Williams asked after the conference room had cleared out.

"I was going to ask the same thing," Crawford said.

"I'm playing a hunch. Something in my gut told me to say it. We'll see if it has an effect." Tanaka grabbed his notepad and walked out of the room.

Waipahu
Tuesday, May 6, 1986

"What are you terrified of?" Lani asked. The response from the seventy-five people—mostly women—crowded in the back room of the Waipahu Public Library was immediate.

"Being murdered."

"Disappearing."

"Rape."

"Kidnapping."

A teenage girl stood up. "I'm terrified that my car will break down and I'll be stranded someplace—my girlfriends feel the exact same way."

An attractive blonde spoke. "I'd like to know more about self-defense courses. This bastard has his eyes on haoles, so that's got me worried. If I'm attacked, I want to have the confidence to be able to hold my own. Go down fighting."

"I'm afraid to be pulled over by the police at night in a remote area. Ya know there's plenty of us who still think a cop may have been involved in the abduction and murder of that young woman a couple of years ago," a thirtysomething woman added.

"I'm sure officers will completely understand if you continue to drive to a lighted area where other people are around," Lani said, her voice measured.

"This killer, this rapist, and others like him are looking for someone vulnerable. They are predators that pursue the weak; they seek out the secluded, and acting tough and confident can give them pause before attacking you.

"However, I ask for forgiveness if my words aren't clear: You absolutely cannot think this will never happen to you. I'm pretty sure that none of the victims expected this to happen to them. Officer Urada is going to provide a list of safety tips—please pay close attention. Be safe, be vigilant, and don't get lazy. We are all targets," Charlie emphasized.

"We want you to keep the following in mind. As Dr. Taylor said, this killer is looking for women by themselves, so don't travel alone. Plan your trips, and make sure that you've informed a family member or friend how you're traveling and when you're departing, even for something as simple as going to the grocery store. Carry some type of device that makes a loud noise and will draw people's attention, like a whistle.

"Next, buy flares and keep them in your car. If your vehicle breaks down, only get out to light the flares and open the hood, and then get back in the car—lock the doors! Do not accept rides from anyone, even if they identify themselves as police officers. Department policy states that a police officer may not transport a woman unless there's another officer present. Next, wait in the car for a police officer to arrive. They will call a family member, friend, or mechanic.

"Know the bus schedule so you don't wait a long time at the stop, and stick to those in high-traffic areas.

"Don't walk too close to the curb. It may be easy for someone to grab you and push you into a waiting car. Be aware of your surroundings always—watch the pedestrian and vehicular traffic. If you see or sense someone is following you, or you see the same car pass by you a couple of times, then run immediately to a safe location.

"Trust your instincts if you start to feel nervous or get a cold shiver running down your spine when it's a beautiful, sunny day. Don't let fear overcome you. You need to keep your smarts about you—turn your fear into action."

A hail of questions followed, and the two hours scheduled for the lecture flew by. "Does anyone have any more questions or concerns?" Lani asked. "On behalf of Dr. Taylor, I'd like to thank you for coming here tonight."

"Good job back there," Charlie said as she and Lani finally made it out of the library.

"Thanks. I'm starting to feel like I'm in my element—I can contribute. I still have a tough time on nights like this, knowing that a killer is out there someplace hunting his next victim." Lani looked up at the clear sky filled with stars.

"I know what you mean. It's been almost a year since Pam was abducted. Rebecca lived close by here, and the bus stop that she was taken from is just up the street."

"Has it already been a year? A year, and we're no closer to catching the killer. Shit, we didn't even know what we were dealing with back then. We were so naïve."

"How can you prepare for something like this? It's completely unprecedented," Charlie said.

"Where's the Mustang?" Lani asked as they approached her car.

"When I'm stranded alongside the road, I want to be more believable," Charlie said, smiling as she admired Barbara's old Honda.

"Is that why you have a new hairstyle and color?"

"I'm trying to fit the part as well as possible."

"None of our decoys have worked so far."

"True, but they probably didn't seem vulnerable enough. Our decoys are police officers in civilian clothes waiting at bus stops. They don't exude anxiousness or impatience, the emotions our killer is looking for. He's out there driving every night, looking for the right one. It's like art to him; the killer knows it when he sees it. He can tell what the victims want to see or believe. He's the cavalry to the rescue, Prince Charming riding up on his horse. I want him to see me as what he wants—an anxious, lonely woman."

"Wouldn't it be better if I go out there? I'm closer in age to the victims than you are." Lani leaned against her car door.

"Thanks for the reminder."

Lani laughed. "I'm sorry. I didn't mean it that way."

"Yes, you did, Punk. I can't pull off eighteen to twenty-five; however, I can pull off thirty-six-year-old Caucasian far better than you can," Charlie said confidently as she unlocked her car door.

"You have me there. Do you want me to come along? I can hide in the bushes or a little ways away, jump out at the appropriate time, and help you apprehend him," Lani suggested.

"Thank you, but I'll be all right."

"What if there are two of them? You've said there might be two of them. Even Detective Tanaka alluded to the idea of two killers."

Charlie paused before she responded. "You're right about that. I still haven't given up on that idea, but I'm not so sure they're working together. More in collaboration, or maybe even in competition. I'll see you tomorrow morning at the station." She closed the door.

She waved in acknowledgment of Lani's honk as she drove away. She reached into her glove box and pulled out her map, looking at all the places she had observed, Xs and notes alongside them. Undecided but determined, she started the car and drove to Farrington Highway. *Left or right?*

She chose left. *He's coming from Ewa.* She recalled her conversation with Kai on their drive around the island.

"Ewa means 'crooked' or 'ill-fitting,'" Kai had said. "Nothing much out there but sugarcane plantations, some villages that are clinging to the plantation days, a few houses that need a fresh coat of paint, railroad tracks, and rusted-out vehicles. For the most part, it's pretty desolate."

Charlie continued along Farrington until she arrived at H-1 and Kamehameha Highway. She decided on Kam instead of H-1, following her instincts. Anxious, she checked the small clock on the dash. *Why struggle with negative thoughts? Because this is a crapshoot, and I'm running out of ideas and time.*

She was tempted by the darkened Aloha Stadium parking lot. The desolate area could be an ideal location, but she decided to continue. *Why am I filled with such indecision? I don't have anything to prove. Screw Williams and his accusations. I just want to make sure that no more women are abducted and killed.*

Charlie made a left turn onto Salt Lake Boulevard and continued alongside the stadium. She was on his grounds and his time. The occasional streetlamps and neighborhoods provided little comfort. She passed a bus stop and was tempted to pull over, but she kept moving forward.

At last she pulled the car to the side of the road and parked. She picked up her map and studied it. Puuloa Road was just ahead. That was a significant route for the killer. It connected to Lagoon Drive—Pam and Rebecca. It connected to Mokumoa Street—Debra. It connected to North Nimitz and Sand Island—Laura. And it was a short distance from the airport bus stops—Juliana. If he was hunting or going back to the dump sites, this would be an ideal location.

The industrial area was dark except for the lights over the doors of the warehouses. Charlie parked on Mokumoa Street, put the hazards on, and raised the hood. She looked around and then made her way to the bus stop on Puuloa Road. The four-lane road had a high volume of traffic during the day but was deserted at this time of night. *All right, Charlie, put on your most vulnerable act.* She thought of her worst nightmares: her gang rape, Annie's death, and possibly her own.

A few cars sped by in both directions, but none slowed down or showed any interest. Charlie looked at her watch and up at the posted bus schedule. She thought about Annie, Josh, Melissa, Barbara, and Kai.

She watched a car out of the corner of her eye. The brake lights went on, and the car came to a stop. Charlie's heart started pounding. *Come on, come on, back up.* The car stayed where it was.

Charlie peered at the windows and tried to get a glimpse of the driver. She felt like she was in a Wild West standoff, each waiting for the other to make the first move. She looked down at her watch and tried to recapture her vulnerable act. *Too late?* The brake lights brightened as the driver put the car into gear and pulled away. *Shit!*

I'll never forgive myself if that was him and I blew the opportunity, Charlie thought. *God, I'm tired and cold.* She looked at her watch and checked for any other signs of life on the barren street. At the intersection of Salt Lake Boulevard and Puuloa Road, there were only a few cars—time to call it a night.

As Charlie walked back to her car, she tried to regain some optimism as she looked up at the evening sky. She tried to appreciate the starlight and the bright moon. She lifted the hood and placed the rod back in place, letting the hood slam shut.

"You okay?"

She jumped at the sound of his voice. A man stood next to a vehicle parked about ten feet behind hers.

"What seems to be the problem?"

"I'm not really sure. I'm not very good at mechanical things, more of a bookworm," Charlie said, trying to recover.

"We can't have you stuck out here all night." He smiled. "Have you been parked here for quite some time? I hate to leave when your car isn't working properly, knowing there isn't much traffic around here at this time of night." He spoke softly.

Charlie strained to hear him and moved closer. "I'll be all right. A bus will show up eventually."

"That'll be hours from now. I wouldn't mind helping you out at all. I'm not very book smart, but I'm pretty mechanical," he said.

"I don't want to be an imposition."

"Don't give it a second thought." He reached into his car and flipped on his headlights and high beams.

Charlie placed her hand above her squinting eyes to shield them from the bright lights.

"I'll wait here while you get into your car. If your car starts up, then there's no harm, and you're on your way. But if it doesn't start, then I can get you to a service station or your house, whichever you prefer." His voice was smooth, reassuring.

"You sure? I really don't want to be a bother," Charlie said. She unlocked her car door. "I'm sure I'll be fine."

"Really, it's no problem at all."

"To be honest, I was getting a little concerned. Wish me luck." She waved goodbye, closed the door, and looked out the rear-view mirror. She turned the ignition key but heard only a clicking sound.

She tried to look out the rearview mirror, but the bright lights prevented her from seeing anything. She could barely make out the outline of the man's vehicle. She turned the ignition key again but could only hear the clicking sound.

She jumped at the knock on the window. "Sounds like the starter. I'm glad that I didn't listen to you," the man said, smiling.

She shivered. She rolled down her window and looked into the man's face. "Hondas are usually pretty reliable."

He looked around and then back at Charlie. "Why don't you grab your things and lock up?"

"You sure?"

"Do you really want to sit out here all night long? Then, in the morning, what are you going to do? You'll still be stuck here. I can get you to wherever you need to go, and then you can call a tow truck in the morning."

"You're a lifesaver," Charlie said as she rolled the window back up. She saw the map with all the notes and folded it up as quickly as possible and shoved it back into the glove box. *Hopefully, he didn't see it.* She grabbed her purse, gave the interior a quick glance, and locked the door.

"My queen, your chariot awaits you." The man bowed with one arm extended, the other wrapped around his waist.

"Not only a lifesaver, but a gentleman too. I can't begin to thank you enough." Charlie smiled and walked alongside the man toward a white van with an aviation logo on the side. In her mind the little boxes of profile indicators were filling rapidly with check marks.

"No, no, trust me. It'll be all my pleasure." He held the passenger door open for Charlie until she was in and then walked around to his side of the van.

"You work over by the airport?" Charlie asked as he got in.

"Ya, I work for a company called Flying Tiger. We deliver items all around the island."

"Do you like your job?"

"It's not bad. I'm not stuck behind a desk all day."

Charlie smiled. "Former military?"

"Ya, how did you know?" He looked at Charlie more intently.

"The tattoo on your forearm. I just took a guess."

"Ya, a bunch of my army buddies and I got drunk one night and thought it would be a good idea to get one. The things that you do when you're young and dumb." He slid his right palm over it and looked back at Charlie with a smile. "So, where are we heading?" He put the van in gear and was about to accelerate when he turned and faced her. "I feel like I've seen you before."

His demeanor started to change. His face turned pale. His eyes became vacant, and his smile dissolved.

"Funny, I had the same feeling, like I know you too," Charlie said, smiling back as her hand slid into her purse.

His hand flew from the steering wheel at Charlie's face. The punch grazed her chin, bringing tears to her eyes. Her ears rang. He was reaching out to grab her by the throat when she pulled the slim canister from her purse and sprayed him in the face. He screamed in agony.

The van slowly rolled into the curb, the man clawed at the door handle until the door opened he fell out. He was on all fours, tears and snot dripping down his face.

"You bitch!" he spat between coughs while his upper body spasmed. "My face is on fire! I'm gonna kill you for this!"

Charlie fought off her own tears and running nose. She walked around the van and sprayed him again. He screamed in pain and rolled onto his back, gasping for air.

"I've been waiting to meet you for such a long time," Charlie said, standing over the man. "I remember seeing you at Wheeler Air Force Base." She heard the roar of a car's engine and the squeal of tires.

She braced herself for another attack. The car stopped within a few feet of her. Lani jumped out of the car. "Are you all right?"

Charlie put her hand on her chin and massaged it gently. "I think so."

"Is this him? Is this really him?" Lani walked over to the man and started to put handcuffs on him. "God, what is that stuff?"

"It's pepper spray, but how did you know?" Beads of sweat formed on her forehead. Her upper body shook, and she doubled over.

"Kai, the psycho stalker, and I take turns covering your backside. Tonight was my night and I'm pumped," Lani said, standing the man on his feet.

"Thanks, I'm glad that you didn't listen to me, but I still was able to protect myself," Charlie said, blowing the clear, slimy snot from her nose.

"I'm surprised if she doesn't come driving up any second now."

"Kai? Why would she show up?"

"You're kidding me, right? She follows you everywhere. For someone who's so observant of others, you have some real blind spots in your own life," Lani said. She called for a patrol car on her handheld radio.

"Seems to be," Charlie said, bent over as she watched a small puddle of sweat and snot form beneath her.

"Hey, Punk. What is that? You guys stink." Kai covered her nostrils and then walked over to Charlie and rubbed her back.

"Really appreciate the cavalry's arrival. What we need is some milk, but I'll settle for water. Do you have any?" Charlie asked.

"Ya, ya, I'm a regular Boy Scout. Isn't that so, Punk?" Kai pulled a couple of water bottles out of her backpack and handed them to Charlie and Lani. Charlie started to pour the water over her eyes and face to flush out the irritant, taking a small swig now and then. Lani tilted the man's head back and flushed his eyes and face.

The man looked over at Charlie. "That wasn't a nice thing to do. I was just trying to help you. Just remember the old expression, 'He who laughs last, laughs best.'"

Honolulu
Wednesday, May 7, 1986

"Hugh Allen Grant, age forty-three, works for Flying Tiger, drives a cargo van for the company, and has no priors," Williams read from his notebook.

They watched Grant through the observation window in the interrogation room. His face and eyes still red, Grant's handcuffs slipped along his wrists as he picked up his soda can and took a swig.

"He's awful quiet for an innocent man—I'd say peaceful," Tanaka observed.

Williams picked up where he'd left off. "He matches the eye-witness accounts: Caucasian, medium build, early forties, and drives a white cargo van with a company logo on it." He closed his notepad.

"Laura Ayres had written his name in her calendar the day she disappeared," Tanaka said.

"Chief, who authorized the search? I checked, and it didn't come through our office," Crawford said.

"I did," Griffith said.

"How about a little cooperation?" Crawford asked, crossing his arms.

"I hadn't seen much from your end, and you're not going to tell me how to run my investigations, let alone my department." Griffith turned and faced him.

"How is the search going at his house?" Crawford asked.

"They've gone through his Ewa beach house and haven't found any incriminating evidence yet. But we're bound to find something eventually," Griffith said.

"I've interviewed his ex-wife and current girlfriend, and they both say he enjoys rough sex. He enjoyed tying them up and choking them. His girlfriend said if she didn't want to play, he would get furious and storm out of the house. She seems to think those were the same nights that our victims were abducted, raped, and murdered," Lani said.

"Dr. Taylor, you've been unusually quiet all morning. Are you feeling all right?" Crawford asked.

Everyone turned and faced Charlie who was standing at the back of the room.

"Thank you. Jaw's a little tender, my eyes are sore, but nothing that can't be solved by getting out of these clothes and a shower. Needless to say, I'll recover."

Crawford nodded. "What are your thoughts?"

"Mr. Grant fits the profile to a T. I think he's our guy."

Crawford walked away from the window and stood in the center of the room. "We're going to have to let him go."

"What are you talking about?" Griffith asked.

"All the information you've provided is compelling—very compelling; however, we don't have any evidence that proves Grant is our guy."

"When are you guys going to grow a pair? You've been breathing down our necks to catch this guy. We've delivered him to you, and now you're going to balk and do nothing?" Williams said incredulously.

Tanaka touched his partner's arm. "What about what he said and did to Dr. Taylor? That's got to count for something."

Crawford looked at Charlie and turned back to Tanaka. "Again, compelling, but it would be 'he said, she said.' Additionally, his lawyer may argue that Dr. Taylor tried to entrap his client."

"Entrapment, that's bullshit," Williams said.

"The defense will argue that Dr. Taylor, by feigning her car trouble and getting in his car, induced him to commit the crime, and since he has a clean record, he would have never committed the crime in the first place," Crawford said.

Williams walked over to the window and pointed at Grant. "He's guilty as sin."

"Again, maybe so, but we do not have any evidence. Additionally, Dr. Taylor's use of pepper spray could be an unlawful use of force. Mr. Grant's lawyer will argue that Dr. Taylor violated his client's civil rights, and since she was acting as a consultant to the state, Grant could sue Dr. Taylor and us. Furthermore, he could press charges against Dr. Taylor for the use of pepper spray, which isn't legal yet in this state, so we may be arresting her instead of him. Suddenly our great case goes down the shitter, so we're going to let him go. Understand where this conversation is going? We have no probable cause." Crawford tried to keep his composure.

Tanaka shook his head. "I've been at this for a long time—this just doesn't make any sense. It's like Mac said, he's our guy."

"What do you want us to do?" Griffith asked.

"As you adamantly told me, I don't run your investigations or your department, so figure it out, but if the search doesn't produce any evidence, then you're going to have to let him go."

"Just like that? We're going to let him go?"

"Yes. Find me more evidence, then I'll reconsider, but in the meantime, I recommend that Dr. Taylor go back on vacation and keep a low profile. Officer Urada goes back to her normal duties, and as for the rest of you, figure it out." Crawford sent the door crashing into the wall and stomped out.

"Let's head back upstairs to your offices and discuss our way ahead. Doctor, Urada, I'd like for you to join us," the chief said.

"Sir, thank you for the vote of confidence, but I don't want to get you in trouble with the DA's office," Charlie said.

"This is my task force, and I'll decide who's on it and what they do—not him. This isn't the first time the DA's office has left us hanging, and it's certainly not my first rodeo. Besides, he can't touch me, so screw him." The chief smiled.

"Sir, I'll be up shortly. I just need a couple of minutes," Charlie said.

"Understandable. Come up when you're ready. By the way, where did you get the spray from?" Griffith asked.

"A friend, an FBI agent, gave it to me. I seem to have a habit of getting into tough spots." Charlie smiled slightly.

"Between all of us, I believe you. That garbage Crawford said about 'he said, she said' was complete and utter bullshit. I'm glad you sprayed his ass with pepper spray—not once but twice. What he did to those women, I'd have given anything to see him scream in agony. Typical perp—can dish it out but can't take it." Griffith nodded. "Ladies. Gentlemen, let's go upstairs." As they left the observation room, Charlie could hear Griffith ask the detectives if they'd ever been pepper-sprayed. "Hurts like holy hell."

Charlie walked over to the window, rested her fingers on the ledge, and watched Grant intently.

"Are you okay?" Lani asked.

"I'll be fine, thanks."

"What are you thinking?"

"Crawford's right. We don't have any evidence, and if we don't find any soon, then he'll slip through our fingers."

"Ya, but he now knows that we know him and will nail him if he ever tries something again."

"Maybe, or he just might wait us out or move to another state and continue where he left off. Let's get upstairs."

As the women walked down the hallway, the detectives and officers moved out of their way, applauding.

"Nice work, Doc."

"Way to nail his ass."

"He got what he deserved."

Charlie and Lani entered the homicide office and joined the others at the bulletin board.

"Now that we have the team all here, let's get started," Griffith said. "Mac, take care of Grant's paperwork so we can get him out of here as quickly as possible, but I want twenty-four-hour surveillance on the guy, so make sure that's in place before he's released. Rice, you and I will prepare our statement for the press. Doctor, as far as I see it, you've got a couple of choices, and I will understand, whatever you decide. You can go back on vacation and terminate your consulting contract with us. Second, you can continue with your consulting. Third, if you think there's a better alternative, I'd love to hear it."

"I would like to stay on, but on two conditions."

"Name 'em," Griffith said confidently.

"First, I will only stay on if Officer Urada is allowed to continue to work with me in the same capacity that she has previously. I told Detective Tanaka when I asked for her that women investigators can get things out of people, especially women and children, that men simply can't. I've been around a lot of investigators, and Officer Urada has the making of an exceptional detective."

"Done."

"Second, only if Detective Williams wants me to."

"I really don't care what he thinks or wants. Mac, what'll it be?"

Everyone turned to face Williams except Charlie.

"I'm rarely wrong and hate to admit it when I am, but I was wrong about Dr. Taylor. We'd be lost without her insights, hard work, and damn! She just plain kicked his ass."

"Did hell just freeze over?" Tanaka said.

Everyone laughed.

"Then it's unanimous," Griffith said. "Doctor, we've discussed among ourselves what needs to get done going from here. What do you recommend?"

"Like Mac, I hate to admit when I'm wrong, but Crawford was right. We don't have any evidence, so we need to build our case. I agree with you on watching him twenty-four hours a day. Maybe the pressure will get to him, and he'll slip up. I also recommend that you send whatever forensic evidence you have to the FBI. They have considerable resources and might find something that our labs can't. We'll continue to look through old cases to see if there are any linkages. If something looks similar or vaguely familiar, then we'll run it to ground."

"Let's keep up the same schedule for the time being. We'll show the public that the investigation is still ongoing and that Mr. Grant was a person of interest. It's been a very long day, so let's call it one, and tomorrow is a new day." Griffith turned around and strode out of the office.

Manoa
Wednesday, May 7, 1986

Charlie parked Barbara's car, picked up her grocery bag, and walked up the drive. When she reached the stairs, the dogs started barking loudly. She looked inside, saw them running around in circles, and smiled. Pepper came rushing toward Charlie when she stepped inside but scrambled away when he got close.

"Pepper, buddy, I'm so sorry," Charlie called. She walked into the laundry room, stripped off all her clothes, and threw them into the washing machine. She took a gallon milk jug from the paper bag, opened it, and poured in a large amount. She threw in some detergent for good measure, turned the dials, and started the machine.

She didn't care if the neighbors got an eyeful as she walked naked across the living room. Salt and Pepper, curious, watched her from a safe distance. She closed the blinds and stepped into the bathroom, shutting the door. In the mirror she saw a woman she hardly recognized. Her hands gripped the sink, and she brought her face closer to the mirror.

Her new hair color seemed out of place next to the dark shadows under her eyes, the crow's feet, and the fine lines just noticeable above her upper lip. She stepped into the bathtub with the jug of milk and applied it to her face, neck, arms, hands, and legs. *What the hell? Why not?* She let the remainder splash onto her head and stream down her body.

"Shit, that's cold." She shivered, but the milk was soothing on her red and irritated skin. She gently spread it all over her body and massaged her scalp. She turned the shower on full blast, and cold water came crashing down on her hot skin.

The water turned lukewarm, then a more pleasant tempera-ture. She soaped up her arms, armpits, and breasts, then rubbed the smooth bar of soap over her stomach and down her legs and meticulously cleaned between her toes. Her spirits began to lift as she rinsed her body off. She spent another five minutes under the shower feeling almost at peace.

She turned off the shower, pulled back the curtain, and patted herself dry with a large, comfortable towel. She wrapped a smaller towel around her head. In her emerald silky robe, she looked closely at her face again. *I had hoped for some improvement.* She generously applied some of her auntie's Oil of Olay. *Like this will make a bit of difference.*

She pulled on panties, cotton shorts, and a white dress shirt. *I haven't worn this outfit since the day I arrived. Well, I haven't been on vacation, either.* She emerged from the bathroom and opened her bedroom door to see Salt and Pepper waiting patiently for her. "Oh, my two buddies." She picked them both up and carried them over to the couch. "Don't say a word to your mom that I let you sit on the couch with me. She'd kill all three of us. I'm expendable, so I'm even more likely to get killed than the two of you."

Charlie flipped on the TV and got comfortable with the dogs. She heard a beeping noise and watched a banner scroll across the screen. "We bring you a special report. Early this morning, members of the HPD brought in Hugh Allen Grant for questioning regarding the murder of the last victim, Laura Ayres. Grant, forty-three, works for the shipping company Flying Tiger near the airport and lives by himself in the Ewa Beach community. The police are not commenting on why Grant was brought in for questioning, nor did they arrest him. Mr. Grant had this to say when leaving the HPD headquarters. 'The police have a job to do, and I'm cooperating with them fully.'" Grant smiled into the camera.

"Ugh, I'm tired of seeing that asshole," Charlie said to Salt and Pepper. She pushed herself off the couch, turned off the TV, looked outside, and watched the cars drive by. "I'll be right back." She stepped out the front door. The dogs leaped off the couch, hopeful for a walk.

Charlie was immediately warmed by the sunshine as she walked down the driveway to the mailbox. She pulled out all the mail and stood there, flipping through the envelopes, mailers, and magazines. The return addresses on three envelopes caught her attention. Charlie's heart started to beat faster, and she got a nasty, dry taste in her mouth. The sun went from warm to hot and uncomfortable. The walk back up the drive and into the house seemed to take forever. Her feet felt as if she were wearing lead shoes. She opened the door and stepped inside, oblivious to the barks and commotion swirling around her legs.

She placed the mail on the kitchen table and made her way to the couch. Salt and Pepper were jumping and scratching, trying their very best to get up. Charlie absentmindedly reached down and picked up Salt and then Pepper and placed one on each side of her. The dogs circled and scratched a few times before they got comfortable next to Charlie and fell asleep.

Charlie looked at the envelopes again. Her stomach started turning, and she felt an urge to rush to the bathroom before she had an accident. She decided to open the easiest one first, the one from the University of Hawaii. She ripped open one end of the envelope, shook the letter out, and carefully unfolded it.

Dear Dr. Taylor,

After reviewing your academic credentials, references, and work experience, we are excited to offer you a position as an adjunct professor. We extend a warm aloha and welina e ka 'ohana (welcome to our family).

One down, two more to go. Charlie looked at the next two envelopes and decided on the one from the University of Michigan's health department. The first letter was good news but paled in importance to this one. This one had so much more at stake—literally life or death. She wasn't sure why, but she said a little prayer. She unfolded the letter and scanned it quickly, her pulse throbbing in her temples.

NEGATIVE at the bottom in bold red letters. She read the entire message, wanting to make sure that she hadn't misinterpreted anything. She took a deep breath and let it out. *God, thank you.* She reread it, but the message was the same—she was HIV negative.

She opened the final envelope. Unlike the previous two, this letter was handwritten. She repeated a prayer.

Hi, Aunt Charlie,

Hawaii looks excellent! I wanted to say that I'm sorry that I haven't written till now. As you explained in all your letters, it has been a very confusing and challenging time for Missy and me with the deaths of Dad and then Mom and then having to move in with Papa and Nana.

Papa and Nana didn't want us talking with you. I've heard them talking with you on the phone, so I know how they've treated you. They didn't want to accept Mom's relationship with you and how she died. It really hurt them so much. Nana would just burst out in tears. Papa said that Mom paid for her sins and that you'll end up in hell too.

It's been really rough, but life is getting a little better. I have a girlfriend now. She's cool and pretty. I love her a lot. We were talking about everything going on in my life and why I'm so angry at times and can't trust. We talked about Dad, Mom, and then Mom and you. I told her about how much fun we used to have. I felt that we were so lucky.

I told her how you've written to Missy and me. She asked what the letters said. I couldn't tell her because I hadn't read any of them. The first batch I just threw away because I hated you so much. I blamed you for everything because I had no one else to blame.

She told me that everything I had told her about you sounded cool. She grabbed the letters away from me and began reading them. After she read the letters, she said that you really loved us. She convinced me that I should read the letters. She said that I should give you a second chance. I told you she was cool!

So I read the letters. Missy read them too, but we had to be careful. We didn't want Nana and Papa finding out, so we hid them because they'd probably burn them.

I don't understand about you and Mom. I don't know if I ever will. I'm starting to understand about love and the sacrifices you are willing to make for someone that you love. I'd do anything for my girlfriend. I kind of understand what you and Mom did for us and how hard it must have been.

I know how happy Mom was when she was with you and how much fun we all had together—some of the best times of my life so far.

Missy and I would love to come to Hawaii and see you. Papa was furious, but Nana said that it would be good for us to get away. Plus, your paying for our tickets helped!

I'll send you another letter to let you know when we'll arrive.

Love,
Josh

PS I want to go surfing.
PSS What's loco moco? Sounds great, I want to have some.

A tear dropped onto the letter, and some of the ink started to spread. Charlie wiped her eyes, and for the second time in a very long time, she thanked God.

"Knock, knock, is anyone home?"

Charlie, Salt, and Pepper looked up. The dogs leaped off the couch and ran for the front door, barking loudly as they went.

Charlie smiled when she saw Kai standing there.

"Get in here quick." Charlie pulled Kai into the house while she nudged the dogs from the entrance with her foot.

"What is it? Something wrong?" Kai asked, looking around.

Charlie held Kai's face and kissed her passionately. "Today has been a great day, and I wanted to do that for a long while."

"Mmm, I don't know what to say," Kai said, looking flabbergasted.

"No need to say anything," Charlie said, taking Kai's hand and leading her into the living room.

"This is a nice place."

"It's my auntie's," Charlie said, squatting to rub the dogs' bellies.

"I can honestly say that you look a lot better than the last time I saw you, and you definitely smell a lot nicer," Kai said, smiling.

Charlie laughed. "God, I've got no makeup on, but I'm sure it's some improvement. Poor Pepper got a nose full when I first came home, and he wasn't too delighted about it."

"I can relate, dude." Kai rubbed his belly vigorously.

"Interested in a glass of wine? I feel like getting a little tipsy." Charlie stood and moved to the kitchen.

"Ya, ya, that sounds good. You've got a reason to celebrate." Kai followed Charlie. "God, I love this house. I'd like to have a place like this myself. Tired of my shitty little apartment. What does your auntie do?"

"She's a professor at the university." Charlie rummaged for the corkscrew. She pulled it out and started to twist it into the cork. "I should've asked, but is white okay?"

"Works for me."

Charlie poured two glasses, recorked the bottle, and handed a glass to Kai. "I thought about what you said about my hair color, and I'd like to change it to maybe a beautiful gray or silver."

Kai raised her glass to Charlie.

"I should be the one raising a glass to you. Your and Lani's timing was excellent, my beautiful stalker." Charlie sipped her wine.

"My pleasure, but I wasn't the only one. You're a popular girl."

"Was that you in the car that stopped and then started back up again?"

"No, no, that wasn't me."

"Then who was in that car?"

"Like I was saying, I was about to sneak up on you and see how you were doing. I even packed Spam musubi in case you'd get angry with me. Then I thought I'd better not. What if I spoiled your stakeout? All the trouble and work you'd put yourself through. For the first time in my life, I showed some patience. I just ducked down in my car when I saw that Grant guy pull in behind you in his van. I started to get really nervous. I could tell that you hadn't noticed him. I was freaking out. Do I yell out? What the fuck do I do?" Kai paused to sip her wine, her hand shaking. "I'm watching all of this when I see another car. The guy in it seems to be watching the both of you." She took another long sip.

Charlie reached out and squeezed her arm. "What did he look like? Make of the car?"

"Sorry, I couldn't get a good look. Like some ancient tutu, I was so far down in my seat that I could barely look above the dash. I don't scare easy, but I was frightened. Do you think there's somebody else out there?"

"It's probably nothing. I'm truly thankful for you checking up on me." Charlie smiled, but she felt a slight twinge in her stomach.

"I don't know what's gotten into me. I've been following you around like you're a dog in heat. I'm usually so confident and move on quickly, but I can't shake you from my thoughts. I'll start styling a customer's hair, and if I don't pay attention, I'll cut it like yours." Kai shook her head in embarrassment.

"Your poor customers, I can't imagine anyone wanting to look like this." Charlie took a long sip of wine.

"Do you ever let your hair down? I mean, get crazy?"

"I know it may be hard for you to imagine, but I can get crazy."

"I'm having a hard time fathoming it. You're always in control. Like, when Grant was talking to you, you let him believe that you needed his help. I'd have kicked him in the balls the moment he came up to the car."

"Believe me, I've had moments when I lost control of my emotions, and it wasn't a pretty sight. As I've gotten older, I've learned to channel my energy and emotions better. My raw emotions weren't healthy or productive."

"I'd like to experience your energy, to see and feel that raw emotion."

"You're getting the best of me. I'm finally starting to accept who I am, and being comfortable in my own skin is wonderfully refreshing and freeing." Charlie lifted her glass and sipped her wine.

"You know, it's all part of your persona. Your education, your job, your control. Look at the way you're dressed! You just captured a psycho. A regular hero, and you're all neat and controlled. Not a hair out of place. Look at me, I'm a mess, and I didn't do shit. I'm Hawaiian ghetto. Cutoffs, tank top, tattoos."

"These are my go-to comfortable clothes. Like my favorite pair of jeans that fit just right, wearing out in the knees and butt, that make me feel good as soon as I put them on. I like your Hawaiian ghetto look. It's very appropriate for you and the island. Hey, I need to talk to you about a couple of things," Charlie said, tucking the bottle of wine under her arm, taking Kai's hand with one hand and the glass of wine in the other and leading her back to the living room.

"Am I going to like this? Suddenly, my heart is pumping, and my palms are sweaty." Kai drained her wine glass.

Charlie poured more wine into both glasses. "Yes, I think so," she said, curling her legs underneath her on the sofa. "I received three letters today, and they impacted me greatly, so that's why I wanted to unwind a little. The first letter was from the University of Hawaii. They've decided to offer me a position—not a full professorship, which I knew was unlikely, but as an adjunct professor."

"That's good, right?"

"Yes, it's good. It just means that I'm on a contract for a specific period of time and that I'm not eligible for tenure. But it's a start in the right direction."

Kai sat up on her knees. "This is the best news I've had in a while. I could kiss you."

"Not yet, there's more." Charlie held up her hand, preventing Kai from kissing her. Charlie watched Kai for her response. Kai sat back on her haunches and took a sip of wine. Charlie placed her hand on Kai's knee and massaged it. "But I do want to talk about us. Well, maybe more about me, but it does have implications for us."

"Is this where you tell me you think I'm a fabulous person, but you're not really that into me?" Kai sat back farther, as if trying to size up Charlie's response.

"Relax, you're way too tense. Nothing of the sort. I wanted to talk about . . . let's go back to the letters. The second letter I received today was from the University of Michigan's health department. My test result for HIV came back."

"Why would you need a blood test for HIV? That's for ass bandits."

"Be kind. It's actually a very deadly virus that can infect all of us—men, women, and children—and have nothing to do with sexual orientation. Straight, gay, lesbian, we can all be infected." Charlie waited to see how Kai was going to respond. "I've told you a little about Annie. You would've really liked her. She was an incredibly beautiful woman. She had this flaming red hair, pure white skin, beautiful hazel eyes, and a smile and laugh that made you feel glad you were alive. She was my best friend and my lover. We both struggled with our sexuality. Annie got married and hid her sexuality because that's what we were supposed to do. I suppressed mine by burying myself in work. We met at a conference and progressed from there. Annie made me feel good about myself. She was nurturing and caring, and when I was with her, I never felt ashamed.

"She was a terrific mother to two beautiful children. Her husband had become infected with HIV through his relationships with prostitutes and eventually died of AIDS. He passed HIV on to Annie. Susan, my sister, is a doctor who studies this disease. She recommended that I get a blood test to make sure I wasn't infected."

"That's great news—I think?" Kai said.

A thousand thoughts ran through Charlie's mind: Annie, loyalty, unfaithfulness, being discovered, safe sex, loneliness, craving.

"What is it? If you're worried about me. I don't hang out with prostitutes . . . I'm not some kind of lowlife," Kai said defensively.

"Honey, I'm not saying anything of the sort, or implying it. I had to make sure that I wasn't infected because I couldn't live with myself if I passed this deadly disease on to someone I cared about," Charlie explained. "You can't tell just by looking at someone if they're infected or not. You'd never have looked at Annie and known. I couldn't tell till after the HIV had transitioned to AIDS—then I saw the real effect. I just wanted to make sure I was clean. I owed it to myself and anyone else I might love." Charlie looked at her wine glass and then back up at Kai. She stood, drained her glass, and placed it on the table.

Kai followed suit and took Charlie's hand as Charlie led her into the bedroom.

"Let me show you crazy," Charlie said mischievously and pinned Kai against the door, pulling her tank top off while she kissed her neck. Her mouth moved slowly along Kai's tattoo, kissing and nibbling the flowers. Kai's nipples grew hard.

Charlie knelt and unbuttoned her blue jean cutoffs and pulled them down and off. Her lips continued to follow the tattoo as it wound down Kai's body. Intoxicated from the wicked combination of Kai's perfume and pheromones, Charlie desired her even more as her lips moved lower.

Kai moaned with pleasure as Charlie brought her to climax. She tried to catch her breath while Charlie retraced her kisses and nibbles as she slowly stood up. She pressed against Kai and whispered, "We've just begun the examination," and pulled Kai on top of her and onto the bed.

Later Charlie and Kai regained their breath and slowed their heart rates. Kai snuggled close to Charlie. "That was insane. I never thought I'd hear myself say I need a break!" Kai stretched. "Whew, Doctor, I like your bedside manner."

Charlie's head rested on her left arm while she gently caressed Kai underneath the sheet. "Thank you. A lot of pent-up desire." She glanced at the clock on the nightstand and leaped out of bed. "Shit!"

Kai tossed the sheet off. "What is it?"

"My auntie will be home soon, and this isn't how I planned to tell her about my sexual orientation. The shower's over there. Let's grab a quick one."

"No, I get it." Kai ran after Charlie into the bathroom.

Showered, dressed, and momentarily collected, Charlie laughed as she opened the bedroom door with Kai close on her heels. She noticed Salt and Pepper with their tails between their legs, eerily quiet and sullen. Charlie stopped in her tracks, and Kai bumped into her from behind.

"Charlie," Barbara said.

Charlie quickly looked over her shoulder at Kai, then to Salt, Pepper, and then back to Barbara. "Yes, auntie?"

"Could you come here, please?"

Barbara's tone was unsettling. "Yes, auntie?"

"I want to know—"

"Maybe I should go so the two of you can talk," Kai suggested, trying to ease toward the front door.

"Maybe it's best." Charlie took her hand and squeezed it.

"Goodbye, auntie." Kai gave Charlie a worried look.

"Goodbye," Barbara answered abruptly.

"Auntie, I'm sorry. I meant to tell you, but I wasn't sure how to go about it . . ." *Shit, this is hard and uncomfortable.* "I don't want you being upset—"

"Upset? I'll tell you why I'm upset. When I came home, I found these two on the couch. Salt and Pepper know they're forbidden to be on the couch, so somebody, namely you, has allowed them to lie on the couch when I'm not around."

"Guilty as charged. I swear it was just this one time, and they both promised me that they wouldn't give our secret away, but so much has happened today that I needed a little tender loving care." *Did I just dodge a bullet?*

"Charlie, you spoil them so much."

Salt and Pepper sensed the danger had passed and crept toward the women. "Where do you two think you're going? Back to your beds," Barbara ordered. They scurried quickly to their beds and looked back at the women sadly.

"Auntie, look at those faces! You can't stay mad at them. Besides, it's all my fault."

"All right, for you two—probation."

Salt and Pepper raced to Barbara and Charlie, running around in circles and yelping with joy.

After the commotion subsided, Barbara asked, "Don't you have something else to tell me?"

Shit, maybe I spoke too soon. "I'm not sure . . ." *I'll be evasive as long as possible until she confronts me directly.*

"The news that's all over campus?"

Okay, maybe this doesn't have to do with Kai and me. "What news?"

"That's what I wanted to know. Kim came bursting in my office and asked if I had heard. She assumed that we had already talked, but I tried to deflect my embarrassment by saying that you were probably too busy to talk. She said, 'Of course, that's probably it,' so I asked what all the excitement was about. She had gotten a call from Frank, and he'd told her how you had risked your life, got in a car with him, and then subdued him by spraying mace in his eyes and face. She said everyone at the department is ecstatic but pissed at the DA for being too chicken to arrest him. I want to know everything!"

"I was planning on telling you tonight when you got home. When I got back here, my eyes were burning, and my nose was running like a faucet. I was pretty whipped from being up all night and crashing from the adrenaline rush. All I really wanted to do was get out of my clothes and take a shower. Poor Salt and Pepper, they got a whiff too. I'm sorry. I did want to tell you, I just didn't think the news would've reached you before I had a chance to tell you everything."

Charlie explained everything that had happened with the apprehension of Grant and why the DA didn't want him arrested.

"My God, Charlie, I could have lost you. He could have killed you. What if he had landed his punch?"

"He could have, but he didn't. I was confident that I knew his actions, and I was prepared for him."

"So what comes next?"

"We'll continue to watch Grant closely and try to find more evidence. Lani and I will start to review previous open cases that might be associated or look like these cases. I'll keep working until something breaks."

Barbara hugged Charlie. "You're so courageous and brave."

"I wish that were true."

"What are you talking about? You caught a killer."

"There were some other reasons that I didn't call you earlier. I received some mail today, and I was trying to process it all." Charlie picked up the letters off the desk. She handed the University of Hawaii letter to her first.

"The deans are pretty predictable—so traditional in their thinking, so political." Barbara hugged Charlie. "I was hopeful they might offer you a full professorship."

"I suspected as much, so I can't blame them. The chancellor's rationale is completely understandable."

"Meaning you're going to stay . . . stay permanently?"

"I don't know if it's permanently, although I don't plan on going back home anytime soon, but under one condition."

"Name it, anything."

"I haven't always been brave or courageous or even truthful." Charlie handed Barbara the letter from the University of Michigan's health department.

"This looks good. Am I missing something?" Barbara put the letter down and looked at Charlie.

Charlie then handed her Josh's letter.

"This is what all the heartbreak has been about? His mother's death."

"Yes." Charlie looked down.

"I take it from Josh's note that you and his mother . . ."

"Annie."

"That you and Annie were involved."

"Yes, we were very much in love."

"I take it this wasn't a passing fancy, that you weren't experimenting like some college women like to do."

"No, this wasn't an experiment."

"The woman that was here . . ."

"Kai."

"Kai . . . Can I assume that she's more than a friend?"

"Yes, we've grown closer over the last couple of months."

"Is she the reason that you want to stay?"

"She's part of it, but I really want to be here with you. I haven't felt this way for a very long time, if ever."

A small tear formed in the corner of Barbara's eye and ran slowly down her cheek, followed by another and another.

"Can you forgive me? Do you want me to leave?" Charlie asked. *I knew I should've kept my mouth shut—stupid.*

Barbara shook her head. She began to sob.

"I'm sorry. I didn't mean to hurt you this way. I just thought that maybe it was a good time to be honest—I'm sorry. I'll go."

"Don't, please, don't. I'm begging you to stay." Barbara grabbed Charlie's hand and pulled her down to the couch. Charlie sat down and looked at her aunt's face—she seemed to have grown old and lost all her vibrancy.

"You've been so strong and so courageous. It's me—it's all my fault. I'm the one that owes the apology and should ask for forgiveness. I'd understand if you wanted to leave on the next plane out of here."

"How could this be your fault? You didn't make me a lesbian. I was born this way." Charlie wiped a small tear from Barbara's face and handed her a tissue.

"Do you know how you got your name?"

"I was named after my father's door gunner who died in the war."

"That's partially true." Barbara wiped the tears away and gently blew her nose. "You know that your mom and I have been best friends all our lives and would do anything for each other. Well, your mom met your dad one day in Waikiki and fell in love— madly in love. Your grandparents weren't happy. They thought that your dad was just after a good time and would break your mother's heart when it was time to leave, so they forbid her to see him anymore. Eventually your mom and I convinced your grandparents that if I went with your mom and dad on their dates like a sort of chaperone, then nothing would happen. Your mom and dad were grateful that they could see each other, but at the same time weren't thrilled to have me along as a third wheel. Your dad's best friend was available, so your dad fixed him up with me. It was better going on double dates. Your mom and I could cover for each other."

"Clever and devious! It's hard to imagine the two of you sneaking around like that. The way my mom talks, I was the second immaculate conception." Charlie shook her head. "So unfair."

"Yes, you're probably right about that. We'd go on dates to the beach, to restaurants in Waikiki, and to the officers' club for dancing and parties. Your mom and I were so excited to be with two handsome men in uniform, with money, having a lot of fun. We were young and in love—it was a dream come true for a couple of island girls. Then it all started to go terribly wrong. I remember waking up early because I had to go to the bathroom. I remember coming back from the bathroom and looking out my bedroom window. It was such a beautiful December Sunday morning, mild temperatures and a clear sky. I thought it was going to be another great day. For no reason, I felt chilled and felt the goose bumps on my arms. I rubbed my arms trying to warm up. What's going on?'

"I saw all the planes flying in the air, and I thought that was strange, especially for a Sunday, because neither my boyfriend nor your father had mentioned anything about it. Then I noticed the smoke, and then I heard the explosions and the air raid sirens going off. I put my hand over my mouth and tried not to scream. The rest, as they say, is history.

"After the Japanese attack on Pearl Harbor, your father and my boyfriend had little time for your mom and me. Understandably, they were busy with war preparation and deployment. If all of that wasn't bad enough, there was something else going on that was just as sinister. There was so much racial hatred toward the Hawaiians of Japanese heritage. As Koreans, your mom and I could understand and appreciate the hate, because we knew what they'd done to our relatives in Korea. But that hatred was extended to any and all Asians. Nobody knew the difference, nobody cared to know—there was just a lot of hate. Before the attack, your father and my boyfriend had been teased plenty about dating Asian women, and now they were being questioned about their loyalty to their country and fellow service members. Fueling the hatred were the reports of Japanese spies hiding in Aiea, reporting on troop movements. We arranged some clandestine visits, but we had to be careful. We all remained hopeful, but we knew that once the boys left the island, there was a good chance they were never coming back. Then, one day, they were gone.

"We knew plenty of girls that were going downtown and hooking up with service members, but we didn't want any part of that. We remained faithful and hopeful that your dad and my boyfriend were coming back to us. Over the next three years, they sent us letters and cards. Your mom and I would sleep over at each other's houses, rereading each letter and card like it had just arrived. We'd talk for hours about our lives after the war. The type of homes we'd live in, where we'd live, the number of kids, order of the kids—boy and then a girl. It was pure fantasy, but it helped pass the time. When we weren't talking about the future, we did everything possible to prepare for it. We studied all the time. Your mom and I were excellent students.

"Then, one day, Christmas of '44, they reappeared magically. The greatest gift that had ever been given. Our prayers had been answered. We did our best to make up for lost time. For those few hours and minutes, our lives almost seemed to return to normal. They'd come back to assist in the planning efforts for the last great battle of the Pacific War—the Battle of Okinawa. Okinawa in spring and then Japan in the fall. Part of the country had already begun to celebrate the defeat of the Germans, but the war still raged on in the Pacific.

"As quickly as they had appeared, they vanished again. Your dad and my boyfriend were part of the Fifth Fleet, and in the spring of '45, and for the next eighty-two days, they were part of the bloodiest fighting in the whole war. Your mom and I, like the rest of the world, were glued to the radio listening to the reports. Crying ourselves to sleep at the news of twelve thousand five hundred service members that had been killed in action and another thirty-eight thousand wounded. Our hatred for the Japanese grew even more because of the kamikaze pilots diving into the ships, sinking thirty-eight and damaging over three hundred more.

"During this time, I found out that I was pregnant. I tried to hide it from my family for as long as I could, but eventually they found out. I was banished from my home for the shame that I had brought. Unmarried, pregnant, no money, and nowhere to go, I was desperate. Your mom found me a tiny studio apartment near campus. She was a lifesaver. I don't know how she did it, but she'd find food, clothes, and even some money for me. She'd go to my classes and gather the notes so I could still study and, by the grace of God, pass my classes. Then one day, your dad returned home. He had been pretty badly shot up and spent a long time in Tripler Hospital recuperating."

"Oh my God, why didn't I know about any of this?"

"Because it was painful. We just wanted to move on. We'd suffered for so long and done without for so long."

"What happened to your boyfriend?"

"Your dad told your mom and me how he had saved your father in a dogfight but lost his life in doing so."

"Auntie, I'm so sorry. What happened to the baby?"

"She was a beautiful little girl. Your parents thought that since they were now married, they could look after the little girl and provide for her better than I could. Your dad owed his life to my boyfriend and thought that was the least he could do to repay him."

"Wait, this is getting a little creepy. Are you saying . . . ?"

"Yes, Charlie. I'm saying that you were named after your real father, Captain Charlie Westin, who died during the Battle of Okinawa, and that I'm your mother."

"Why didn't someone say something? It explains so much."

"We thought it was in your best interest that you didn't know. When you keep telling the same lie, you begin to believe it."

"Did Uncle Bennie know?"

"No, he never knew, but I think he always suspected something. The way I would go on about you and have all your pictures and report cards. How happy I was when you came to visit and how I would cry for the next three days when you'd leave."

"Why didn't you and Uncle Bennie have your own kids?"

"We couldn't. I couldn't go to a real hospital or doctor, so there were complications after your birth, and I couldn't have any more children. I'm thankful that you came out okay, but poor Bennie had been injured during the war and couldn't father children. So it was convenient for both of us. Neither could produce a child, so we had a good marriage—no hard feelings between us."

"I'm dumbfounded. I don't know where to begin or what to say."

"You don't have to say anything. I know what a miserable and lousy mother I've been all these years. For so long I wanted to tell you that I was your mother and let you know how much I loved you, but I was the one that had lied all this time and lacked courage. I can only ask for your forgiveness and understanding." Barbara got up and went to her bedroom.

Charlie could hear the sobs from the other side of the door.

Aiea
Saturday, May 10, 1986

"That bad?"

"What?"

"Did it go that bad with your auntie? You look like the wind has been taken out of your sails. Even your hair seems lifeless and dull."

"I'm sorry. Just some totally unexpected news. I have a pretty strong intuition, and I always suspected something, but when you're confronted with the truth, and it was what you expected, but you can't fathom it, either? You know what I mean?"

"No clue, but I do know coloring and styling, so let's get you back to normal." Kai turned Charlie's chair around and slowly adjusted the seat so she could begin to wash her hair.

Honolulu
Saturday, May 10, 1986

"How many years have you been on the island, and you've never been to the top of Diamond Head? Slow down, Leinani, wait for uncle and me."

"Hurry up. Uncle, catch me."

"Boy, she's a handful. I guess I was saving the climb for the right woman." Dempsey squeezed Lani's hand.

"Do you think I'm going to believe that line?"

"You don't seem to believe anything else I say, so does it matter?"

"You're right, for once in your life. I don't believe a word you say, so it doesn't matter." Lani slipped her hand out from Dempsey's grasp.

"Do you guys really think Al was the killer?"

"Who's Al? You mean Hugh Allen Grant?"

"Yeah, Al."

"Yes, we think the bastard's responsible for all the killings."

"He just doesn't seem the type. I can't imagine him being able to convince any woman to get in his van."

"Why? Because he's not sophisticated and doesn't have the come-on lines that you do?"

"That, for one, but he just doesn't seem to have enough smarts or initiative to get anything done. He's lame."

"You seem to know a lot about him. Did you spend a lot of time with him?"

"Well, we'd occasionally go out for a beer, but that's about it."

"You sure?"

"Wait, are you grilling me? Would you like me to take a lie detector test?"

"The thought has crossed my mind, but then I'm afraid of what I might learn."

Manoa
Sunday, May 11, 1986

Charlie knocked lightly on the door and opened it to a darkened room. The morning sunlight slivered through the cracks in the curtains. Barbara was sleeping, her eyes swollen. The sheet was pulled up to her chin, and the bedspread lay on the floor in a pile. Charlie tiptoed to the other side of the bed, lay down next to her, and put her arm around her.

"Auntie, you must not know me well. How could I ever stop loving the woman that I always admired and wanted to be with? I'm not going to lose you now."

Ewa Beach
Friday, May 16, 1986

Charlie and Lani were greeted at the door with a warm and friendly smile and welcomed into the home. Charlie sat down and looked around the living room: wood paneling, orange plaid sofas and chairs. Crucifixes and Catholic icons were used not only as a statement of devotion but for decorative purposes too. Charlie observed all the pictures of a happy family hanging on the walls. The oldest pictures were of Dad, Mom, older sister, and four little brothers. She stood up and walked over to one of the walls and looked at the smiling face of the eldest child.

Ruth drew a deep breath and began. "That date is etched in my memory forever. October 7, 1984, when Hana, my daughter, disappeared from a bus stop in Waipahu. The police keep telling me that Hana's case is not related to these murders because there are slight differences, but I can't help thinking that they're wrong."

"Tell me about her," Charlie said as she returned to the couch and watched the two distraught parents.

"They keep pointing out her physical and mental disabilities— her handicaps. She had cerebral palsy, and her intellect was not much more than a third grader's, but she was tough. Hana was akamai."

"Akamai?" Charlie asked.

"It means smart," Lani answered.

"Ya, ya. My daughter had a street smartness about her, just like the other women," Moses added.

"The detectives say because she wasn't one hundred percent Caucasian, was part Filipino, and short and heavy. Gosh, she was only about five feet one, and she weighed about a hundred and fifty pounds," Ruth said.

"Grant, that guy who was brought in for questioning, he lives just a couple of blocks away. It gives us the creeps," Moses said.

"I don't understand. Hana was the same age as the other women. She was only twenty-two and was last seen at a bus stop in Waipahu around seven thirty or seven forty-five in the evening. She was sexually abused—just like the others," Ruth pleaded.

"Officer, I'm sorry. We're glad that you're here, but your buddies downtown, those cops, they like to speak out of both sides of their mouths. They always want to point out the differences. They found our Hana in an irrigation ditch in a Kunia cane field. Ya, just like the others, near the water. What differences? Tell me, Officer, is it the same person that murdered our Hana who murdered these other women?" Moses said.

"I understand and appreciate your frustration. The circumstances and evidence surrounding cases are rarely the same, so it's difficult to discern what is pertinent and what's not," Charlie said.

"Every time I hear or read about the disappearance of a woman and it's just a little paragraph, it brings me to tears. I'm filled with anger. It's small and petty, but I can't help myself. At least I was able to bury Hana and lay her to rest. I can't imagine how parents who've lost children and never get their bodies back cope. Please don't forget about our baby—please don't." Ruth broke into tears.

"We're doing everything we can," Lani said.

Moses followed Charlie and Lani to the front door. "Hana's death has been hard on her. It's been hard on all of us. I just don't understand. Why her? Why us? We're good people."

Mililani
Monday, May 19, 1986

"Mary, thank you for seeing us," Charlie said to the attractive woman across from her.

"Doctor, no problem, I see you all the time in the paper and on the television news. I'm glad that you're here, but I don't know how I can be of assistance."

"As you may know, Officer Urada and I are part of the task force investigating the murder of the five women. As part of our investigation, we go back and look at unsolved crimes that match specific details of these crimes to see if there are any correlations. I don't want to get your hopes up, but I'd really like to hear what you have to say about Madison."

"Wade, my ex-husband—Madison's father—was in the military. We moved here about sixteen years ago when he went on his tour to Vietnam. We liked it so much that we decided to stay. When Wade returned from Vietnam, he was not the same man. Eventually we got divorced, and I remarried, and we settled in Mililani."

"Was Madison born here?" Lani asked.

"No, she was born at Fort Campbell, Kentucky, and compared to that place, this is really paradise. Madison, like most teenage girls, was a challenge. She'd fight with me and her stepdad tooth and nail, but other times she could be so sweet and thoughtful. She wrote poetry and composed music too."

Charlie analyzed Mary as she continued. "She was a very thoughtful and selfless young lady. Madison turned sixteen and graduated high school early. She had just started to attend Leeward Community College. She wanted to be a doctor. She wanted to help people with disabilities. On the night that she disappeared, she called the house from school and spoke to her sister to say that she was on her way home. She was going to catch the bus in front of the school. I think her last words to me that morning were something like, 'I'll see ya later, alligator,' and I cornily replied, 'After a while, crocodile.' The next time I saw her was in a black-and-white police photo. It looked like she was sleeping peacefully. She was stretched out on a pile of dirt in a Kunia cane field. The police officer told me that she'd been tied in a way that if she moved her legs, she'd choke herself."

"A terrible death," Lani responded.

"The same officer told me that they thought she'd been picked up by someone she knew or forced into a passing car on the dark road she was walking on from the college to the bus stop." Mary gently blew her nose.

Charlie patted Mary's arm. "Thank you for meeting with us, and we're so sorry for your loss."

Waipahu
Tuesday, May 20, 1986

"Kathy Grevinck, age thirty-six, lived alone on North Shore in Haleiwa. She was last seen arguing with an unidentified man on Kupuna Loop in front of the Village Park subdivision, here in Waipahu. Her body was found on the shoulder of Kunia Road near the Hawaii Country Club, apparently beaten and strangled." Lani closed her notepad. "Do you think this could all be Grant? It's frightening—the similarities—and the cases keep piling up."

Charlie surveyed the modest residential area and then unfolded her map on the hood of the car. She marked on the map where Kathy had disappeared and where her body was located. She visualized the sugarcane on both sides of the desolate route as her finger traced Kunia Road, Route 750, down from Wheeler Air Force Base and Schofield Barracks, across H-1 to Route 76, and into Ewa.

"We have Madison, sixteen, murdered on November 17, 1975; Kathy, thirty-six, April 4, 1984; Hana, October 7, 1984; Pam, May 29, 1985; Rebecca, January 15, 1986; Debra, January 30, 1986; Juliana, March 26, 1986; and Laura, May 3, 1986." Charlie pointed to each location where a woman's body was found. "I understand Hawaii is an island, but that is a lot of women in an even more confined geographical area, with more similarities than contradictions in their cases." She looked up from the map.

"Now that we know or have at least strong convictions that Grant was responsible for the murders, do you still think there is someone else involved? A military guy?" Lani asked.

"It would be interesting to trace Grant's movements around the other murders and see where that leads us," Charlie thought aloud.

"But why the separation in time and the differences in women?" Lani asked.

"Could be for several reasons: he was working, on vacation. I've seen enough—let's head back to town." Charlie folded the map.

Honolulu
Tuesday, May 20, 1986

Charlie and Lani walked into the homicide office and found Tanaka at his desk.

"Good afternoon, Detective. How is the surveillance coming along?" Charlie asked.

"He's a model citizen. All he ever does is go to and from work." Tanaka started shuffling through the logs on his desk. "He also seems to have found God. He is now attending church every Sunday and Bible study on Tuesday nights. What do you think about that?"

"He may be trying to build his defense so that people see him in another light. But I assure you he isn't doing it for any spiritual reasons." Charlie took some of the log sheets and started to peruse them.

"We think he may be leaving the island—permanently," Tanaka said.

"What? Can he do that?" Lani asked.

"Legally, we have nothing to hold him on, so I guess he's free to go." Tanaka sat back in his reclining office chair, pushed off his desk, and rolled a couple of feet back.

"Is the DA comfortable with this?" Charlie asked.

"Privately, I'm being told that everyone is elated. Once Grant's off the island and some semblance of normality returns, we can get back to busting tourists for engaging in prostitution. Basically, he becomes someone else's problem," Tanaka said.

"A scary thought. On another note, I've been looking at the cold cases and missing persons, and one stands out to me: Madison Humberto."

"I don't remember that one." Tanaka began to leaf through his notebook again. "The guys downstairs thought there might be some similarities with Ichika Sato, age twenty-one, who disappeared on November 27, 1985, when she was walking back from a convenience store to the motel she and her family were staying at."

"I saw that one too, but I don't agree with the logic. Ichika was Japanese, so her description doesn't match the others. She has no connection with the center of the island, and we never found the body. Why I'm interested in Madison is she was sixteen, Caucasian, blond, and had just departed class at Leeward Community College and was on her way to the bus stop."

Tanaka stopped what he was doing, looked up at Charlie, and sat back in his chair.

"We've spoken with her mom and looked at the old files. She'd been raped, hands tied behind her back, tape on her, and a rope around her neck in a sadomasochistic bondage manner—in such a way that if she moved her legs, she'd be choked. The report stated they thought she might have been picked up by acquaintances or forced into a passing car. It's not acquaintances because no other sixteen- or seventeen-year-old would have that knowledge of sophisticated knot tying. So being tricked, forced, or coerced into a passing car sounds familiar. She was found on a dirt road in an abandoned pineapple field. Venture a guess where her body was located?"

"Waipahu?"

"Kunia, but close enough."

"Strangled too?"

"Yes."

"Okay, our killer is tying the victims' hands behind their backs, but he isn't using a sophisticated knot."

"This may have been a younger version of our serial killer—testosterone kicking in, more rage, more impulsive, and over time he becomes more mature, careful, and deliberate in his thought process, so he ditches tying the knot around their necks and ankles."

"Near water?"

"Plenty of irrigation ditches in the area."

"Sounds like a stretch."

"You're missing the point. Take into consideration the victim's description and location. He's matured. He's changed." Charlie began to lay out her map on Tanaka's desk.

Tanaka looked annoyed at first but began to take an interest. "When do you go back on vacation?"

"Wishful thinking. Mac finally getting to you? Too many unanswered questions. Too many loose threads to pull on." Charlie smiled.

Honolulu International Airport
Tuesday, May 27, 1986

"You look good in uniform. I almost didn't recognize you, except for the vague memory of a patrol officer disturbing my sleep on the beach." Charlie grinned.

"I forgot how uncomfortable this thing could be. I was getting to like my own clothes when working, but if there's a bright spot, it does save me money on having to buy new clothes all the time—it was hard to keep up with a fashion horse like you."

"Nonsense, woman."

"Can I ask you something?"

"When haven't you?"

"Are you and my sister, like . . . you know, a couple?"

"Never ask a question of a suspect that you don't already have the answer to. You'll never catch them in a lie. You'll never make detective with bold assumptions like that. You've got to follow the evidence." Charlie smiled.

"I've learned from you, the best there is, and I did follow the evidence, and the evidence clearly states that something is going on."

"Does it matter? Does it bother you?"

"At times it seems a little strange or unordinary, but I love the both of you and want the very best. Besides, I'll make detective before you know it."

"I know you will."

"I'm glad to hear the university president changed his mind. I miss the banter, and I couldn't handle Kai in a constant state of depression."

"My auntie can be pretty determined—when middle-aged Korean women get something in their mind, stay out of their way." Charlie reflected on when she had arrived to the airport, seeing Barbara, and the time that has raced passed.

"There he is." Lani nudged Charlie.

They watched Grant make his way to the airline counter at the gate. He smiled pleasantly at the attendant as he handed her his ticket and identification. He looked around the waiting area at the other passengers waiting to board the flight. He nodded his head toward Charlie and Lani in acknowledgment of their presence.

Grant picked up his boarding pass, put it in his sport coat pocket, and took a seat against the wall. He opened his Walkman, checked the cassette, and closed it. He adjusted his headphones, reached in his bag, pulled out a package of Whoppers and a paperback book, and began to read intently while occasionally popping candy into his mouth.

"Should we go over and annoy the arrogant prick? We could sit on either side of him," Lani said.

"We'll wait until he starts to board, which should be any minute," Charlie responded.

"Passengers for United Flight 604 to San Diego, we will begin boarding now."

Charlie and Lani watched as Grant gathered his belongings and made his way toward the line, boarding pass in hand. They walked up alongside him. His head was nodding to the music. He looked over and lifted one headphone off his ear.

"Doctor and Officer, what an unexpected but most pleasant surprise. What do I owe this honor to?"

"We just wanted to make sure that you're really leaving and that, hopefully, you'll never come back." Charlie smiled.

"Doctor, you don't have to ever worry about me again. I've found God. I'm a changed man." Grant dropped his bag and put his hands together in an attitude of prayer.

"I don't know about God, but I'll make sure that you find hell someday," Charlie said coolly.

As Grant approached the gate, he handed the attendant his ticket. As he passed, he leered at Lani and Charlie. "He's got a special treat for you, the both of you."

Charlie and Lani could hear Grant's laughter fade away as he walked down the boarding bridge.

Tantalus Lookout
Saturday, May 31, 1986

The winding and scenic drive brought Charlie, Josh, Melissa, Barbara, and Kai to the Tantalus Lookout in Pu'u Ualakaa State Park. Josh was in white pants with a navy-blue Hawaiian shirt, and the women wore wedge heels and flowered dresses. All of them wore leis.

They set the packages they'd been carrying on the grass. They paused, overcome by the breathtaking view, and looked out over the city to the beautiful blue ocean, Diamond Head in the foreground, and wisps of white clouds with a tint of pink in them. A gorgeous sunset was in progress, a fiery red ball slowly dropping to the horizon.

"Aunt Charlie, thank you. This is a wonderful spot, and my mom would've loved it here," Josh said. His eyes were filled with tears, but there was a smile on his face.

"It's a little chilly, but I can feel her warmth. You know how she always would find a way to make you feel warm inside," Melissa added.

"I know how much she loved you," Charlie said to them. "Your well-being and happiness were always on her mind and in her heart, even to the very end. I look at the sky, and I can see and feel your mom. The color of the sun matches her hair color, and the clouds are the color of her skin. When I look at Diamond Head, I can see her hazel eyes and the sky turning the light purple of her favorite blouse."

The slight breeze tousled their hair, and Charlie thought about Annie's zany character. She, Josh, and Melissa told their favorite stories about her. Charlie opened the wooden box and handed a turquoise ceramic urn to Josh. He and Melissa looked at each other.

"You go first—you're the oldest." Melissa looked at Josh with pride.

"Why don't we do it together?" Josh suggested. They both looked at Charlie. "Aunt Charlie, please join us. I know how much she loved you, how much you loved her, and how good you were to all of us when we didn't always reciprocate the love."

Charlie came closer and stood next to Annie's children. They opened the urn and, together, slowly shook it back and forth. The breeze caught the ashes and carried them toward the sun.

Annie's wish had finally come true—she had always wanted to see a Hawaiian sunset with Charlie. So full of energy and love, she could now rest in peace. Charlie wiped the tears from her eyes as she said goodbye to her soul mate.

Barbara and Kai put their arms around Charlie and the teens. Barbara handed them leis to toss high into the sky. They watched the wind take them and carry them away.

They stood with their arms around each other as the sun set. When the city lights began to twinkle against the dark sky, they headed back along the cement path toward their cars.

"Where's Lani?" Charlie asked Kai.

"I don't know. I'm astonished she's not here. Lani knew how important this was to you, and she wanted to be here."

"Maybe she got called away to work," Barbara said.

"This doesn't feel right." Charlie stopped.

"Aunt Charlie, what is it?" Josh asked, concerned.

"Honey, it's nothing. Sorry, something just popped into my mind." *He's got a special treat for you, the both of you.*

Afterword

The 1980s were known for many things. Some refer to it as the decade of greed because many countries moved from planned economies toward laissez-faire capitalism. I could make the argument that the 1980s should be called the first personal computing decade. In 1981 MS-DOS and the first IBM PC were released; in 1983 the first commercial cell phone was made; in 1984 Steve Jobs introduced the first Macintosh computer; in 1985 Microsoft introduced Windows; and in 1989 the internet went global. And technology made big leaps in other areas: in 1987 DNA was first used to convict criminals and exonerate prisoners on death row.

The decade was also known for big and bold: hairstyles, clothing, perfume, and music; however, nothing was bigger or scarier than the recognition of the HIV/AIDS epidemic, marked by panic, shame, and ignorance. It raged through the world, killing thousands. "With no effective treatment available in the 1980s, there was little hope for those diagnosed with HIV, facing debilitating illness and certain death within years," says Dr. Gottfried Hirnschall, director of the HIV/AIDS Department of the World Health Organization.

December 1, 1988, was the first World AIDS Day, created to raise awareness about HIV and the resulting AIDS epidemic. Since the outbreak, more than seventy million people have been infected, about thirty-five million people have died, and today around thirty-seven million worldwide live with HIV. Approximately twenty-two million are in treatment.

References

Newspaper Sources (Listed Chronologically)

Police Beat. 1985. "Woman Found Dead at Keehi Lagoon." *Honolulu Advertiser*, May 31, A15. Microfiche.

Police Beat. 1985. "Gail Purdy, 25, of Mililani." *Honolulu Advertiser*, June 1, A15. Microfiche.

Mayer, Phil. 1985. "Isle Police Warned of Probability of Hillside Strangler Type of Crime." *Star-Bulletin*, September 13, A3. Microfiche.

Honolulu Star-Bulletin. 1985. "Double Murder in Wahiawa." December 17, A3. Microfiche.

McMurray, Terry. 1985. "Two Women Stabbed to Death in Wahiawa Adult Book Store." *Honolulu Advertiser*, December 17, A1, A4. Microfiche.

Tswei, Suzanne. 1985. "Police Find No Motive So Far in the Slaying of the Pair in Wahiawa." *Honolulu Advertiser*, December 18, A12. Microfiche.

Honolulu Star-Bulletin. 1985. "Police Seek Leads in Wahiawa Knife-Murders." December 18, A9. Microfiche.

Tswei, Suzanne. 1985. "Police Still Searching for Clues in Fatal Stabbing of 2 Women." *Honolulu Advertiser*, December 19, A7. Microfiche.

Honolulu Star-Bulletin. 1986. "Student Slain." January 16, A14. Microfiche.

Police Beat. 1986. "Body of Woman Found on Stream Bank." *Honolulu Advertiser*, February 2, A2. Microfiche.

POLICEFIRE. 1986. "Police Await Identification of Murdered Woman's Body." *Honolulu Star-Bulletin*, February 3, A8. Microfiche.

Police Beat. 1986. "A Young Woman Found Dead." *Honolulu Advertiser*, February 4, A2. Microfiche.

Honolulu Star-Bulletin. 1986. "Police See Links in Murders of 3 Women." February 5, A3. Microfiche.

Phillips, Robin. 1986. "Police Task Force to Probe Murder Link." *Honolulu Advertiser*, February 5, A3. Microfiche.

Police Beat. 1986. "The Murder Victim Found Saturday Near Moanalua Stream Was Identified." *Honolulu Advertiser*, February 6, A8. Microfiche.

Honolulu Star-Bulletin. 1986. "Third Murder Victim Is Identified by Police." February 6, A10. Microfiche.

Honolulu Star-Bulletin. 1986. "Reward Triples in Woman's Slaying." March 12, A10. Microfiche.

Lynch, Kay. 1986. "4th Murder Victim in Streambed." *Honolulu Advertiser*, April 3, A1, A3. Microfiche.

Honolulu Star-Bulletin. 1986. "Police See Possible Link in Killings of 4 Women." April 3, A3. Microfiche.

Adamski, Mary, and Catherine Enomoto. 1986. "Slaying Victim Identified by Police." *Honolulu Star-Bulletin*, April 4, A3. Microfiche.

Enomoto, Catherine. 1986. "Isle Police Contact Force Probing Seattle Slayings." *Honolulu Star-Bulletin*, April 5, A3. Microfiche.

Hoover, William. 1986. "Serial Killer Theory Reinforced." *Honolulu Advertiser*, April 5, A3. Microfiche.

Honolulu Advertiser. 1986. "Makiki Woman Found Slain." April 9, A11. Microfiche.

Hoover, William. 1986. "Mother's Crusade: Find Killer." *Honolulu Advertiser*, April 9, A1. Microfiche.

Chang, Lester. 1986. "Victim Was Apparently Waiting for Bus." *Honolulu Star-Bulletin*, April 9, A1. Microfiche.

Yamaguchi, Andy. 1986. "Makiki Woman Found Murdered." *Honolulu Advertiser*, April 10, A3. Microfiche.

Honolulu Advertiser. 1986. "Murder Victim Identified; Cause of Death Strangulation." April 11, A9. Microfiche.

Honolulu Advertiser. 1986. "Too Many Murders." April 11, A20. Microfiche.

Hoover, Will. 1986. "Police Watch Bus Stops, Advise Women to Be Alert." *Honolulu Advertiser*, April 12, A3. Microfiche.

Hoover, Will. 1986. "HPD Will Keep a Lid on Related Killings." *Honolulu Advertiser*, April 16, A1. Microfiche.

Hoover, Will. 1986. "Profiling a Serial Killer." *Honolulu Advertiser*, April 17, B7. Microfiche.

Hoover, Will. 1986. "Criminologist Warns Women: Misplaced Trust Can Be Fatal." *Honolulu Advertiser*, April 30, A7. Microfiche.

Police Beat. 1986. "Report of a Missing Woman Draws in Special Task Force." *Honolulu Advertiser*, May 1, A5. Microfiche.

Honolulu Advertiser. 1986. "Services to Be on Kauai Saturday for Murder Victim Louise Medeiros." May 1, A3. Microfiche.

Morse, Harold. 1986. "Autopsy Fails to Find Cause in Fifth Serial Murder." *Honolulu Star-Bulletin*, May 5, A3. Microfiche.

McMurray, Terry, and Jay Hartwell. 1986. "Body Is Identified as Linda Pesce's." *Honolulu Advertiser*, May 5, A3. Microfiche.

Honolulu Star-Bulletin. 1986. "Victim Identified." May 5, A3. Microfiche.

Honolulu Star-Bulletin. 1986. "Missing Isle Woman: Foul Play Suspected." May 6, A4. Microfiche.

Dingeman, Robbie, Hildegaard Verplogen, and Harold Morse. 1986. "Police Arrest Suspect in Linda Pesce Death." *Honolulu Star-Bulletin*, May 6, A1. Microfiche.

Adamski, Mary, and Lee Catterall. 1986. "Police Release Man Arrested in Pesce Probe." *Honolulu Star-Bulletin*, May 6, A1. Microfiche.

Hoover, Will. 1986. "Portrait of Hawaii Serial Killer a Caucasian Man in His Late 30s." *Honolulu Advertiser*, May 6, A3. Microfiche.

Dingeman, Robbie, and Mary Adamski. 1986. "Serial Killer Pictured as an 'Opportunist.'" *Honolulu Star-Bulletin*, May 6, A6. Microfiche.

Adamski, Mary. 1986. "Serial-Killings Suspect Profiled." *Honolulu Star-Bulletin*, May 6, A4. Microfiche.

Dingeman, Robbie. 1986. "Women Told to Avoid Risks, Trust No Strangers." *Honolulu Star-Bulletin*, May 6, A4. Microfiche.

Yamaguchi, Andy. 1986. "Police Review Missing-Person Case as Tips on Serial Murders Pour In." *Honolulu Advertiser*, May 7, A3. Microfiche.

Yamaguchi, Andy. 1986. "No Serial Murder Suspect Yet." *Honolulu Advertiser*, May 8, A6. Microfiche.

Ryan, Tim. 1986. "Honolulu's Serial Killer: A Special Report, Serial Killers: Usually, They Just 'Blend In.'" *Honolulu Star-Bulletin*, May 9, A1, A5, B1. Microfiche.

Manuel, Susan. 1986. "The Victims." *Honolulu Star-Bulletin*, May 10. Microfiche.

Wright, Walter. 1986. "FBI Lab Will Examine Pesce Slaying Evidence." *Honolulu Advertiser*, May 16, A12. Microfiche.

Antone, Rod. 2001. "Breakthrough in Bustamente Murder Raises Hope for Another Unsolved Case, the Mother of a Mililani Girl Killed in 1975 Hopes for a Break in the Case." *Honolulu Star-Bulletin*, May 14, 1986. Retrieved August 27, 2019. http://archives.starbulletin.com/2001/07/21/news/story3.html.

Other Sources (Listed Alphabetically)

"1980s Timeline." 2013. *National Geographic*, April 10. Retrieved January 24, 2020. http://www.natgeotv.com/int/the-80s-the-decade-that-made-us/the-80s-timeline

Bonn, Scott A. 2015. "Serial Killers: Modus Operandi, Signature, Staging & Posing." *Psychology Today*, June 29. Retrieved February 26, 2019. https://www.psychologytoday.com/us/blog/wicked-deeds/201506/serial-killers-modus-operandi-signature-staging-posing.

Christie, Agatha. 1958. *Ordeal by Innocence.* New York, New York: William Morrow.

Dees, Tim, and Christopher Hawk. 2014. "Let Me Ask You This: Do Detectives Really Pin Pictures on a Board when Investigating a Crime?" *Independent*, August 16. Retrieved October 16, 2019. https://www.independent.co.uk/news/uk/crime/let-me-ask-you-this-do-detectives-really-pin-pictures-on-a-board-when-investigating-a-crime-9667488.html.

Dias, Gary A. and Dingeman, Robbie. *Honolulu Homicide, Murder and Mayhem in Paradise.* Honolulu, Hawaii. Bess Press.

Earhart, Amelia. 2014. "In Her Own Words: Amelia Earhart's Record-Setting Flight—Plus a Bold Prediction." *National Geographic*, July 28. Retrieved April 20, 2019. https://www.nationalgeographic.com/news/2014/7/140727-amelia-earhart-history-flight-airplanes-adventure-explorer/#close.

"Explosion of the Space Shuttle *Challenger* Address to the Nation, January 28, 1986, by President Ronald W. Reagan." 2004 (updated). NASA History Office, June 7. Retrieved January 24, 2020. https://history.nasa.gov/reagan12886.html.

Fisher, Mary. 1996. *My Name is Mary.* New York, New York: Scribner.

Gil, Natalie. 2019. "Thousands of Women Told Us What They Call Their Vaginas & Vulvas—Here Are the Results." *Refinery29*, March 12. Retrieved October 28, 2019. https://www.refinery29.com/en-gb/2019/03/226652/names-for-vaginas.

"How to Body Surf Like a Pro." 2019. Pod, May 1. https://www.podware.com.au/blog/how-to-body-surf-like-a-pro/. Retrieved September 27, 2019.

Larsen, Eliza. 2019. "Hawaii's Remarkable Women: Lucile Abreu." KITV 4 News, April 25. Retrieved January 6, 2020. https://www.facebook.com/KITV4/posts/one-of-hawaiis-remarkable-women-lucile-abreu-her-legacy-now-lives-on-through-her/10155959697421861/

"The Lord's Prayer in Hawaiian." 2015. *Makanalani* (blog), September 18. Retrieved June 13, 2020. https://makanalani. com/fresh/the-lords-prayer-in-hawaiian/?doing_wp_cron=1 592069892.6607151031494140625000.

Pruit, Sarah. 2016. "5 Things You May Not Know about the Challenger Shuttle Disaster." History.com, January 28. Updated October 19, 2018. Retrieved January 24, 2020. https://www. history.com/news/5-things-you-might-not-know-about-the-challenger-shuttle-disaster.

Seattle Times. 2011. "Timeline of the Green River Killer Case." February 18. Retrieved March 5, 2019. https://www.seattle-times.com/seattle-news/timeline-of-the-green-river-killer-case/.

Swancer, Brent. 2019. "Hawaii's Most Mysterious Death and Unsolved Mystery." Mysterious Universe, May 15. Retrieved January 3, 2020. https://mysteriousuniverse.org/2019/05/ha-waiis-most-mysterious-death-and-unsolved-mystery/.

Thomas, Brendon. 2010. "Bodysurfing with Mark Cunningham." *Surfer*, July 22. Retrieved September 27, 2019. https://www. surfer.com/features/surf_tip-bodysurfing_with_mark_cun-ningham/.

World Health Organization. n.d. "Why the HIV Epidemic Is Not Over." Retrieved January 24, 2020. https://www.who.int/news-room/spotlight/why-the-hiv-epidemic-is-not-over.